Accidentally *In Love*

DANICA FLYNN

ACCIDENTALLY IN LOVE

A MACGREGOR BROTHERS BREWING COMPANY BOOK

DANICA FLYNN

Accidentally In Love

Ebook ISBN: 978-1-7342012-6-0
Print ISBN: 978-1-7342012-7-7

Cover Design: Emily's World of Design
Cover Photography: Volodymyr Tverdokhlib/ Deposit Photos
Editor: CamRei Editing

Content Note: This book is an accidental pregnancy trope, so mentions of pregnancy and miscarriage are throughout the book. As this is a sensitive topic for most, I want to be upfront that it is talked about at length in the book.

To Neshaminy Creek Brewery, thanks for the inspiration, but also RIP The Borough Brewhouse :(

CHAPTER ONE

AVERY

SEPTEMBER

One thing I loved about living in the small town of Drakesville, Pennsylvania, was the annual Fall Arts Fest. I loved walking up into the town square and seeing all the booths for the local businesses lined up together—like the bakery, the paint and pottery place, and my favorite brewery. The MacGregor Brothers Brewing Company.

Being ten miles north of Philadelphia and in a generally safe area, Drakesville gave you that small-town feeling without being too far away from it all. Not that I went into the city all that much. Only when I was going on yet another horrible date.

My current date, Greg, had agreed to meet me at the Arts Fest. He lived a few towns over and was happy to come check out the festivities with me. We met on a dating app and had been talking for a couple of weeks, but this was our first in-person date. Greg wasn't my typical type. I preferred my men thick and bearded, and he had that clean-cut look about him. He also looked like he went to the gym five times a day. I tried not to judge him too harshly because, at thirty-five and perpetually single, I couldn't be picky anymore.

I pushed my hair behind my ear and bent down to admire a crystal necklace at one of the jewelry booths. I didn't believe in the power of crystals. That was my sister Gemma's thing, but I thought they were pretty.

I was cramming the last of a donut into my mouth when I spied the disgusted look on Greg's face.

"What?" I asked, thinking I had chocolate smeared all over my face.

"Nothing," he snapped.

I reeled back at that because, until now, he had been the perfect date.

"What's wrong?" I asked.

He sneered at me and wrinkled his nose. "You would be prettier if you lost a few pounds."

My mouth hung open in shock at his bluntness.

I knew I had some curves on my petite frame. Most people wouldn't even consider me plus-sized, though. I just liked a side of cheese fries with my cheesesteak and beer every once in a while. What was wrong with that?

"Excuse me?" I stuttered out once the shock wore off.

He shrugged and put his hands in his pockets. "No wonder you're still single. Men would be more interested in you if you put in the effort and got fit."

Wow.

I knew men were garbage, but I'd never had a man be so rude to my face. I stood there blinking at him in shock for what felt like an eternity. Finally, I clenched my teeth together and chose my words carefully. "Why did you agree to go out with me?"

He shrugged, and we continued to walk down the street. "You looked thinner in your profile picture."

WOOOOOOW!

"Did you ever wonder why you're still single?" I asked.

He shrugged as if he didn't care.

"Because you're an asshole," I seethed at him. "I need a beer."

"You know there's a lot of cal—"

I fixed him with a glare. "Greg, go fuck yourself and never call me again."

With that, I stormed off down the road until I reached the booth for the tattoo shop where my friend Lizzie worked. Lizzie stood at the booth with her toddler, Matty, on her hip. She cocked her head to one side, and her lavender-tinted hair hung down at me like a question mark. Her son pulled at her hair, and she nuzzled her face against his nose, which made him giggle. That made me smile. Her kids were cute.

"Hey Avs, how's the date?" she asked, but I think she knew since I was alone.

"Bad," I groaned.

She frowned and shifted Matty onto her other hip. "What happened?"

"He told me I would be prettier if I lost a few pounds."

"What an asshole," a deep voice came from behind me.

I turned around and came face-to-face with Lizzie's husband, Wyatt. Or rather, face-to-chest, because Wyatt was a freaking blonde giant compared to my five-foot-five frame. I smiled when I saw their new baby girl sleeping soundly strapped to his chest.

"Oh, my ovaries!" I cried and put a hand on my chest.

Wyatt gave me a funny look. "Erm, what?"

I gestured to him, holding his baby. "That! A hot guy with a baby. Sorry to ogle your man, Lizzie, but I'm jealous."

The couple laughed.

"She's so cute!" I said to them, and Lizzie beamed at me.

"We make cute babies," Wyatt agreed. He put a hand on my shoulder. "You need me to rough the guy up?"

I rolled my eyes at him. "Thanks, but no. What I really need is a beer."

Lizzie and Wyatt shared a look.

"What?" I asked.

"I'm sure Nolan would be happy to see you. He was grumpy when I was over there," Wyatt said to me.

Nolan was always grumpy. It was kinda his MO.

Nolan MacGregor was the co-owner and brewmaster of the local brewery and a good friend—with whom I happened to occasionally fall into bed, but that was a secret.

With his burly physique and big bushy beard, Nolan was one hundred percent my type. He exuded that whole lumbersexual thing, over six feet tall and a little round in the middle. Thick men with big beards were my weakness. It was too bad he was only looking for an occasional hookup.

I looked over at the booth across the way and spotted the big man in question. We locked eyes, and he held up a plastic cup. "Beer?" he mouthed. I smiled and nodded.

When I turned back to Wyatt and Lizzie, they were smirking at me. "Guys, it's not like that," I tried to argue.

Lizzie rolled her eyes. "Sure, it's not…"

"We're just friends," I insisted.

Friends with some benefits, but it wasn't like they knew that. Nobody knew. Not even my baby sister, Gemma, knew, and she worked at the brewery. I didn't think Nolan's brother Declan knew either, and they were business partners.

Wyatt snorted and shook his head.

I glared at them. "Goodbye, you jerks!"

They both laughed as I headed in the direction of the brewery's booth, where Nolan and my sister were doling out beer. Nolan handed me a beer, but shook his head when I tried to give him some cash. "No, Avery, your money's no good here."

My sister scoffed, and she tossed her cotton-candy pink hair over her shoulder. "Um, false, boss man! That's how we lose money. She's family... give me ten dollars."

"Ten dollars? That's more than the sign says!" I argued.

Gemma gave me a cheeky grin. "You're family. You get charged extra."

"Six," Nolan said to my sister firmly.

Gemma rolled her eyes. "FINE."

I handed the cash to my sister and took the beer from her before downing it in one big gulp. Like the classy lady I was.

Nolan cackled out a big, booming laugh. "That's my girl!"

My heart jumped at hearing him call me 'his girl,' even though I knew that wasn't how he meant it. Nolan MacGregor might be good in bed, but I'd never be 'his.'

Gemma smiled, but it quickly dropped into a frown. "Wait, I thought you brought a date to the Fest?"

I shook my head. "Shut up and beer me, woman."

"What happened?" she asked.

I grimaced. "He said I would be prettier if I lost weight."

A scowl formed across Nolan's face. "Fuck that, guy! He doesn't know what he's missing."

A small smile curled up on my lips. "Thanks, Nol. It's fine. I'm used to assholes."

His jaw ticked, and the scowl stayed on his face. "It's not fine. That guy's a dick, and you deserve better. I have something that might cheer you up, though."

"What's that?"

"We finally released that pumpkin beer I was talking about."

"Oooh! I love pumpkin beers!" I cheered.

"I know," he said with a grin.

"Basic bitch," Gemma muttered under her breath.

I handed her more money and took the beer. "What's this one called?"

"The Drake Pumpkin Ale."

Gemma made a face. "I'd rather have a Drakesville Lager any day. Or the 611 IPA."

"I didn't make it for *you*," Nolan snapped at her.

Gemma nudged him in the ribs. "Grouchy! Go take a break, boss man. I see Declan coming back. We'll handle it."

Nolan rolled his eyes at her, but did as he was told. He came around the table and joined me on my stroll around the square. We came to a stop at the dumpling truck.

"You want one?" he asked while he studied the menu thoughtfully, like he didn't have it memorized already.

"No," I lied.

Of course, I wanted a dumpling. I loved that the dumpling truck was always here for the Arts Fest. Right now, I wasn't thinking about how much I wanted to eat a dumpling. Instead, I was thinking about what that jerk said to me. Maybe he was right. Maybe I could afford to lose a little weight.

"You sure?" Nolan asked. He looked down at me with concern in his whiskey-colored eyes.

"I'm sure," I lied again and took a sip of my beer.

He frowned but didn't push the conversation and went up to the truck window while I waited off to the side and drank my beer.

Nolan startled me when he came back over to me. "Open your mouth," he grunted.

"What?"

I was used to him grunting that demand at me, but usually, it was in the bedroom, and I was on my knees.

He held a dumpling in his big hand. "Open," he demanded again.

I opened my mouth and let him gently place the dumpling inside. I bit into it and moaned at the taste of buffalo chicken wrapped up in crisp dough.

He grinned down at me and popped a dumpling into his mouth. "Love that sound."

"Nolan!" I hissed.

He shrugged and swallowed. "What? Why do you care if people know we occasionally hop into bed together? We're both adults."

I glared up at him. "Because our siblings would start planning our wedding."

He made a non-committal grunt in response.

Nolan wasn't a man of many words. Unless those were dirty words and he was growling them while I was underneath him.

"What's wrong?" he asked after a few minutes had passed without further comment. "You never turn down carbs."

"Do you think I need to lose weight?"

He raised a dark eyebrow at me. "Is that a trick question?"

"No..."

"Avs, lose weight if you want to, but don't do it because some asshole told you to. I've never complained about your doggy-style hand grips." His eyes trailed down my body, and it was like tiny fires licking across my skin. "I always have a good time."

I put a hand over my face. "Jesus, Nolan."

He gave me that naughty grin that I loved and popped another dumpling into his mouth.

"Open," he commanded again and held another one up to my mouth.

"What flavor?" I asked.

"Apple pie," he said, and I let him feed it to me. I bit down on the delicious dessert and moaned again.

"Avery..." he trailed off and ran a hand through his thick beard.

"Yeah?"

"Any guy would fall over themselves to be with you. You deserve a man who treats you like his queen."

"Then how come I haven't found him yet? I'm getting too old for this. I feel like I'm gonna die alone with my cats."

"You don't have cats," he argued.

I glared again. "Not the point."

He squeezed my hand. "You'll find the right guy, probably when you aren't even looking."

I nodded but didn't believe him. I was pretty sure the man I wanted a future with was standing right in front of me. It really sucked when you were hopelessly in love with your friends with benefits.

"You want to come over tonight?" he asked.

"I've got nothing going on."

He smiled at me. "Avs?"

"Yeah?"

"Wear the red lingerie."

CHAPTER TWO

NOLAN

I smiled from my end of the couch as I watched Avery laugh at something my brother said. I hadn't been paying attention to the conversation one bit. My horny brain was more focused on waiting for everyone to leave so I could get Avery underneath me.

I met Avs two years ago. I was done with my shift at the brewery and headed home when I saw a pretty brunette crying into her beer. I asked the bartender to send her another on the house. One beer led to two, which led to her underneath me, moaning my name. It was supposed to be a one-time thing, but it kept on happening. Somehow along the way, we became friends.

Since my divorce a couple years ago, I wasn't one for relationships. I never wanted to fail someone the way I failed Kath. That's why I told Avery we could only be casual, even though I was pretty sure I caught feelings for her the very night we met. I learned to tamp those feelings down because I knew she didn't feel the same way.

"Right, Nol?" my brother's voice cut through my broody thoughts.

"Hmm?"

"Buddy! What a Space Cadet." Declan laughed and drank down the rest of his beer.

I shrugged.

Gemma sighed and finished her glass of water. "It's late. I better get going."

"You okay to drive?" Avery asked.

Gemma held up her water. "I'm good. I had one beer an hour ago."

Avery stood up and hugged her sister. "Text me when you get home, okay?"

The younger woman rolled her eyes. "Yes, mom!"

Declan stood up, too. "I'll walk you to your car."

"You don't have to," Gemma said in protest.

"I'd feel better about it," he argued.

"Dec, you live in Drakesville. I feel much safer walking at night here than in South Philly, and I do that all the time. I'll be fine."

Avery sighed. "Gem, let Declan walk you to your car, okay? It's on his way home."

I walked Gemma and Declan to the front door and locked it behind them. When I walked back into the living room, Avery had her head tipped back against the couch, and her eyes were closed.

"You want me to walk you home?" I asked.

Drakesville was such a small town that the walk to her apartment on the other side of town wasn't that far. I never timed it, but it was maybe ten minutes, probably a little less. Sometimes it was just easier to drive over there, but I didn't like to drink and drive. I might have only had two beers since Avs got here, but that was enough.

A drunk driver killed my parents. I didn't fuck around with that shit.

She shook her head. "I'm not tired."

"You look tired," I said while I stalked over to her. I lifted her chin, and she gave me a sly smile. Then she reached a hand up and rubbed it across my crotch. "Oh, I see."

"Do you?" she asked and looked up at me with those big blue eyes. The kind of eyes a man could get lost in.

"C'mere you," I growled and lifted her into my arms. She giggled while she wrapped her legs around my waist. I slid my hands under her dress and stumbled up the stairs into my bedroom. It shocked me when I came across bare flesh.

"Naughty girl, not wearing any panties."

I put her down when we got into my bedroom.

"I had to take them off," she said.

"Why?"

"Because I'm so ready for you, they were already soaked."

I bent my head down to capture her lips, and I grabbed onto the luscious flesh of her ass—her perfectly round ass. Fuck that guy who said she needed to lose weight. I wanted all that delicious weight on top of me, underneath me, and on display while I took her from behind. My big hand hovered on her mound while we kissed.

"Please, Nolan..." she begged.

Fuck, I loved when she begged for it. I kissed her neck. "Are you sure you want to have sex tonight?"

She groaned in annoyance and pushed my hand against her pussy. I felt her slick arousal on my finger as I lightly grazed across her slit. "Does that answer your question?"

"No. We've been drinking. I want to make sure you won't regret it."

She cupped my bearded face in her smaller hands. "Baby, I never regret it. I always love it."

I knew it was just casual sex between us, but when she looked deep into my eyes and called me baby, I pretended she was mine. Pretended that I *could* be enough for her. I had already disappointed my ex-wife, and I couldn't bear to disappoint Avery, too.

"You sure, Avs?"

"Nol, I had two beers. I'm not drunk. Now gimme that big dick."

I slid my middle finger through her slickness. "That's my girl. You like it when I touch you like this?"

"Mmmhmm," she moaned. "I'm aching for you, Nol. Please."

"Greedy girl. I want you out of these clothes and naked on my bed."

"Yes, sir," she said and gave me a sarcastic little salute.

"Brat," I teased, giving her a light tap on her ass.

I loved when she called me 'Sir,' even if she was a cheeky brat. I removed my hand from her dress, turned her around, and slid the zipper of her dress down until the material fell to the floor. With a quick flick of my wrists, I had her bra off, too. She stepped out of her clothes and got onto the bed, lying back, ready and waiting for me.

I got rid of my clothes and crawled into bed next to her. I devoured her mouth, and she let me. She allowed me to dominate her until I rolled onto my back and she straddled my thick thighs.

"Get up here and sit on my face," I growled.

She grinned and scooted up the bed. She put her knees against my ears, and settled her pussy level with my mouth.

I loved face-sitting, and she loved when I let her ride my beard until she coated it with her cum.

I flicked my tongue out, sliding up her slit until I zeroed in on her clit. She ground her hips against me, begging me with her body to bring her over the edge, to give her the one thing she needed more than anything.

"That's a good girl," I cooed. "Fuck my face."

"I love beard rides," she moaned and gripped the headboard above me.

There were permanent nail marks etched into the wood from all the times we had been in this position. My inner caveman loved when I made her lose herself like this. I loved the feeling of her delicious curves on top of me while I drowned in the sweet taste of her pussy.

She ground herself on my face and screamed above me as she tumbled down into the depths of her orgasm. I held her in place while I gave her one last lick as she came down from it.

"Good girl," I cooed from below.

"I want to ride your cock," she panted.

"Do it."

She scooted down my body until she had my cock lined up with her entrance. In the back of my mind, I knew we were forgetting something, something really important. I forgot about everything else when Avery was riding me while I sucked on her tits, though. I loved her tits, her ass, and everything else. I loved her curves, especially when they were on top of me.

Man, the guy she went out with today was a douchebag. He didn't know what he was missing out on. My inner caveman beat his chest again at the fact that she ended up in my bed tonight and not his.

"Yes..." she moaned as she rode me faster, her fantastic tits bouncing up and down with her every movement.

I gripped her ass and thrust up into her hard and fast.

"Nolan," she sighed in ecstasy as she arched her back and let the pleasure take control of her.

It was in these moments, when she unraveled to pieces, that she was the most beautiful. She looked like a queen when she was bouncing on my dick and coming apart at the seams. There was nothing sexier than a woman in the throes of passion. Especially when it was this woman.

She yelped in surprise when I pulled out and rolled her onto her back. "I want to be in charge," I growled.

She could only nod in response.

I kissed my way down her body until I tasted her on my tongue again. She gripped my hair while I licked and sucked her to another orgasm.

"Oh my god," she cried out.

"You don't have to call me god," I teased.

She cradled my face in her hands and gave me a loving look. "C'mere, big guy, and give me what I want."

I made my way back up her body and gave her a long, lingering kiss. I pressed inside her, and she wrapped her legs around my waist, pulling me in deeper. I squeezed my eyes shut and tried to hold off from blowing my load right then and there. I was glad I gave her a couple orgasms already because I wouldn't last much longer.

"Nolan, please," she begged while I slow-stroked her, and she arched her hips to meet my every move.

I pumped inside her slowly, my large body moving above her petite frame. I cradled her face in my hands and kissed her while I got lost in her. Lost in the feeling of becoming one with this woman.

I slid my hand down and stroked her clit softly while we

unraveled together. "I'm gonna come," I whispered in her ear while my thrusts got more erratic.

"Please, baby, take what you need from me. I'm yours," she moaned.

I wished that were true.

She dug her nails into my back while my orgasm wracked through my body. I came in long, hot spurts until it dripped down her thighs. Warning bells went off at the sight, but in the aftermath of my orgasm, I wasn't thinking about the consequences.

I groaned against her chest and laid my head there for a moment while I caught my breath. She ran her fingers through my short-cropped black hair and sighed in contentment.

I pulled out of her and didn't register something was missing—something super important that we *never* forgot, especially since Avery wasn't on the pill. I pulled her onto my chest, and we passed out naked in my bed.

In the morning, she was gone, but that wasn't unusual. I didn't recognize it as a sign that anything was wrong. I didn't know then that our lives were about to be turned upside down.

CHAPTER THREE

AVERY

NOVEMBER

2 MONTHS LATER

My period was two whole months late. I was never late. Ever.

When I started waking up and getting sick last month, I knew something was wrong. I was old enough to recognize the signs of pregnancy, but I didn't want to admit it. When my period didn't come again this month, I convinced myself it was because Thanksgiving was a couple of weeks away, and I was already feeling stressed about the holidays.

I didn't want to admit I was pregnant with Nolan's baby.

"Are you sure you don't have the flu or something?" Gemma asked from across the kitchen table, stirring her burrito bowl in thought.

Gemma lived in South Philly but commuted to the

brewery in Drakesville. When we could, we'd have dinner together before her shift. I tried to cancel tonight, but she insisted. My sister could be needy.

I shrugged and pushed my untouched bowl of food out of the way. I had zero appetite tonight.

"PMS?" she asked.

I stared back at her in silence.

"Avs, when did you last get your period?"

"Not since before the Arts Fest," I admitted in a low whisper.

Her eyes turned to saucers. "That was two months ago!"

I cringed. "Maybe it's stress?"

Gemma looked horrified.

When Gemma was in college, she had a pregnancy scare, and I drove all the way up to State College to be with her. She didn't want kids, and an unplanned pregnancy hadn't been in the cards. She ended up not being pregnant and got her period the next day, but to this day, she was always stressed if it was late. If Gemma had been in my shoes, she wouldn't have ignored the signs. She would have taken a pregnancy test the day her period was late.

She stood up and put on her coat.

I furrowed my brow at her. "Where are you going?"

She glared at me. "Going to the pharmacy to get a pregnancy test."

Before I could argue, she ran down the steps and out of my apartment. I cringed at my door slamming shut behind her.

Gemma was gone for maybe fifteen minutes before she clomped back up the steps and waved a bag of pregnancy tests in my face.

"Come on, let's take these," she said and led me into my bathroom.

Ten minutes later, we stared down at the third and final pregnancy test and waited for the results. The first two tests were positive, so I didn't have a good feeling about this one. I knew I was pregnant before those pink lines showed up on the first test, but I didn't want to accept it. I ignored what my body told me and tried to will the pregnancy away. I had even been avoiding Nolan because if I had seen him, I would have burst into tears and told him everything.

My timer chimed, and I handed the testing stick to my sister. "Please look. I can't."

She gave me a sympathetic smile. "Oh, Avs," she cooed and squeezed my hand in comfort.

"I'm pregnant, aren't I?" I sobbed.

She reached out and grabbed my hand. "What do you want to do?"

"What do you mean?"

"Avery, do you want to keep the baby? Or do you want to, you know..."

"Get an abortion?" I snarled at her. I pulled my hand out of her grasp and put it protectively over my stomach.

I had no problem with women who wanted to choose that route, but I didn't think I could do that. I had always wanted to be a mother, just not like this.

Gemma blew out a breath. "Okay. Does the father know?"

I shook my head.

"Do you... know who the father is?"

My mouth hung open at her question.

"What the fuck?" I snapped.

She held up her hands in surrender. "You go on a lot of dates. I'm not slut-shaming you, sis. But..."

"There's only been one guy in the last two years," I admitted but couldn't look at her.

Nolan and I had kept our affair quiet. That was the point when you had a secret friend with benefits. No one was supposed to know.

"Okay, how about we talk to him?"

I shook my head. "He's gonna hate me."

Gemma glared at me. "This is his fault too."

"We usually remember to use a condom."

My sister held up her hand. "Wait, a second. You sleep with this guy on the reg? Not a one-night stand?"

I nodded.

"Who?"

I stared blankly at her.

Gemma's eyes widened as realization dawned on her. "Oh my god!"

"He's gonna hate me. He doesn't want to be tied down. He's always made that perfectly clear."

"You and Nolan have been fucking this whole time?"

"Off and on, not all the time."

"Avs, you gotta tell him."

I cried into my hands.

She came over and wrapped her arms around me. "Nolan's a good man. He'll stand by whatever you want to do."

"Gem?"

"What?"

"I don't want to baby trap him."

Gemma wiped my tears away. "Oh, Avs, you have feelings for him, don't you?"

I nodded. "Gem, I've been in unrequited love with Nolan freaking MacGregor for over a year."

She squeezed me tighter. "Oh, sis. I had no idea. I thought you were just friends. I hoped you'd both realize you were meant to be eventually, but I had no clue you were sleeping together."

I shook my head and let the tears fall to the floor. "That was the whole point. It was supposed to stay a secret. He's never gonna feel the same way, and now we're gonna have a baby, and he's gonna hate me.'

"He won't hate you, but you have to tell him how you feel."

"Why?"

No way Nolan felt the same way. He made it perfectly clear he had zero feelings. He said his divorce had been amicable, but I got the feeling his ex-wife ripped his heart out of his chest and never gave it back.

I shook my head. "I can't."

"You have to tell him about the baby at least," she urged.

"Gem... what if he doesn't believe me? What if he wants nothing to do with us?"

She raised an eyebrow at me. "Are we talking about the same Nolan MacGregor? He may have that whole stoic lumberjack thing going on, but he's a good man. He'll want to provide for you and the baby."

I wasn't convinced.

"He raised Declan when their parents died. He knows how to take care of people."

I shook my head. "That's not the same thing. Declan was twelve, and this is a baby. A baby we didn't plan for."

My sister put a hand on my belly. "If he doesn't want to be involved with you and the baby, I've got you. We can do this. You want to be a mom, right?"

I nodded. "I thought I would have a husband first."

She shrugged. "Sometimes the universe is an asshole, and you have to roll with the punches."

"Gem, we haven't talked since that night. I've been avoiding him."

"Why?"

I squeezed my eyes shut. "Because I knew I was pregnant weeks ago, but I was in denial. I could stay blissfully ignorant if I didn't have to face him."

She shoved my phone at me. "Call him. You need to speak to him."

My hand shook as I took my phone from my sister and dialed Nolan's number. It rang until it went to voicemail, and I hung up.

Gemma gave me a sad smile. "He might be in the hops room or doing inventory. It's almost time for my shift. I better get going. You want me to say something to him?"

I shook my head. "Please don't."

She hugged me one last time. "I love you, big sis. You're gonna be a great mom, and I highly doubt Nolan will abandon you and the baby. He's not that kind of guy."

"I wish mom were here."

Gemma frowned.

Our mom died of cancer when Gemma was eight and I was eighteen. I had been away at college when she died, but Gemma had been so young that I didn't think mom's death affected her as much as it had me. It was moments like this that I wished my mom were here. She would have put a comforting arm around me and told me everything would be okay. Even if I was sure nothing would ever be okay again.

Gemma straightened her spine. "Mom would say that everything's gonna work out in the end. No matter what, I'm here for you."

I hugged her tightly. "Thank you."

"But not right now. I need to go to work."

I waved her off. "Go, don't be late."

I watched my sister walk out of my bathroom and heard the front door slam as she left.

Sighing, I stared down at the positive pregnancy test. I couldn't believe how irresponsible I had been.

I went back into my kitchen and tried to eat the rest of my dinner, but I felt too sick to my stomach to keep anything down. Instead, I crawled into bed early and cried myself to sleep.

Around midnight, I woke to my phone buzzing on my bedside table. "Hello?" I said into the phone groggily.

"Did I wake you?" Nolan's voice asked.

"S'okay," I said sleepily.

"Sorry, I've been buried in inventory spreadsheets, but Gem said you needed to talk to me."

I sighed. Of course Gemma would go against my wishes.

"Can you come over?"

There was a beat of pause.

"Now?"

"Now, Nolan. It's really important," I cried.

"Avs, are you okay?" he asked. I heard the worry in his voice.

Nolan hated when women cried. I think it was why we became friends. We met after a man left me with the check at the brewery and I cried into my beer over another unsuccessful date. Nolan had the bartender send me another beer on the house, and that's how this whole affair started. I knew one day it would end. I just didn't think it would be because I got pregnant.

I sighed. "No."

"Avs, what's wrong?"

"It's... can you just come over?"

"Okay..." He sounded unsure, but I couldn't tell him I was pregnant with his baby over the phone. "Are you gonna explain why you've been avoiding me?"

I cringed. I hoped he hadn't noticed. Nolan wasn't a clingy guy, but I guess it was obvious when I'd been leaving his texts unanswered and avoiding the brewery at all costs.

"Yes, but I can't do it over the phone."

"Okay. I'll be over in a bit," he said in a whisper and then hung up.

I lay back on my bed and tried to think about the best way to tell him. How was I supposed to tell a man who never wanted to be tied down that I was about to complicate his life? That we would be inexplicably connected for the rest of our lives?

I jolted at a loud knock on my door. I hadn't realized how long I had been lying in my bed trying to figure out my next move. The brewery was a short walk to my apartment, so it didn't take Nolan that long to get here.

I got out of bed and walked down the steps to my front door. When I opened the door to find Nolan furrowing his brow in concern, I burst into tears.

He wrapped his arms around me and held me to his big, burly chest. "Hey, hey, what's going on?"

I felt the tears falling down my face again, and I tried to shake them away. Okay, this might be pregnancy hormones. I had never been this weepy before.

"You're gonna hate me," I cried and clung to his flannel jacket.

He tipped my chin up to look at him. "Let's go inside so you can tell me what's wrong."

I wiped my tears away but felt queasy. I wasn't sure if that was the pregnancy or my nerves. Maybe a little of both.

I pulled away from Nolan and walked back up the

stairs. His loud footsteps followed behind me. I walked into my bedroom at the back of the apartment and sat on my bed in defeat. Nolan toed off his shoes and sat on the bed next to me.

"Tell me," he urged.

"I'm pregnant," I sobbed.

He was silent beside me, but he didn't storm out or call me a liar, so that had to be a good sign. I couldn't look at him, though. I couldn't bear to see the look of disappointment on his face.

"Are you sure?" he asked after what felt like a full minute passed.

I nodded. "It's why I've been avoiding you. I took three tests tonight."

"Oh. Oh, Avs."

My vision swam from the tears that I couldn't stop coming. I looked over at him, and he didn't look mad, but his brow was still furrowed.

"You're not mad?"

He looked taken aback at my question. He cupped my face in his hands and wiped my tears away. "Avery, no. You should be mad at me."

"Why?"

"Because I forgot to wrap it up. I never do that because I know you're not on the pill. It was so irresponsible. I wanted to talk to you about that, but you've been ignoring me."

"I was in denial. I couldn't talk to or see you when I didn't want to believe what was happening."

"What do you want to do?" he asked.

"I want a baby. This wasn't exactly how I planned on having one, but I'm thirty-five. This might be my last chance to become a mother. I'm having this baby."

He slid a hand between us and placed it on my stomach. "I want to be involved. We're in this together."

"Really?"

"Of course. I promise I'm here for you, okay? Both of you."

"Will you stay the night?" I asked. "I want to be held."

"Whatever you want."

I nodded but stood up and went into the bathroom. The pregnancy tests were still on the counter, so I tossed them in the trash. I splashed water on my face, but it was still splotchy and red from crying. Nolan reacted better than I thought he would. I thought he would never want to speak to me again. Gemma was right. He was a good man, and I wasn't sure why I had been so worried.

When I came back into my bedroom, Nolan had stripped down to his boxers and was lying in my bed. If I didn't feel so sick, the sight of his deliciously thick body in my bed would have made me horny. Sex was the last thing on my mind, though. Sex was the reason we ended up in this situation. I didn't want that tonight. I wanted Nolan to tell me everything was going to be okay, that we would be okay.

I got into the bed beside him and lay down on my side. He held me tight, his hand firmly on my stomach like he was trying to protect both of us already.

He kissed my temple. "Avery?"

"Yeah?"

"I'm not mad, okay? We'll figure this out together."

"Okay," I whispered, but I wasn't sure I believed him.

CHAPTER FOUR

NOLAN

I jolted awake at the sound of retching from the other room. I jumped up and ran into the bathroom to find Avery kneeling over the toilet.

"Oh, Avs," I sighed.

I bent down and gathered up the ends of her hair so it was out of her face. I rubbed her back until she finished. She got to her feet with a groan and wiped her mouth.

"Can I make you breakfast?" I offered.

She peeled off her clothes and turned on the shower, not acknowledging my question. I tried not to stare at the generous curves of her body, but my dick thickened against my leg as if in spite.

She fixed me with a glare and pointed at my crotch. "First, get that thing away from me. Second, I don't think I can keep anything down."

"Toast? You gotta eat something."

She grimaced. "I feel like I'm gonna throw up again."

"Try, okay?"

She nodded and stepped into the shower. My lizard brain definitely would have loved to be in there with her. Instead, I walked into the kitchen and started making her toast.

It broke my heart last night when she asked if I was mad about the pregnancy. We had both been irresponsible that night. Of course, I wasn't mad because it was both of our faults.

Deep down, the prospect of being a father excited me. Part of the reason my marriage failed was that I wanted kids, and Kath didn't. It took years to figure out we wanted different things. Avery and I might not have planned the baby, but we could have the family I always dreamed of together.

The toaster dinged, and I took out the bread before spreading a little butter on each slice. I made coffee, even though I wasn't sure if Avery could drink it. Could pregnant people drink coffee? I was looking it up on my phone when she came into the kitchen with a towel wrapped around her.

"Oh, you made coffee, thanks," she said and poured herself a cup.

"Can you drink that?" I asked and raised an eyebrow.

"One cup a day, and I'm going to need it if I have to deal with eleventh graders today."

I handed her the toast.

She squeezed my bicep. "Thanks. Sorry, I'm moody this morning."

I placed a hand on her stomach. "Come on, Peanut, give your mama a break, huh?"

Her eyes got all shiny. "You want to call the baby 'Peanut'?"

"Aw, Avs, don't cry over that."

"I'm sorry," she muttered and shoved the toast in her mouth. "It's the hormones."

I rubbed her belly again. "We don't know if it's a boy or girl yet. I feel like 'Peanut' is good enough for now."

She pulled away and set her half-eaten toast down on the counter. She ran her hand through her hair and grimaced while she stared down at the piece of bread.

"What's wrong?" I asked.

She sighed. "Nothing, I just gotta get to work."

"Okay..."

She stared at me expectantly.

"Oh. You want me to leave?"

"Yeah, sorry, I need to get ready for work."

I frowned and noticed she looked a little pale. Maybe the toast was a bad idea.

"Are you okay?"

She shook her head. "Can you please leave? I want to throw up again, and I don't want you to see."

I reached out and brushed her hair behind her ear. "I don't mind holding back your hair."

"Please, Nol?"

"Let me help you."

She sighed. "Can you just go? We'll talk about everything later."

I nodded, but I didn't like that she was dismissing me. I wanted to be there for her. Even if that meant holding back her hair while she hurled. I didn't mind the hard stuff, but she had to let me help.

"Okay, call me later?" I asked, hopefully.

She nodded, and I reluctantly walked out of her apartment.

We still had a lot to talk about. Last night, she needed to be held and told everything was going to be okay. This morning, that wasn't enough. I had to do right by her. I had to provide for her and the baby. I couldn't do that if she was living in her tiny duplex apartment. I had to convince her to move in with me. Somehow. Her kicking me out so quickly this morning didn't make it easy, though. Even if it was because she felt like she was going to throw up again. I would have held her hair and rubbed her back through that. I didn't like that she was pushing me away.

I walked down the street to my house on the other side of town, but I made a detour to my brother's apartment first.

Declan lived in an apartment above the tattoo shop. When our parents died, I inherited our childhood home. Dec moved out a couple of years ago because he wanted his own space. I think he just liked that it was literally two doors down from the brewery.

Normally, I would have waited since we both worked late last night, but this was serious business, and I needed his advice. I keyed into the outer door and walked up the steps. I banged on the front door to his apartment and waited for him to answer.

"What?" my brother snapped when he swung open the door wearing nothing but boxer briefs. He squinted at me, a sign I woke him up too early, and he hadn't put his contacts in yet.

"I need to talk to you," I urged.

"It couldn't wait until later?" he growled.

I shook my head.

He must have seen the look of anguish across my face, because he let me in and led me over to his couch. "You need coffee?" he asked.

"Please," I said as I slumped onto the couch.

He went into his bedroom and came back with more clothes on and his plastic-rimmed glasses shoved on his face.

He sent me an annoyed look, but walked into his tiny kitchen and started making coffee.

"What was so urgent you needed to pound on my door so early?" he asked from the kitchen.

"Avery's pregnant."

He rustled around in the kitchen and came back with two cups of steaming coffee. He raised an eyebrow at me and handed me a cup as he took a seat beside me.

"What does that have to do with you?" he asked.

I took a sip of coffee and then put the mug down on the coffee table. "Let me rephrase... Avery's pregnant with my baby."

"Oh... oh fuck!" he exclaimed, and then he glared at me. "I knew there was something up with you two."

"I..."

"You were so weird with her at the Arts Fest."

"What do you mean?" I asked and scowled.

I wasn't weird with her. What did he mean by that?

He rolled his eyes. "Gem said you had been a grouch all morning, and as soon as Avs came over, your entire demeanor changed. Then we watched you feed her dumplings."

"She was being moody and not eating carbs like I knew she wanted to. That asshole she went out with said she needed to lose a few pounds. Fuck that guy."

"It was kind of intimate, man."

"Dec, it wasn't a one-time thing."

He narrowed his eyes at me. "What?"

"We've had a casual thing going."

"Seriously?"

I nodded.

Declan frowned at me. "How long, Nol?"

"Two years," I admitted and took another sip of coffee.

Declan's eyes widened. "Two years?"

"Not consistently. We'd hook up occasionally."

My brother steepled his hands in front of his face. "Why was it casual?"

I furrowed my brow. "What do you mean, why?"

"Why have a secret casual thing?"

"Because she deserves someone better. Someone who won't fail her, like I failed Kath."

He scoffed. "You and Kath got married way too young. You wanted different things. That doesn't mean you 'failed' Kath. And it doesn't mean you need to close yourself off from love."

"I..."

"You love Avery, don't you?"

I stared at him. Of course, I loved Avery. That was the problem. She didn't love me back.

He kicked me. "Tell the truth. Has there been anyone else since her?"

I rubbed the back of my neck. I didn't want to get into this with him. He didn't need to know about my sex life or how Avery had been the only woman in my bed for the last two years. There had definitely been some offers, but I wasn't interested. Not unless they were the petite, raven-haired school teacher.

"Nolan!"

"No. She's been the only one," I whispered.

I never admitted that out loud before. Not even to myself.

"It sounds like you've been dating without the title."

I shook my head. "No. She doesn't want me that way. She only wants me for a good time."

"Why do you think that?"

"She goes on all those dates."

"You don't see how she looks at you with stars in her eyes, do you?"

I shook my head at him. He was full of shit. She didn't look at me that way. Whatever the fuck that meant, anyway.

"What are you gonna do?" Declan asked and sipped on his coffee, waiting for my answer.

I drank my coffee in thought.

I wanted to support her and the baby. I wanted to give her what she had been searching for. I could do that if I asked her to marry me. That way, she didn't have to raise the baby in her tiny apartment. We could be happy together as a family. She wanted a husband and family so badly, and I could give her everything she wanted. If she let me.

I stroked my beard. "I'm gonna ask her to marry me."

Declan held up his hand. "Whoa, timeout. I think that's rushing things. Just because you got her pregnant doesn't mean you need to marry her."

He was wrong. The more I thought about it, the more I knew I had to marry her. It might just take some convincing.

"It's the right thing to do."

He pinned me with a glare. "Is it the right thing to do or what you *want* to do?"

"I want to do it. I can make her happy."

He kicked my foot. "Dude, you need to tell her how you feel. Asking her to marry you because you don't know how to express your feelings isn't the way to go. She'll think you're just doing it for the baby. And you're not, are you?"

I shook my head. "No. Not just because of the baby. Because I love her, and I know I can give her the family she's always wanted."

"Then you have to tell her that, asshole! You're perfect for each other, but you have to actually use your words."

I put my coffee down on the table and let his words

wash over me. I still had a lot of thinking to do about the whole situation. I could give Avery what she wanted, but the way she kicked me out today made it feel like she'd never want that from *me*. We could be happy together. I just had to figure out how to convince her of that.

"I better go. I have some things to think through before going to the brewery," I told my brother with an air of finality.

"Nol..." Declan trailed off with a sigh. He took his glasses off and rubbed the bridge of his nose.

"I'll see you later," I said and stood up.

He didn't argue or stop me from leaving. I walked out of his apartment and down the steps, walking the short block home in thought. I was still mulling it all over when I stepped into the house.

I went into the office and pulled my mother's ring from the safe. Instead of a diamond, the center stone was an emerald with two tiny diamonds on each side. I hadn't given it to Kath when I proposed because she liked flashy things. Mom's ring hadn't been meant for Kath, but maybe it could be for Avery. At forty, this might be my last chance to find someone to share my life with. My last chance to become a father and have a family.

I sighed and put the ring back in the safe. If I was going to support my baby mama, I needed to make sure the brewery was producing the best beer we could. I owed that much to Avery and the baby.

CHAPTER FIVE

AVERY

"How are you feeling?" my doctor asked as she looked up from my chart.

"Exhausted."

"That's normal. Morning sickness?"

I nodded. "Yes. Will it ever stop?"

The Asian woman laughed. "I don't want to lie to you and say yes, but some women have it the whole time."

I groaned. "You said I was at high risk. Should I be concerned?"

She looked at my chart. "Because of your age, you're technically referred to as having a geriatric pregnancy."

I made a face at that phrase.

She laughed. "It's just a medical term. You're healthy, and everything looks good so far. Is the father involved?"

I nodded.

"How's he feeling?"

I shrugged. "I don't know. He wants to support me, to provide for the baby. We're not exactly together."

"Ah."

I shrugged again.

"Complicated relationship aside, you're relatively healthy, so I think you'll be fine. Do you have questions for me?"

I stared at her, bewildered. I had a lot of questions, but I didn't know which one to ask first. This was my first pregnancy. I never even had a pregnancy scare before. I wasn't sure what to ask.

"Is sex on the table?" I blurted out. A crimson blush crept up my neck. I didn't know why that was the first question I asked.

She laughed. "Yes, but be aware of any pain. You can always readjust if something is uncomfortable."

"Okay."

"Make sure you take your prenatal vitamins and lean on the baby's father. Let him be your support system. Even if you aren't together."

I chewed on my lip. It had been a couple of days since I told Nolan about the baby. I'd been a little abrupt with him when I told him to leave. After he left my apartment, I felt like such a bitch, but I was so nauseous I just wanted him to go away. He was trying to be there for me, and I was cold and callous to him. That wasn't fair of me. I hoped I hadn't hurt his feelings, but maybe I should have asked him to come to this appointment with me.

Doctor Lee handed me a printout, and I took the grainy photo of the early sonogram from her. When I looked at the image, my heart climbed up into my throat. That tiny bean was growing inside me. Nolan and I had made this little life together.

"Oh..." I sighed as I looked at the image in my hands.

Doctor Lee smiled at me again and squeezed my hand.

"You're gonna do great. Make sure you're taking care of yourself, okay?"

"Okay."

I left the office, and my heart felt like it was going to burst. I drove back to my tiny apartment and realized I was exhausted and hungry. I cut out of school early to get a later appointment, and now I was too tired to make dinner. I got out of my car, and instead of going upstairs, I made the short walk over to the brewery.

The brewery was probably the coolest place in Drakesville. It used to be an old Rolls Royce showroom bought by another brewery before Nolan and Declan bought it. The old owners spent all their money on decor and ended up going under. When the MacGregor Brothers bought it, they didn't have to do a lot of remodeling. There was already a bar, bathrooms, and a place for Nolan to brew beer. He just had to bring in his own equipment. At first, they only had beer, but they turned it into a fully functioning brewpub with a full kitchen over the past couple of years. It was my favorite place in town, and all my favorite people worked there.

I spied my sister's pink hair behind the bar when I walked inside. My sister and I couldn't be more different. Where I was petite with dark hair, Gemma was tall and lanky and had been dying her hair bright pink since she was a teenager. She had a sleeve tattoo of black and grey flowers down one of her arms, so paired with the bright hair, she stood out.

I walked over to the bar and sat down on a barstool. Gemma gave me a brief wave while she poured beers for a group of rowdy co-eds. One of the other bartenders, Felix, came over and dropped a coaster in front of me. Felix had that edgy tattooed bad boy look about him, but he was a total softie. And also a huge flirt.

He leaned on the bar, and Gemma made an annoyed face behind his back. For whatever reason, my sister and Felix didn't get along, and I didn't know why. Any time I pressed her, she changed the subject. I'd get it out of her one day.

"Hey, Avs, you want that new pumpkin beer?" Felix asked and gave me a wink.

"No," I said with a frown. I really wished I could have enjoyed more of that beer before its creator knocked me up. "Can I get a water and a menu? I'm so hungry."

His eyebrow quirked up in confusion. "No beer? But Nolan made that one specifically for you."

I wrinkled my nose. I didn't think that was true. Nolan liked to experiment with different beers. My liking pumpkin beers was just an excuse for him to make one.

Gemma came over to us and shot Felix a glare. "Felix, fuck off. I need to talk to my sister."

He held up his hands in surrender. "Touchy, touchy."

Gemma nodded her head at the two women seated at the other end of the bar. "Go help those two. I got this."

He winked at her sardonically and walked to the other end of the bar. Gemma plunked a water down in front of me and handed me a menu.

I perused it with a groan. "I don't think I can eat any of this stuff."

"Get a salad. The goat cheese one is so good!"

"I can't!" I cried.

"Why not?" Gemma asked, twirling her pink hair around her finger.

"No soft cheeses! Or sushi. Or fish at all. Or deli meat."

"No hoagies?" Gemma asked in shock. "Remind me to never get pregnant."

"Zero out of ten, do not recommend," I said. I scanned the menu again. "Can I get the burger, but make sure it's well done?"

Gemma smiled at me. "You got it."

I watched her put my order into the system, and my eyes scanned up to the TV screen above my head. The hockey game was on, and the Bulldogs were getting creamed by New York. Our mutual love for hockey might have been the reason Nolan and I became such good friends in the first place. Not liking hockey was practically against the law in my house; dad was a Bulldogs fiend.

I checked my phone to see what time it was and realized it wasn't late enough for me to be this tired. Incubating a baby was exhausting, and I wasn't even that far along yet. I pulled the printout from my pocket and looked at it again.

"You look like you're glowing!" Declan's voice pulled me from my thoughts.

"Hey, Dec."

He nodded toward the piece of paper in my hands. "Did you show that to Nol yet?"

"You know?" I asked.

I hadn't told Nolan not to tell anyone about the pregnancy, so it wasn't a shock his brother already knew.

Declan nodded. "Nol told me the next day after you kicked him out of your apartment."

I cringed. Maybe I had hurt Nolan's feelings when I dismissed him like that. Pregnancy mood swings were no joke.

I looked down at the grainy image of our baby. "No, I haven't shown him yet. We haven't spoken since I told him about the baby."

Declan's gaze slid over to the windowed wall on the other side of the bar. Nolan and one of the other brewers looked like they were in a heated argument.

Declan's whiskey brown eyes connected with mine. "Actually, seeing you might cheer him up."

"Cheer him up?"

Declan sighed. "We found out the tank's calibration was off and had to dump a whole batch."

"Oh, no!"

He nodded. "Yup. Safe to say, Nol's not in the best mood."

I cringed. "I'm probably the last person he wants to see then."

Declan gave me a funny look, but we were interrupted by Gemma cursing loudly at Felix while he laughed in her face. "Christ, those two."

"What's the deal?" I asked.

"Beats me, woman! They're either gonna kill each other or..."

"Or what?"

Declan waggled his eyebrows at me.

"Gross!" I scoffed.

We were interrupted again when one of the food runners brought my burger. I cut into it to make sure they cooked it thoroughly and then bit into it with a low moan. Declan walked off to go break up the argument between my sister and the other bartender.

One day Gemma would tell me why she couldn't stand Felix. I didn't get it because Felix was her type of man with his sleeve tattoos and piercings. Most of the women she dated looked like that, too. Felix seemed so nice; I wished she would just tell me what was up with that.

I was cramming fries into my mouth when I turned and

saw Nolan sitting next to me. His grumpy face turned up into a smile, and his broad shoulders shook with laughter as he watched me fight to swallow.

"Hi," I finally greeted after I wiped my mouth with a napkin.

He ran a hand through his beard. "Hey, you. How are you feeling?"

"Like hot garbage?"

He frowned. "I'm sorry."

"S'okay. The doctor said it's normal. Pretty sure I'll throw this up tomorrow."

His brow furrowed. "You went to the doctor?"

"Yeah? I had to make sure it was a real pregnancy. Everything looks good." He frowned at me, so I slid the sonogram over to him. "Here."

He took the printout, and his face immediately transformed into a grin again. "Oh... oh. Is that our little Peanut?"

That was growing on me. It was cute that he had a nickname for the baby already.

I nodded.

He placed a hand on my belly while his finger traced the tiny bean-sized figure on the image. "I would have gone with you."

"It was a long appointment."

"I want to be there."

"I know. You can come to the next one."

He beamed and kissed my temple. I froze at that. He never made any type of public display of affection with me before. It must have shocked a lot of his workers because Felix's eyes narrowed as he watched Nolan massage the back of my neck. I melted into Nolan's touch because I was sore and achy, and his big hands felt good on my skin.

"Did you drive over?" he asked and handed the photo back to me.

I slid it into my purse and shook my head. "Walked."

"I'll drive you home."

"I can walk."

"I don't want you to."

I rolled my eyes at his protectiveness. "Walking isn't going to hurt the baby."

He grunted at me. "Just let me, okay?"

"Stop treating me like glass. I'm pregnant, not dying."

"Avs, don't be like that."

I motioned for my sister to give me the check. She raised an eyebrow in concern but went to get it for me. I signed the check and left her a hefty tip.

"Avery," Nolan tried again.

Tears stung my eyes. I was being a bitch to him for no reason. I could blame it on my hormones, but maybe I was being unreasonable.

I turned and looked at him, and his face crumbled when he saw my tear-stained cheeks.

He pulled me into his arms and wiped my tears away. "I want to be involved. I want to know how the baby's doing."

"The baby you don't want."

He slanted his eyes at me in confusion. "When did I say that? I never said I didn't want the baby. Stop pushing me away."

"I think I better go before you resent me even more."

"I don't resent you."

"You will," I muttered.

He gingerly pushed my hair behind my ear and cupped my face in his hands. "I don't resent you, okay?"

I shook my head.

"Avery," he sighed. "I know we didn't plan for Peanut, but I'm here for you and the baby. You know that, right?"

"Okay," I muttered.

He shocked me when he slanted his mouth over mine, right there at the bar in front of everyone. All our kisses before had been in secret. In the shadows and behind closed doors where nobody could see. This was out in the open like he didn't care who saw us. He kissed me slow and tenderly, and I faded into his touch like I always did. Like I always would. It was the kind of kiss that made me feel safe and warm. Made me feel loved.

"Come to my place so we can talk?" he asked when he pulled away.

"It's a school night."

"I'll drive you home afterward."

"Okay," I conceded, and I wasn't sure why I did.

Maybe it was because when he kissed me, my heart wanted to pretend it meant he felt the same way I did. But my head knew better. Nolan might want me in his bed, but never in his heart.

CHAPTER SIX

NOLAN

*A*very was quiet on the walk over to my house. I hated her living in that tiny upstairs apartment. It was right across the street from the school where she taught, but I had a big house all to myself. It would be the perfect place to raise our child. I needed to figure out a way to convince her to marry me and move in.

I held the front door open for her, and she walked inside. She took off her shoes while I locked up. She looked exhausted, as evidenced by how she flopped down on my couch. I went to grab her a glass of water, but when I walked back into the living room, her eyes were closed, and she had passed out. So much for having that talk tonight.

I bent down to carry her upstairs. She stirred. "Nolan?"

"Yeah?"

"What are you doing?"

I huffed as I walked up the steps with her in my arms. "You passed out on the couch. I'm taking you upstairs to bed."

"Mmm. Growing a baby is tough work."

I smiled down at her and kicked open the bedroom door. I gently set her down on the bed. "You're doing amazing, okay? You want to get out of these clothes? I can give you one of my shirts to sleep in."

"I love sleeping in your shirts. They smell like you and make me feel like you're hugging me," she slurred sleepily.

Her words struck me in the chest, but I knew she didn't mean it the way I wanted her to.

She slid her dress pants off, and when she unbuttoned her blouse, my eyes widened at how her tits spilled out of her bra. "Don't even think about it. They hurt so much."

"Aw, Avs. I'm sorry."

She unclipped her bra with a relieved sigh, and I went over to my dresser to pull out an old t-shirt. My 2XL t-shirt would look like a long dress on her petite frame, but I wasn't about to let my baby mama sleep in her work clothes. I went to hand it to her, but she had already crawled underneath the covers and was fast asleep. I smiled at that; she looked good naked in my bed. I wished she could always be there, wished that I could wake up every morning to her cute sleepy smile.

I left the t-shirt on my side of the bed and tip-toed downstairs. I sat in my living room reading the pregnancy book my brother had thrown at my head yesterday. If I was going to do right by her, I wanted to be prepared for the baby to come. The mood swings were normal. I just had to roll with the punches. Hopefully not literally.

An hour later, I slid into bed beside Avery. She must have woken up at some point because she was now wearing my shirt. As I expected, it fell to her knees. She was such a little thing.

She stirred and curled herself into my arms. "Nolan?"

"Shush, go back to sleep," I whispered and kissed the top of her head.

"I'm so tired, Nolan. I've never felt this tired before."

I slid my hand over her stomach. "I know. Peanut needs all that energy to grow."

"What if I'm bad at this? What if I'm a terrible mother?"

I tilted her chin up. "Hey, you're gonna be a great mother."

"Promise?"

I kissed her forehead. "Promise. Now go to sleep."

She settled into my chest, and I felt her breathing getting steady as she fell back asleep.

Sleep was a challenge for me. I lay in bed with her curled around me and thought of my next step. I wanted to prove to her I could be worthy of her, but instead, I had given her an unplanned pregnancy and a lot of uncertainty.

I woke with a start to the sound of someone throwing up. Immediately, I rushed into the bathroom and found Avery once again hugging the toilet and crying.

Did pregnant people cry all the time?

I kneeled down beside her and rubbed her back. "Shush, it's okay, get it all out."

"It's like this every morning. I hate this so much, Nol," she sobbed over the porcelain bowl.

I hated that. I hated that she was feeling awful because of the growing baby inside her. I didn't know how to help her, so I rubbed her back until she finished.

She wiped her mouth and took a swig of mouthwash.

"You get sick every morning?" I asked.

She nodded.

"Avery?"

"Yeah?" she asked while she walked back into my bedroom and started putting her clothes on.

I tried not to stare at her tits popping out of her bra while she attempted to put it on. She might not look that pregnant yet, but her tits had definitely gotten bigger.

"I have to ask you something, and I don't want you to freak out."

She raised an eyebrow at me in confusion. "Okay..."

"Move in here?"

She stared at me. "What?"

"Your apartment's too small to raise a baby in. I have this house all to myself. We can raise the baby here, and it won't feel cramped."

She rubbed her fingers between the bridge of her nose. "I know you feel you need to do right by me, but I don't have to move in here."

"Why not?"

"We're just friends who're having a baby together. How would we explain it when they got older? That Mommy and Daddy live together but aren't together?"

I sighed and went into my sock drawer and pulled out the ring. She was putting on her blouse and wasn't paying attention until she looked down and saw me kneeling in front of her.

"Will you marry me?" I asked.

"Nolan..." she breathed.

"Come on, Avery. We're gonna have a baby. Let's become a family too."

She shook her head. "We don't have to get married because you got me pregnant."

"Why not?"

"Because you told me you'd never get married again. I'm not trapping you into a loveless marriage because we made a mistake one night, and now we have to live with the consequences!"

"Avs, please."

She gestured to the ring in my outstretched hand. She took it but placed the box on the nightstand. "You're gonna be a great father, but it doesn't mean you have to force yourself into a marriage you don't want."

I'd forgotten I told her all that stuff about never wanting to get married again or how I wasn't a settle-down kind of guy. That wasn't true. I just didn't think I deserved it. Until I met her. One small smile from Avery could pull me from the depths of the foulest of moods. She unearthed all those feelings I locked away after my divorce. She made me yearn for something more.

Her saying no to my proposal was like Kath ripping my heart out all over again. It reminded me why, before Avery, I drowned myself in casual hookups.

I stood up from my kneeling position. "You still want a ride home?"

She nodded, and I saw the emotions swirling across her face. I didn't know what that expression meant. I steeled myself and threw on some clothes, trying not to think about how she crushed my heart into a million pieces. It wouldn't have been a loveless marriage for me, but I wouldn't force her into something she didn't want.

I went down the steps and grabbed my keys while I waited for her. We drove across town in terse silence.

"Thanks," she said in a quiet voice when I parked in front of her apartment.

I grunted in response.

She frowned but leaned over to kiss my cheek. "Do you want to come to my next prenatal appointment?"

"Yes."

"Okay..." she muttered meekly. "I'll call you later."

She got out of the car without another word. I wasn't sure why she sounded so sad. She was the one who rejected me.

I watched her cross the street and climb the stone steps until she reached the porch of the duplex. She waved, but I didn't return the gesture. I waited until she was safely inside before I banged my head on the steering wheel.

I drove home to sleep off my anger until I had to go into the brewery. Hopefully, I could fix the fuck up that happened yesterday with the tank calibration. Allen, my right-hand brewer, had mentioned something to me previously, but I had waved him off, saying it was fine. It wasn't fine, and now we were going to lose a lot of money because we had to dump a whole batch of beer.

When I got to the brewery, I was my usual grouchy self all day. Someone must have told Declan I was in a shit mood because he made me take a break with him in the office.

"Dude, what's your problem?" he asked through a mouthful of fries.

I picked at my food. "I asked Avery to marry me this morning."

He stared open-mouthed at me. "Oh."

"She basically told me to go fuck myself."

"Ohhh. Bro, all of this is coming at her fast. She just found out she's pregnant. She's probably scared and needs someone to support her."

"That's what I was trying to do," I argued and shoved some fries into my mouth.

"Sure. But what are you offering her? A marriage and a home, but love? Avery's a hopeless romantic. She wants to find her soulmate."

"I want to give that to her too."

He kicked my boot. "She doesn't know that! She thinks you only did it out of obligation. Man, you're really smart with brewing beers, but you're a dumb fuck when it comes to women."

"Are you any better?" I snapped back.

My brother had no room to talk. His bedroom had a revolving door because he still wasn't over his high school girlfriend breaking his heart years ago.

He shrugged. "Not about me right now. Give her time and show her it's not just because of the baby."

"But she doesn't want me!"

My brother ran a hand down his clean-shaven jaw in frustration. "Nol, why did you ask her to marry you?"

I sighed. "You know."

He glared. "Say it out loud."

"I already told you," I growled.

"Christ, you need to learn to talk about your feelings. Why did you ask Avery to marry you? Not because of the baby, right?"

"No, of course, not. It's because I love her, and I want to be worthy of her."

He stared at me for a long time. Declan had long accused me of being an emotionless robot. He said the only time he ever saw me show any emotion was when Kath finally left.

"Tell her how you feel."

"She already rejected me."

He groaned and banged his head on the desk. "Bro, you're dumb! She said no because she thinks you only asked because of the pregnancy. She has no clue how you feel about her. You have to tell her."

I mulled over my brother's words, but I wasn't sure how to do any of that. I thought I had done that when I offered Avery what she wanted more than anything. When she rejected me, it was clear she'd have my baby, but she'd never be *mine*.

CHAPTER SEVEN

AVERY

I cut a glare at Nolan as his knee bounced up and down while we waited for my OBGYN to start my check-up.

"Nol, stop," I snapped.

He gave me a sheepish look. "Sorry."

I gave him a tight smile. I shouldn't have snapped at him, especially since things had been off with us since I rejected his proposal a couple of weeks ago. Gemma said he had been moodier than usual and had made one of the new guys quit on the spot yesterday. Thanksgiving was tomorrow, and Nolan despised the holidays, so he was probably just being his typical Grinch self.

"Sorry, I'm moody," I offered.

He raised an eyebrow and pressed his lips to a thin line but was silent.

"Nol—"

I couldn't complete my thought because Dr. Lee came into the room. She looked at Nolan first since he hadn't been with me at the last appointment. She walked over to him and firmly shook his hand. "Hi, I'm Dr. Olivia Lee. You must be the father."

"Nolan MacGregor," he said as he broke the handshake.

"It's good to meet you," Dr. Lee said to him. Then she looked over at me and asked, "How are you feeling?"

"Okay," I lied.

"Avs, don't lie," Nolan cut in. He turned to my doctor while I glared at him. "She's been dealing with a lot of morning sickness. I got her one of those relief bands, but I'm not sure it has helped."

I fidgeted with the band around my wrist. Nolan had shown up at school during my free period one day to give it to me. When I expressed my surprise, he shrugged and said, 'you were complaining,' and then he left as quickly as he had come. That grumpy bear of a man confused me sometimes.

My doctor wrote something down on her chart. "Okay, that's normal, but maybe once you hit the second trimester, you'll be out of it. If the band works, use it."

I nodded. I knew that, but feeling sick and tired all the time sucked. I was supposed to hit the second trimester in December, and I had been counting down the days, hoping once I hit it, I would feel better.

She ran a couple of tests as we went through the rest of the check-up. She said everything was looking good, despite me being at high risk because of my age. Other than my morning sickness, which she thought would go away soon, she felt like we were in good shape. I wasn't having any further complications, so she wasn't worried.

"Do you have any other questions for me today?" she asked.

"Um... sex is a no, right?" Nolan asked.

I felt myself get flushed at that. I couldn't believe he asked that. We hadn't had sex since we conceived the baby, but it wasn't like we had it all that often beforehand. We only occasionally fell into bed together. I asked her that already, but I hadn't been keen on telling Nolan her answer.

"Nolan," I hissed in annoyance.

Dr. Lee tried to hide her smile. "Yes, if Avery's feeling up to it, sex should be okay. With a partner or on her own."

Little did Nolan know how much I had been using my vibrator.

"Everything looks good, you two. Have a happy Thanksgiving," she said to us before she left.

"Did you have to ask that?" I snapped.

He shrugged but was tight-lipped again.

"Nolan..."

"Whatever. I gotta get back to the brewery. I need to hire another new guy, and we're swamped."

"Hey, what are you doing for Thanksgiving, anyway?"

"Working," he grunted in a way that told me it was the end of the conversation.

I frowned.

I had hoped to ask Nolan to come to my dad's for Thanksgiving. Maybe I'd have the courage to finally tell my family about the baby if he came with me, but he didn't even give me the chance to ask. My sister and I were ten years apart because my mom had a couple of miscarriages in between us. I was scared of telling my dad I was pregnant on the off chance I lost the baby.

"Okay, I'll see you later," I whispered in defeat.

He nodded and then left me to get dressed by myself.

Even though we occasionally slept together, Nolan and I had always been friends first. I knew the baby would present some challenges, but I didn't like how grouchy he had been with me. I think I hurt his feelings when I said no to marrying him.

I got dressed and went back to work, but I could barely concentrate. I used my lunch and free period to make the appointment, so I didn't get a break between classes today.

After school, when I got back to my apartment, I checked my phone for the first time and saw a string of texts. I checked the ones from my sister first.

GEM: *What did you do to Nolan??*

GEM: *He's a supreme grumpy bear today!*

I typed back a shrug emoji. Her guess was as good as mine.

I scrolled through to the texts from the man himself.

NOLAN: *Sorry about today.*

I typed back a response. ME: *S'okay.*

I saw the dots of him typing, and I set my phone down to make dinner. My phone buzzed again while I waited for the water to boil for my pasta. I picked up my phone again and saw a second message from Nolan.

NOLAN: *No, it's not.*

ME: *You're right. It's not. You were a dick.*

NOLAN: *I'm sorry. I'm stressed, but I shouldn't have taken it out on you. Forgive me?*

I set my phone down on the counter and stared at the pot on the stove as I thought about how to respond to him. I knew this time of year wasn't his favorite, and I hadn't exactly been nice to him today, either. The stress of the baby was getting to both of us, but we needed to learn to not take it out of each other. I knew I wasn't doing the best job at that lately, either.

I picked my phone back up and sent him another text.

ME: *You're forgiven.*

NOLAN: *I'm here for you. For you and Peanut. Always.*

His words meant everything to me, even though I knew they weren't quite the ones I wanted to hear. Nolan would be a good father, but I wished I could have more from him.

"Is the bird done yet?" my dad called from the living room as I took the turkey out of the oven.

Today was Thanksgiving, which meant my favorite time of year was quickly upon us. Once we got through today, it would be time for me to break out my mom's recipe book and start making all my Christmas cookies. I loved the holidays, and making cookies with my mom had been a favorite pastime when I was a kid. I kept up the tradition after she passed, mainly to keep her memory alive. Someone had to continue the family traditions. God knew my sister had no interest.

My Aunt Karen and I rolled our eyes in unison at my dad's nagging. He had been asking that all morning. Yes, we were one of those weirdo families that ate Thanksgiving dinner at two o'clock in the afternoon.

I opened the oven and pulled out the turkey. Aunt Karen helped me check it was done.

Since mom died, my aunt and I tag-teamed Thanksgiving. Mainly because Dad and Gemma were useless in the kitchen. The same went for my cousin Mason and Uncle Bill.

"Almost!" I yelled back.

"We want to eat!" Uncle Bill called back.

Aunt Karen shook her head. "That man, I swear."

I laughed and wiped the sweat from my brow. It was hot in here, and I felt nauseous.

I was still dealing with morning sickness, which sometimes wasn't just in the morning. The relief band Nolan bought me had helped a little. Yesterday he came over to my apartment with ginger tea that he read might help too. That had been sweet of him, and I was grateful for it. Ever since my last appointment, he had been going out of his way to atone for being such a dick to me. I still felt like things were tense between us, and I wondered if our friendship could survive this pregnancy.

"I'm used to it. Bird looks good to me. Let's get the table set," I said to my aunt.

"GEMMA! MASON!" Aunt Karen yelled to my sister and my cousin. "Come in here and help set the table."

I gave her a small smile. "Thanks, Aunt Karen."

"They're doing the dishes tonight," she said with a grin. She gave my hand a little squeeze. "Your mother would be so proud of you, Avery."

"Thanks."

Aunt Karen could tell I was having a hard time today, but it wasn't for the reason she thought. She probably thought I was missing my mom. I missed my mom; I missed her every day, but that wasn't why I was off today. It was because the smells in the kitchen were making my morning sickness worse. I hadn't told my family I was pregnant yet, so I couldn't even complain about it. I didn't want to explain that I was pregnant and the father and I weren't together.

My sister and cousin set the table while my dad and uncle strolled in with MacGregor Brothers Brewing Company beers in both of their hands. Dad loved that Gemma worked at the brewery and we had befriended the owners. I wasn't sure how he'd feel when I told him one of them had knocked me up.

My Aunt said grace for everyone, and then we all dug in... except for me. I pushed my food around on my plate and had two bites of plain turkey with no gravy. Which sucked, but I didn't want to throw up again.

"You okay, Avery?" my aunt asked.

I didn't have to explain myself because my sister nearly jumped out of her chair. "Hell yes!" she cheered as she looked at her phone.

"What's up?" Dad asked as he gently pushed her back down in her seat. My sister could be a bit excitable.

"We got the tree lighting ceremony."

"The what now?" Uncle Bill asked.

"In Drakesville. You know how they do the tree lighting ceremony in the town square? The brewery applied for a booth this year, and they said yes."

"Really?" I asked.

That might have explained why Nolan looked super stressed lately. Some of the local restaurants sold hot chocolate and cider during the ceremony. Still, I don't remember the town ever letting any beer be sold before. I would have figured Sullivan's, the oldest bar in town, would have gotten that deal before the brewery.

"It was my idea," Gemma explained. "Nolan was so grumpy about it, but Declan always likes my ideas, and he's still handling the marketing."

"Nolan hates Christmas, that's why," I said as I tried to eat some of my potatoes.

I loved mashed potatoes, and Aunt Karen made them so good. Mine were usually okay but had lots of lumps. Aunt Karen's were always perfect, and it pissed me off my pregnancy wasn't letting me enjoy all the tasty food we made together.

"Such a Grinch," my sister agreed with the shake of her head.

"When is that?" Dad asked.

"Saturday," Gemma and I said in unison. We always went to the tree lighting ceremony together, but she was probably working if the brewery had a booth.

"That's kinda soon to put up the tree, isn't it?" Aunt Karen asked.

Gemma laughed. "Not for Avery! She usually puts her tree up after Halloween."

I ignored her and the rest of my family while I took out my phone and texted Nolan.

ME: *Congrats on the tree lighting ceremony.*

NOLAN: *I didn't want to do it.*

ME: *You just didn't want me to drag you to it again.*

NOLAN: *I'll see you there, tho, right?*

ME: *You know it!*

I put my phone away and tried to eat more of my dinner.

"You okay, honey?" my aunt asked.

I nodded and gave her a fake smile. "Just tired."

"Don't worry, Avs, we'll do the clean-up," my dad said as he took a sip of his beer. "I really like this holiday beer."

I was glad my dad thought I was tired from mine and Aunt Karen's work in the kitchen today.

"You want a beer, Avs?" my cousin Mason asked as he got up to grab another Holiday Hops from the fridge.

"Nah, too hoppy for me," I told him.

Luckily, I could use that excuse because my dad didn't have any of the MacGregor beers I liked in his fridge. Gemma got her taste for hoppy beers from him, but he usually kept some lager in the fridge for me. When we got here this morning before Aunt Karen arrived, Gemma found all of those and hid them in the extra fridge in dad's garage.

"It's so good!" Gemma argued. "Avs is such a basic bitch."

We shared a conspiratorial look, but no one noticed when she and Mason were teasing me mercilessly. I was grateful she hid those beers, and I'd rather endure the teasing than have to admit to the rest of my family the real reason I wasn't drinking.

After dinner, I scraped my food into the garbage disposal, which didn't go unnoticed by my aunt. "You sure you're okay?"

"Yeah, just exhausted. School has been busy lately."

She peered at me and studied my face. "You sure that's it?"

I nodded.

She squeezed my arm. "Okay, Avery, but you know you can talk to me, right?"

"I know. Thanks, Aunt Karen."

My sister rescued me by saying she wanted to drag me out to the mall for Black Friday shopping. I groaned, but she pressed me until I agreed. We said our goodbyes to our family, and when we got into my sister's car, she drove me to my apartment instead. We carpooled together, but I hadn't realized 'Black Friday Shopping' was a ruse.

"What did Aunt Karen say?" Gemma asked when she parked her car outside my apartment.

I groaned. "I think she knows I'm pregnant."

"You still don't want to tell them?"

I shook my head. "Not yet."

My sister flicked her pink hair behind her shoulder. "You should have invited Nolan."

"I tried. He's not interested."

She pursed her lips. "Is that why you don't want to tell them yet?"

"I'm afraid of losing the baby."

Gemma's face fell. "Oh, Avs. Because of what Mom went through?"

I nodded.

She pulled me into a big hug. "You're not gonna lose the baby. Everything's gonna be fine."

"What if I do?" I cried.

She hugged me tighter. "The doctor said everything's fine, right?"

I nodded.

"Then stop worrying! I know you're scared because Mom went through that, but I'm here for you no matter what. Nolan's here for you, too. Remember that."

I squeezed her tighter as she hugged me. "Thanks, sis."

"Hey, I know what will help you get your mind off of this."

"What?" I asked and pressed a hand against my cheek to wipe away the stray tears. My fears about miscarrying like my mom weren't helpful when I cried at everything lately.

Gemma clapped her hands excitedly. "Let's watch those cheesy Hallmark movies you love so much!"

I smiled at my sister; she knew exactly how to cheer me up. I loved Christmas, and one of my favorite things to do as the holidays got around was to melt my brain with those silly movies. Gemma teased me about how predictable they were, but I was a hopeless romantic. I loved a happily ever after.

Gemma nudged me. "Well?"

"You know I do!"

"You can pay me in cookies later."

I shook my head at her. She knew she would get a whole batch of her favorites, no matter what. "Thanks, sis."

"Come on! I want to find the most ridiculous one and make fun of it!"

I laughed and got out of the car, following her up to my apartment. Gemma was a lot of things—flighty, eccentric, and excitable—but when I needed her, she knew when to show up. It was okay if things with Nolan were off because I knew I had my sister to lean on.

CHAPTER EIGHT

NOLAN

"Go get the other keg. This one's kicked," I barked at Gemma.

She arched an eyebrow at me and flipped her pink hair over her shoulder, but she walked away and did what I asked without complaint.

"Nol, you gotta stop snapping at Gem," my brother chastised.

I finished pouring the last beer from our current keg and handed it off to a customer. The customer gave me his money, and I placed it in the lockbox while Gemma returned with the other keg. I hadn't expected to sell so much beer at the freaking tree lighting ceremony.

"Is your sister coming tonight?" Declan asked Gemma when she started setting up the new keg.

She shrugged.

Declan elbowed me. "Get out of here."

Gemma hip-bumped me out of the way as she took over

taking orders. I scowled and stood off to the side while looking out into the crowd gathered in the square tonight. Twenty minutes ago, the town lit up the Christmas tree, and now there was a local band playing music while the townsfolk milled about. When I looked out into the crowd, I realized I was looking for Avery.

I spotted her in front of the tree, talking to her friend Lizzie. Her smile shone brighter than the lights behind her like she was glowing. Maybe it was the pregnancy glow, or maybe it was because every time I looked at her, my heart felt like it would burst out of my chest.

I growled when I felt a jab in my ribs. "Go talk to her," Declan urged.

"You need my help," I told him with a hard look.

Declan gestured to Gemma and Felix, who were handling the customers while he supervised. He gave me a little shove. "Get out of here and take that grumpy attitude with you."

I scowled at him.

"Go talk to Avery," my brother insisted.

"Why?"

"Because she's the only one who can get you out of that grouchy mood. Go, dude, you being all growly is driving away customers," Gemma said as she poked my chest.

"Fine."

"And don't come back!" Declan yelled back at me.

If there weren't a bunch of kids around, I probably would have given him the finger while I walked off. Instead, I clenched my jaw and strode over to Avery and Lizzie. Avery jumped when I came up to her, but then her face softened when she saw it was me. Her smile split her face, and I felt my chest constrict at the sight. When she smiled at me like that, it melted my bad moods.

"Hey, can you hold her for a second?" Lizzie asked when she noticed me and thrust her baby into my arms.

I took the baby as Lizzie searched for something in her bag. Almost immediately, the baby pulled on my beard, and it made me laugh. I wondered what it would be like when I held my own baby. Avery's eyes got shiny when she watched me with Lizzie's kid. She must have been thinking the same thing.

"Sorry!" Lizzie offered, and then she took the baby back from me. She put a pacifier in the baby's mouth. "She's getting fussy. I better find Wyatt and get out of here. Avery, call me later so we can plan a girls' night."

Avery nodded and sipped on her hot chocolate quietly while Lizzie took off in the other direction.

I smoothed down my beard. "Should I shave my beard?"

Avery's eyes widened. "Hell no!"

A grin spread across my face. "I mean when the baby gets here."

She reached out a hand and rubbed her thumb across my beard. "I can't picture you without this. It would look... wrong. I want Peanut to know their bearded daddy."

"Okay... I'll keep it, but only for you."

She gave me a tight smile.

It wasn't lost on me that things between us were awkward. Since she rejected my proposal, I was trying to show her I was here for *her*, not just the baby. I wasn't doing a good job because I was a dick to her at our last check-up. I was stressed about the brewery and money, and I shouldn't have taken it out on her. She didn't need the extra stress.

"How are you feeling?" I asked.

She frowned. "Tired."

I noticed she wasn't wearing the morning sickness band anymore. "No more morning sickness?"

"I don't want to say it's passed yet, but I've been feeling okay."

I pulled out my phone and checked my calendar app. "We're not quite in the second trimester yet, but soon."

She beamed at that. "Why, Nolan MacGregor, are you keeping track?"

I nodded. "I told you, I want to be there for you and Peanut. Are you gonna hang out here much longer?"

She shook her head. "I think I want to head home."

"Oh," I said and hoped she didn't hear the hint of disappointment in my voice.

"I kinda want to cozy up on the couch and watch Christmas movies."

"Okay, I'll walk you."

She made a face. "Nolan, we live in Drakesville. I'm perfectly safe walking home alone."

"Avery, it's still a couple of blocks away, and it's dark out," I growled.

"I walk home by myself all the time."

I scrubbed a hand down my face in frustration. "Appease me, okay?"

"Fine," she spat, and she walked off to toss her empty hot chocolate cup into the trash. She didn't wait for me as she sped off down the street.

I caught up to her, and we walked the couple blocks to her apartment in terse silence. When we got to her apartment, I stopped in front of the steps leading up to the porch. I wanted to make sure she got home all right, but I didn't think she was going to invite me in.

She peered up at me with a guilty look. "Sorry, I'm moody."

I put a hand on her stomach. "Avs, it's all good. I told you, I'm here for you."

She squinted up at me. "Do you want to come inside? Or do you have to get back to the brewery?"

I scowled. "Declan dismissed me."

"Was your grumpy bear face scaring away customers?" she teased with a laugh.

"Yes," I gritted out between clenched teeth.

"Are you too moody to come upstairs and hang out with me?"

"You want company?"

She nodded and looked down at her feet. "But I want to watch cheesy Christmas movies. I know you hate that, so you don't have to come in."

"If that's what you want, we can do that."

Her face lit up, and her smile was brighter than any bulb on any Christmas tree. "Really? You'd do that?"

I groaned but nodded. I would suffer through those dumb movies for her. I would have done anything she asked me to if only to be with her.

She grabbed my hand and led me upstairs into her apartment. I helped her take her coat off and hung it on the back of one of her kitchen chairs. She went into her bedroom to get dressed into something comfy.

I went into her living room, kicked off my boots, and I sat back on her futon. Her uncomfortable futon. More and more, I was uneasy about this arrangement. I wanted more for Avery and the baby, and I certainly didn't want them living in this cramped space I didn't like that her stairs didn't have a railing either. I worried about her falling. What if something happened to the baby?

Avery walked back into the living room wearing a pair of Christmas-themed leggings that made her ass look fantastic and a matching long-sleeved top. The shirt clung tight across her middle, showing off the bump of our baby growing inside her. She was starting to show a little more, but only if you were really paying attention. She had been wearing clothes to hide it, but tonight, I saw the evidence of the life we created together. My inner caveman beat at his chest because that was *my* baby.

She situated herself beside me on the futon and pulled a blanket around her legs. I put one arm around the back of the futon and laid my other hand on her stomach. I didn't think we could feel the baby yet, but I ached for that connection with my child. Avery didn't know how much I wanted to be a father. Sure, raising my kid brother had been hard, but I always wanted a family of my own.

"Thanks for hanging out with me tonight. Being pregnant makes me boring. I mostly sit on my ass anymore," she said.

She put the rest of the blanket over my lap, and she pressed herself into my side. It was nice cuddling on her futon with her, but it made my heart get big, stupid ideas. It made me imagine we were an actual couple cuddling up together for a night-in.

"Tell me about this ridiculous movie you're making me watch."

I felt her laugh against my chest. "You really want to watch this with me?"

I rubbed my hand over her belly. "I'm here for you, and if that means watching some cheesy movie, I'll do that for you."

She looked up at me with that bright smile that made my chest constrict. "Really?"

I nodded.

She paused the movie before we got past the credits. "Okay, it's like the parent trap."

I raised an eyebrow.

"She looks like this Princess, and the Princess wants to enjoy being a normal person for a day. So they do the whole switcheroo thing."

I groaned. "Avs, this sounds so dumb!"

She pinched my side. "Appease your baby mama, ya Grinch!"

I turned and smiled at her. "Okay, Avs, for you."

Her face lit up with that beautiful smile again as she pressed play. When she smiled at me, I wanted nothing more than to keep it on her face. To do everything in my power to make her happy. I'd give her the world if I could.

"Why haven't you put your tree up yet?" I asked when I noticed her apartment wasn't decorated yet. Avery usually started her decorating the day after Thanksgiving. It was now two days after Thanksgiving, and it wasn't like her to be behind schedule. Especially since last year, she had it up before Halloween.

She shrugged. "Eh. Incubating this baby made me too tired to do it yet. I'll get to it."

"I'll help if you want."

"Okay," she whispered as she laid her head against my shoulder and glued her eyes to the TV.

"I'm serious. You love Christmas. Let me help you set it up."

"Thanks, Nolan. I appreciate it. I've just been too tired."

I kissed the top of her head. "I'm here for whatever you need."

"I haven't even started making my Christmas cookies yet."

"What? Woman, you're behind!"

She laughed. "I know, but I've been exhausted."

We cuddled together on her shitty futon for twenty minutes before I realized she had fallen asleep.

"Avs, come on," I whispered.

"Hmm?" she asked sleepily.

"You want to go to bed? You fell asleep."

"Oh, no! I'm so tired, Nol."

"It's okay, you gotta rest for Peanut."

I stood up and offered her my hand to help her up. She took it, and I walked her back into her bedroom. I watched her get into the bed, and she glanced up at me with hopeful eyes. "Nolan?"

"Yeah, Avs?"

She bit her lip, and there was a downcast sadness in them I hadn't noticed before. "Will you stay here tonight?"

"You want me to?" I asked. I was more than surprised by her request.

She nodded and laid her head against her pillow. I stripped down to my boxers and slid into the other side of her bed.

"Nolan?" she asked. She turned to look at me with those bright blue eyes of hers.

"What do you need?"

She shook her head. "I'm glad it was you."

"What do you mean?"

She yawned. "You're gonna be a wonderful daddy. I can't wait to see you hold Peanut in your arms."

I felt the corner of my lips upturn into a smile, and I rested my hand on her stomach. "I can't wait to meet Peanut."

She nodded and closed her eyes again. I pressed a kiss to her forehead, and we fell asleep together.

In the morning, I left without saying goodbye. She

wouldn't have remembered her moment of weakness when she asked me to stay over. It had been nice holding her in my arms as we slept, but I couldn't entertain the fantasy. Avery didn't want me that way, but I would take whatever morsel of attention I got from her. Even if it pained me later.

CHAPTER NINE

AVERY

After weeks of enduring morning sickness, I finally felt much better. I had a couple more days before I officially hit the second trimester. Nolan was the most supportive non-partner I could have asked for. We hadn't spoken again about the morning he asked me to marry him. Or about how he stayed over last weekend because I wanted the comfort of his big body beside me in my bed. When he was gone the next morning without so much as a 'goodbye,' I had to admit it stung.

Sometimes I caught him staring at me, and I didn't recognize the look in his brown eyes. It looked a lot like love, but I was pretty sure that was for the baby. I may love the man who would give me my first child, but I knew he didn't want to settle down.

Outside of our siblings, I hadn't told anyone else I was pregnant yet. My dad still didn't know, despite that my sister kept nagging me to tell him already. I was thirty-five and pregnant, and I was too scared to tell my dad.

"Seriously, did you do something different to your hair?" Helen, one of the other English teachers, asked me after the faculty meeting. She pushed her waist-length box braids over her shoulder. A suspicious look came across her dark complexion as she peered at me.

I unconsciously rested a hand on my stomach as I thought about my answer.

Helen's dark eyes widened as she noticed my hand on my stomach. I had been wearing flowy dresses and blouses lately to hide the pregnancy, but it was harder to conceal. One of the older male teachers had asked me if I was pregnant the other day. Even though that was really rude, I couldn't hide it much longer. Especially since come Monday, I would officially hit the second trimester.

"Oh my god! Are you pregnant?" Helen shrieked.

I nodded.

"I didn't know you were seeing anyone. Wait, did you do one of those sperm donor things?"

It didn't surprise me she asked that. When I bemoaned all the terrible dates I had gone on and how much I wanted a family, she told me I didn't need a man to do that anymore. Props to women who did the single mom thing, but I always wanted the devoted husband to go with the family I dreamed of.

I shook my head with a laugh as we walked out of the school building and down the street. "No. Just forgot to wrap it up. The father's a good friend."

"Really?"

"Yeah."

"Wait... who?"

I put a finger to my lips.

Helen's husband Allen was Nolan's right hand at the brewery, so I was a bit surprised she didn't know. Although

Allen was the type of guy who kept things close to the vest.

"Why is it a secret?" she asked.

I glared. "Because we live in a gossipy small town." I peered across the street and saw my sister sitting on my front porch. "I gotta go. My baby sis is waiting for me."

"It's Nolan MacGregor, isn't it?"

I gave her a shocked look.

She waved me away with her hand. "Girl! You two eye-fuck each other all the time. It took me like two seconds to figure it out."

I cringed.

"Good for you. I didn't realize you liked them thick."

I grinned. "And bearded."

She laughed and hugged me. "Well, congrats! You and Nolan will have the most ridiculously cute baby. He's so hot."

"Helen! You're married."

She laughed. "Yeah, but I got eyes. Plus, I do like a bigger guy."

That was true. Allen had a similar build to Nolan. I think he might be taller than Nolan, too.

"Say hi to him for me. I gotta go," she said.

Helen got into her car and waved goodbye to me. I walked across the street and up the steps to the porch where my sister sat. Gemma greeted me with a big hug.

In all the stress with this surprise pregnancy, my sister had been the shoulder I leaned on the most. Even though I was having a baby with Nolan, who was such a supportive baby daddy, I didn't want to rely on him too much. I didn't want to continue to confuse my feelings.

I keyed into my apartment, and we walked up the steps

inside. I took a load off in one of my kitchen chairs and rubbed my stomach.

My sister frowned at me while she looked around. "You haven't put your tree up yet."

That was unusual for me. I hadn't even taken the box of decorations out of the living room closet yet. Usually, my apartment looked like Christmas had blown up in it by now. I wasn't sure I felt like putting up my tree this year. Pregnancy was exhausting.

I groaned. "Oh, I know, but I've been too tired to do it. Nolan offered to help, but you know how much he hates Christmas. I didn't want to bother him about it."

"But he wants to do it. He asked me if I had helped you because you haven't brought it up again."

"He did?" I asked in surprise.

She nodded. "Yeah! He told me he voluntarily came over here and watched a cheesy Christmas movie with you after the tree lighting ceremony."

"He's overcompensating for being a dick to me at our last doctor's appointment. I know he didn't want to do that, but he's been doing little things like that for me."

Gemma rolled her eyes at me. "Of course he is. He wants to make it up to you. You gotta let him help you. He wants to."

I shook my head. "I can't continue to complicate my feelings for him."

She squinted at me. "What aren't you telling me?"

"It's none of your business," I said flatly and gave her an annoyed look.

"Woman, tell me!" she begged.

I sighed. Little sisters sure were annoying.

"He asked me to marry him."

"What?" she screeched. "Oh my god, Avs! Why didn't you tell me?"

"I said no. It was right after we found out I was pregnant."

She glared at me. "Is that why he's been so moody? He's been insufferable."

I shrugged. "You know Nol, he's a grump."

She shook her head. "Nah, this is something else. He's been in a *foul* mood. He made another guy quit yesterday. Why did you say no?"

"He only did it because of the baby. I can't marry someone who doesn't love me. Besides, he doesn't want to be tied down."

"How do you know that?"

"He told me. It's not like I've been the only woman in his bed lately."

She studied me for a second. "Are you sure about that?"

I frowned. Actually, I wasn't sure; I just assumed. We hadn't had sex since we conceived the baby, so I figured he was getting it elsewhere.

He didn't want to be tied down. He made that perfectly clear to me on several occasions. I wasn't naïve. I saw how other women looked at him. Nolan might not have six-pack abs, but he had that hot lumberjack thing going on. Some women were into that. *I* was very much into that.

Gemma shook her head. "No wonder he's been so snippy lately and miserable as all hell."

"Why would you say that?"

She rolled her eyes, and I resisted the urge to tell her that her eyes would stay that way one day. Holy crap, was I turning into my mother? Is that what happened when you got pregnant?

Gemma fixed me with an annoyed look. "The big guy loves you!"

I shook my head. "No way, Gem."

"That man wants to give you what you've been searching for. You want your happily ever after, but when someone offered it to you, you said no."

"Because he doesn't love me!" I screeched at her.

How did she not get it? Nolan was just doing what he thought was 'right.' I didn't want to marry someone who only did it because they had to. I wanted big love like in all the romance novels I read, but all I got from Nolan was a strained friendship and an unplanned pregnancy. Of course, I wanted to get married and have a family. That's why I was going on all those terrible dates while I was still sleeping with Nolan. Deep down, I loved the idea of marrying him, but I didn't want to trap him into a marriage he didn't want.

Gemma crossed her arms over her chest. "What if he wants what you want? What if you tried? You know, really gave it a go? That man only smiles when he sees you."

That was true. Nolan's demeanor was usually gruff and dominating. Still, I've seen his scowl completely transform when he saw me from across a room. I used to think that was because I was one of the few people he tolerated. Did Gemma see something I didn't?

"You think we should try it?" I asked.

"Yes!" my sister screeched.

I chewed on my lip.

"I think you should marry Nolan."

I ran a hand down my face and groaned. "Gem, why are you pushing this?"

She put a hand over mine and squeezed it. "He's such a

grouch, but when you come into a room, his whole face lights up."

"But he only wants to marry me because he thinks he has to," I argued again.

"Avs, when he looks at you, all the grouchy broodiness falls off of him. I never see him like that with anyone else. Like..."

I frowned at her while I rubbed my pregnant belly in thought. "Like what, Gem?"

Her eyes got wide with excitement. "Like you're his light."

I rolled my eyes at her.

She poked me in the arm. "Seriously, Avs. I think you're meant to be. Maybe the pregnancy wasn't an accident. Maybe it was the universe's way of pushing you together."

I chewed on my lip in thought. I wanted to have the husband and babies and maybe the white picket fence, too. I think Nolan would give that to me if I told him that's what I wanted. He had been willing to marry me right after I told him about the baby. And he was so protective of me and provided for me even when I didn't ask for it.

Gemma gave me an exasperated look. "Okay, so maybe you don't have to say yes to his proposal, but I know he cares about you, and I know you could be happy together."

"What if it doesn't work out?"

"Then it doesn't work out. What's the worst thing that could happen? I've been waiting two years for you two to get your heads out of your asses."

Gemma had a point. We didn't have to get married, but the truth was, I wanted that more than anything. That was why I had been on the apps for so long, with no luck. I wanted a husband who would love me and care for our children and me. Nolan could be that for me. He knew what I was searching for, and he was willing to give it all to me. Maybe it was enough that we could try to have a life together.

"Okay," I said quietly.

If I didn't say it out loud to my sister right now, I would chicken out and continue to keep Nolan at arm's length. After listening to Gemma, I was seriously considering accepting Nolan's marriage proposal. Was that weird and irrational? Absolutely! Did we need to get married just because we were having a baby together? That was a big nope. But it was time for me to take a risk for the man I loved. Then maybe I would be brave enough to tell him all I ever wanted was his love.

One day. Preferably before our baby turned thirty. I hoped.

"Okay, what?" Gemma asked, but she had a hopeful look in her eyes. Like she already knew what I was going to say. She rubbed the rose-colored crystal she wore around her neck between her fingers as she stared back at me in anticipation.

"I'm gonna tell him yes," I said firmly and then nodded my head in confirmation.

"YAY!" Gemma cheered and hugged me again.

"I'm going to marry Nolan MacGregor."

"For real? You're really going to do it?"

"Gem," I whispered and brushed away happy tears from my eyes. "He wants to give me everything I've ever dreamed of. Something's telling me I have to try."

"It's a sign from the universe, Avs!"

I tried not to roll my eyes at that. God, I loved my sister, but she definitely was into her healing crystals and 'signs from the universe' a little too much. And yet, maybe my pull to marry Nolan *was* the universe telling me what to do. Not that I'd ever admit it to Gemma.

Gemma grabbed my hand and gave it a little squeeze. I smiled at her through my tear-stained eyes. "Avs, everything is going to be perfect. Nolan already dotes on you, and he'll give you that happily ever after you want."

I really hoped she was right. This was a huge risk. Who decided marrying their baby daddy was a good idea? Often, that didn't work out, but something told me I had to take the chance on Nolan. I really hoped this didn't all blow up in my face later.

CHAPTER TEN

NOLAN

"Hey, Boss Man, you got a visitor!" Allen announced as he came back into the tank room, where I was finishing up the fermentation of a new batch of beer.

"Busy!" I roared over the noise.

A smirk came across Allen's dark complexion. "Too busy for your baby mama?"

I jerked my head up and immediately assumed the worst. "Avery?"

I never planned to blab to everyone about Avery's pregnancy. Still, Allen had been at the brewery the night she showed me the sonogram. Allen kept things close to the vest so he wouldn't say anything. Although we lived in such a gossipy small town, I was sure word would get out soon, anyway.

He shooed me away and took over my work. "Go talk to her, man!"

I wiped my hands on my apron, went out to the floor, and saw Avery laughing with my brother. She turned at my loud footsteps and gave me a big smile.

I felt something warm spread across my chest when she smiled at me.

"Hey, is everything okay?" I asked.

She stood up, and I saw Gemma give her a thumbs up from behind the bar. I wondered what that was about. I smiled as Avery walked toward me.

"Okay," she said firmly and with a bit of conviction.

I raised an eyebrow. "Okay, what?"

She smiled up at me and pulled my face down to her level. She shocked me by kissing me hard on the mouth. Instinctively, I wrapped my arms around her waist, pulling her closer to me. I only pulled away at the sarcastic cheers from my employees. A cute blush crept up across Avery's face.

"Okay, I'll marry you," she said, and her mouth curved up into a sweet smile.

"Really?" I asked in surprise. That had been the last thing I expected to come out of her mouth.

She nodded. "Yes."

"Why? What changed?"

"My sister told me that if you're offering me what I've been searching for, I should take it. That we should really try."

Okay, not exactly her telling me she had feelings for me, but if she wanted to get married and let me try to be the man she deserved, I would take it. Maybe in time, she would come to love me, too.

I put my hands on her growing belly. "Avs, I promise I'll do everything in my power to make you happy. You and the baby."

She put her hands over the top of mine like she was telling me how much we were in this together. "I want a courthouse wedding. Can we do that?"

"Whatever you want."

I kissed her again, and she didn't freeze up or care that we were in front of people. I didn't know if she loved me like I loved her, but it was a start. People had shotgun weddings all the time and fell in love. Maybe this would be like that. We already had amazing chemistry and knew how to make a baby. How hard could marriage be?

"Come on, let's go home," I said when I pulled away from the kiss.

"We have a lot of things to talk about," she agreed.

I kissed her again and felt her melt into my arms. I only pulled away because a rag hit me square on the back of the head. I looked over at the bar where Gemma and Declan were giving us shit-eating grins.

Avery smiled up at me with an *I told you so* look.

"They're planning our wedding, aren't they?" I asked.

She nodded. "That's why I want to go to the courthouse."

"Get out of here!" Declan yelled at us.

I gave him the one-finger salute and walked out of the bar with Avery's hand in mine. When we got to my house, I sat her down on the couch and ran upstairs to grab my mother's ring.

"Where are you going?" she called up to me.

I went into the office and unlocked the safe. I took out the box with my mother's ring and locked the safe back up. I rushed back down the stairs and into the living room, where Avery still sat on the couch. She gave me a perplexed look while I kneeled in front of her and opened the box to her.

"Avery Jensen, will you marry me?"

She laughed. "I told you, I would. You didn't have to ask again."

"I wanted to do it right."

She held up a finger. "Wait a second, that wasn't her ring, right?"

I shook my head as I slid the ring on her finger. It fit her perfectly, like it was made for her. "It was my mother's."

She put her hand on her heart. "Oh, Nolan."

I put my hands on her stomach and kissed her growing bump. "I can't wait to meet you, Peanut."

"Nol, you're gonna be such a good dad."

"I want to be a good husband," I admitted.

"You're the best friend a woman could ask for."

That wasn't exactly what I was going for, but I would take it. "Will you move in here now?"

She nodded.

"Okay, let's go get your things."

She laughed. "Slow your roll, buddy. One thing at a time. I have to call my landlord and give him my notice, but I'd like to stay here tonight... with you."

I kissed her again. "Perfect."

I shook awake at the sound of whimpering. When I slid my eyes open, I smiled at the woman in my arms. Avery was clutching onto me. Her arms were thrown over my bare chest, and one of her legs was tangled against my meaty thigh. She was whimpering in her sleep. No. Moaning. And grinding against my leg.

Was she humping my leg like a dog in heat?

I squinted at my phone in the dark and saw it was one

in the morning. I wanted to let her sleep, but hearing that noise made my dick lift in interest. I nudged her softly. "Avs, wake up."

"Nolan," she moaned.

"Hey, I'm right here. What's wrong?"

Her eyes slid open and then widened when she realized her hand was reaching for the very thing that loved her moans. She shifted onto her back.

"You okay?" I asked.

She shook her head but wouldn't look at me.

"What's wrong?"

She put a hand on her face like something embarrassed her. "Nothing's wrong."

"You were whimpering in your sleep. Did you have a bad dream?"

"Not a bad dream," she said, her words muffled by her hand over her mouth.

"Okay..."

She pulled her hand away from her face. "I was having a sex dream."

"Oh."

"I'm very horny."

"How horny?"

A sheepish look crept across her face, and even though it was dark in my bedroom, I knew she was blushing. "Like I need to charge my vibrator every single night, horny."

I slid a hand down her body, and she shivered at my touch. I gently caressed her tits, and she bucked against me.

"What do you need?" I whispered huskily.

"You. I need you," she whispered back with a needy whimper.

She was wearing one of my t-shirts to bed again. What

looked tight across my gigantic body looked like a dress on her. I pushed the shirt up and dipped a finger inside her panties.

"Oh, fuck, so wet," I hissed while I slid my finger across her clit.

"I lied," she blurted out as she arched her pussy up into my hand.

"About what?"

"About how horny I am. I'm so horny I broke my vibrator."

"Why didn't you tell me? I could have helped you."

She moaned as I pushed one finger inside her pussy and then another. "Yes. Oh god, yes."

I kissed her neck. "Tell me what you need."

"Fuck me."

"You sure?"

She nodded.

I pulled my hand out of her and licked her juices off my hand. "You should be on top. I don't want to hurt the baby."

She smiled at me. "The Doctor said missionary is okay, but if I feel any pain, we should switch positions."

I gave her a sheepish smile. "I still don't want to hurt you or the baby. The books I read said not to do it."

"You've been reading the baby books?" she asked, looking surprised by that.

I nodded. "Well... Dec threw one at my head when we found out you were pregnant."

She laughed. "Sounds like Dec. They say not to because it can be uncomfortable once I get bigger."

"I'm afraid of hurting you. I'm so much bigger than you; I don't want to crush you."

She cupped my face in her hands. "You won't. But I kinda want to do doggy, anyway."

I grinned at her. "Course you do. It's your favorite."

She caressed my beard. "I love it, especially when it's with you."

She sat up abruptly and tore the t-shirt off, exposing her tender, enlarged breasts to me. Her tits were perfect before, and now they looked terrific. She kicked her panties off, turned around on all fours, and I nearly came in my pants.

My new fiancée was sexy as hell.

I stripped off my boxers and got behind her, kissing up her spine until I was at her ear. "You're so sexy."

"No, I'm not."

I ran my hands down her wide hips, and I clenched them in my hands. "Shush. You were sexy before and even more now that you're carrying my child. Let me give you what you need."

"Please, I need your big dick."

"What the lady wants, she gets," I said with a chuckle.

I kneed her legs apart and lined up with her entrance. I teased her clit with the head of my cock, loving the feeling of being bare against her.

"Please, Nol. I need it," she begged, and she rocked her ass back into me.

I leaned over and peppered her neck with kisses while I pushed inside her. I tilted her face up to kiss her from behind. We kissed in time while I moved inside her, nice and slow.

"Yes..." she moaned as she broke off the kiss and rocked her ass back into my groin. She met me thrust for thrust, begging me with her body to give it to her hard and deep.

I rocked into her, and grinned when she gripped the sheets, and I noticed the emerald engagement ring on her hand. I loved seeing her wearing my mother's ring. I didn't care why she changed her mind or why she took a chance on me. I was just grateful this goddess let me be near her. That she was allowing me to prove to her I could be worthy of her love.

I slid one hand around her and down the length of her stomach until I found her clit. I stroked it in time with my movements inside her.

"Yes, oh yes," she moaned beneath me. "Fuck me with your big cock."

"I am," I laughed and increased the tempo the tiniest bit.

I kissed her neck and continued the slow motions, savoring her. I was two seconds away from blowing my load, but I wanted to tend to her needs first. She was all that would matter for the rest of my life, and I intended to make good on that promise.

"I got you. Be a good girl and come all over my big dick," I growled into her ear while I bucked behind her.

I felt her walls clench around me, and she moaned uncontrollably as she came. "Nolan!" she cried out as her orgasm wracked through her body.

I clutched her hips in my hands and lost myself in the feeling of her. "Avery," I moaned into her ear when I finally gave in and came.

It took me a couple of seconds for my brain to come back online, but when it did, I gave her a quick kiss before pulling out. I collapsed on my back in exhaustion.

She turned on her side and gave me a small smile. She ran a red, manicured hand across my bushy beard. "Thank you."

"Gotta admit, fucking you raw is amazing."

She laughed at that. "Oh, hard agree."

I ran a hand down her side and held onto her hip. "You felt so good."

She grinned at me. "You're not so bad yourself."

"Brat," I teased, but I grinned back at her.

I got up from the bed and took a leak. I brought back a warm washcloth to clean up, but she went into the bathroom instead. I didn't bother putting clothes back on, and she didn't either when she crawled back into bed.

I slid down under the covers and kissed her bare stomach. "I can't wait for you to get here, Peanut. You be good for your mama in there, okay?"

Avery stroked my hair while I kissed my way up her body until I was kissing her lips again. I leaned my forehead against hers, and my smile cracked my face.

I held her face in my hands. "Thank you."

"For what?"

"For accepting my proposal and carrying my child. I promise you, we're going to be happy together."

Her eyes got shiny.

"Aw, Avs, don't cry."

"I'm pregnant! I cry at the drop of a hat now."

I pulled her against my chest and pulled the comforter over our naked bodies. "Let's go to sleep. If you wanted sex, you could have told me before we went to bed. You didn't have to hump my leg until I woke up."

She glared at me. "I was *not* humping your leg!"

I kissed her neck and nuzzled into her. I wrapped my arm around her and laid my hand on her belly protectively. "You were totally humping my leg. You gonna tell me about the sex dream?"

"Ha! You wish!"

I kissed her neck again. "Goodnight, future Mrs. MacGregor."

She sighed and snuggled down into my chest. My chest felt tight as I watched her fall asleep, curled up beside me.

Her in my arms, in my bed, and wearing my mother's ring was like something out of a dream. I had to keep pinching myself to make sure it was real.

CHAPTER ELEVEN

AVERY

The sunlight shone through Nolan's bedroom and forced me awake, but I didn't want to open my eyes. I heard a soft murmuring of whispers and felt a hand rubbing across my stomach. I slid one eye open and looked down to find Nolan talking to my pregnant belly. I didn't have the heart to tell him that the baby couldn't hear him yet or recognize his voice. Instead, I strained my ears to hear what he was saying.

"Your mama and I can't wait to meet you, Peanut. I'm gonna be the best daddy I can be. Maybe then I can prove to your mama that I'm good enough for her." He kissed my belly, and I tried not to flinch.

I didn't understand what I overheard. How could Nolan think he wasn't good enough for me?

I shifted in the bed, and Nolan's brown eyes slid up to look at me. I placed my hand on my stomach, right next to his bigger one. The engagement ring on my finger glinted in the sunlight and reminded me that last night I agreed to become Nolan's wife. He was willing to give me everything I wanted. I just had to take a chance on him.

"You awake?" he asked.

I nodded.

He slid up the bed, threaded his hand through my hair, and kissed me good morning. If this was how our marriage would be, I could get used to it. When he slanted his mouth on mine, it felt like we fit, like our lips were made to be locked together.

"How do you feel?" he asked after he pulled away. He shifted onto his side, but his hand stayed on my belly.

"Tired. Sorry, I woke you up for sex last night."

He chuckled. "I didn't mind. You tell me anytime you want this dick, it's yours."

I laughed. "You're a dirty old man."

He ran a finger across my cheek lovingly. "You love it."

I gestured to my growing belly. "Clearly. That's how this happened."

"No, we created Peanut because you wanted to ride my cock, and I wasn't stopping you."

I laughed. "Sorry, beard rides melt my brain."

He rubbed said beard against my neck, which made me laugh. "When do we find out the sex?" he asked.

"After the new year. Do you want to find out?"

He nodded as he peppered my neck with kisses. It felt like an arrow shooting down to my core when he touched and kissed me. Pregnancy was so weird. I'd never been hornier in my life. I shifted onto my side, so my back pressed against his chest, and his enlarged cock poked my ass. I was grateful we never put our clothes back on last night because I wanted his dick inside me again right now. Like right fucking now. I needed him to fill me up and press deep inside me, or I was going to explode.

I ground back against him, and he chuckled low into my neck. "You need something?" he whispered in my ear. I placed his hand on my breast, and he massaged it lightly. "S'okay?"

I nodded and moaned while he continued to kiss my neck and massage my tender breasts. "They feel so heavy," I groaned.

"Damn, I didn't think your tits could get bigger. They're amazing."

"Ass!" I teased.

"What? They're awesome," he argued as he brushed a thumb across one nipple. His touch felt wonderful, but that wasn't where I wanted his hands.

"Go lower," I growled.

I felt his grin on my neck, and his hand danced down to find my clit. "Tell me what you need."

"You."

He slid a thick finger across the nub of my clit, brushing gently at the sensitive spot. I was already coming, and he hadn't even fingered me yet.

"That good, huh?" he said into my ear in a low growl.

God, I loved when he growled at me during sex. It was such a turn-on, and it made me need him even more.

"So good," I purred back.

He slid his finger down to find my entrance. I moaned and clutched his bicep while his thick fingers pumped in and out of me. He had amazing hands. And tongue. And cock. No wonder he got me pregnant.

"Turn around," he growled and pulled his fingers out of me

I shifted so we were face-to-face and whimpered when I

watched him lick his fingers. He gave me a wicked grin and kissed me. I melted into the kiss, letting his tongue inside as he devoured my mouth. I would let this man eat me up whole if he could.

He gently pulled my thigh over top of his bigger one and pulled me closer. He teased me by dragging the head of his cock across my sensitive clit, but he wasn't sliding home yet.

I wrapped my hands around the back of his neck. "Please."

He held my face in his hands and looked deep into my eyes. I felt like he could see into my very soul, like he could see how much my heart was bursting for him.

"I'm here. Whatever you need," he whispered.

"I need you inside me, now," I begged.

He entered me slowly until he was buried to the hilt. He kissed me for a while and kept up the slow tempo of his thrusting. The slow, intimate pace was exactly what I needed this morning. He held my face in his hands lovingly as our eyes connected, my blue ones bored into his dark brown ones.

"This is nice," I said as I clutched onto his big shoulders.

"Nice?" he asked with a laugh as he continued to pump inside me. "It's fucking awesome. Slow morning sex... any sex with you is my favorite."

My eyes watered at his sweet words. I knew he was just saying he'd have sex with me no matter what, but the way he paced himself and held me close made me feel loved. It made me feel like maybe he could feel for me what I felt for him. My emotions were too much of a mess to ask him about it. Not yet.

"Be a good girl, and come for me," he growled as he pressed a hand between where we were joined. He slid his thick finger across my clit and rubbed in soft circles while he rocked his hard length inside me.

"Yes..." I moaned.

I loved when he called me a good girl in bed. I yearned for it sometimes.

He wound his free hand through my hair and pulled me as close as he could, and held me as we made love. I realized as I came again that's what he was doing. He was making love to me in the morning light after I agreed to become his wife.

When I came down off the high of my orgasm, he studied my face. "What?" I asked.

He grinned at me. "I love watching you come."

"Ass! That was a really sweet moment, you perv."

He nipped at my bottom lip and continued the soft stroking inside me. "I'm gonna make you come again."

"Nuh-uh, old man. Your turn," I teased.

I threaded my hands through his hair and thrust back against him, urging his hard length to press deeper inside.

He kissed me hard, but I felt him holding back.

"Come for me," I whispered.

"You feel so good," he groaned into my neck. "I don't want to stop."

"Let go, baby. Fuck me like you mean it."

"Now you're gonna get it," he growled and quickened his pace.

"Give it to me," I purred as I tipped back my head and let him take me.

We ground against each other, our bodies pressed tightly together as we became one. He tilted my head down to meet me in a searing kiss, and then he was off, coming in long, hot spurts.

We panted together as we came down from our high.

Nolan pressed his forehead against mine and held my face in his hands like he wanted to say something profound. The sound of the doorbell ringing and his phone buzzing across the bedside table killed the moment.

"Goddamnit," he groaned.

"Who's that?"

He sighed and reluctantly pulled out of me. He looked at his phone and opened his security app. I saw the image of his brother and my sister standing at the front door on the screen, with shit-eating grins on their faces.

Little siblings were so annoying.

"At least they weren't complete cockblocks," I said with a shrug.

He laughed and pulled me toward his chest for a cuddle. He kissed the top of my head. "They can wait. Let's go get cleaned up."

"Why are they here?" I asked.

He slid out of bed and picked me up in his arms. "To help you move in."

"Should we let them in?" I asked as I wrapped my arms around him while he carried me bridal-style to his bathroom.

He set me down in the shower and turned on the water. "No. Dec has a key. He was being polite by ringing the doorbell."

We showered together as quickly as we could, but Nolan kept getting distracted by my naked body. I felt insecure about my growing belly, but the way he put his hands on it protectively and talked to the baby filled me with so much love. I think if our siblings weren't waiting for us, we would have done it again in the shower. Although it didn't stop him from going down on me until the water got cold.

Oops! I wasn't sorry about that at all.

When I toweled off and walked back into the bedroom, I found a set of clean clothes for me on the bed, probably from Gemma. I was thankful my sister left me leggings and a sweatshirt because I was having a hard time fitting into my jeans. I heard laughter from the kitchen, and I smelled coffee brewing. I really wanted coffee, but I was trying to limit myself as much as I could.

When I turned around, Nolan stared at me. "What?"

"Damn, your ass looks fantastic."

"What? It looks huge!"

He came up behind me and gripped my hips. "It's awesome. I loved your body before, and you look great now." He kissed the side of my neck. "Come on, let's go downstairs."

We walked down the stairs, and when I found my sister in the kitchen, I hugged her tightly.

"Coffee?" she asked.

I squinted at her. "Why are you here?"

"To help you move," Dec said and flipped a pancake on the stove.

I took a seat at the table, and Nolan sat next to me. He put my feet in his lap and rubbed them. "Oh... that feels amazing. Thanks."

He smiled.

"Oh my god, Avs! He hasn't even married you yet, and he's already whipped!" my sister squealed.

Nolan smiled but didn't argue with her.

Declan scoffed as he brought me a plate of pancakes and a coffee. "Nah, he was like that before he knocked her up. You could have told us you were dating."

"But we weren't," I argued and crammed pancakes into my mouth.

"That's true," Nolan said in agreement.

Declan doled out food to everyone else and pushed the bowl of fruit my way. I wasn't paying attention anymore because shoving pancakes into my mouth was more important.

"Mom's ring looks good on you," Declan said with a nod of his head.

I swallowed my pancakes sheepishly, but my sister grabbed my hand. "Oh, it's so pretty! Nol, did you get it resized?"

He shook his head. He had stopped rubbing my feet but had one hand rested on my stomach while he ate with the other. "Nah. It just... fit."

My sister's eyes got wide and twinkled with excitement. I fixed her with a glare. God, I loved my baby sister, but she believed hard in the fate of the universe. She looked at me like she was the heart-eyes emoji. "Oh my god! It's fate!"

I shoved more food into my mouth and moved onto the fruit so she didn't see me roll my eyes. I looked up at one point, and both of the MacGregor brothers were looking at me with impressed looks on their faces.

"Damn, woman!" Declan exclaimed with a laugh.

Nolan rubbed my stomach, and his chest puffed out in pride.

"What? I can finally eat without throwing it all up."

My sister was still swooning. "Aw, Dec, aren't they so cute?"

Declan winked at her. "Bout time these two figured out they're perfect for each other."

Once I finished eating, I turned to Gemma. "We better start getting my stuff together. I have papers to grade this weekend."

"Yay! Let's go!"

I think she literally skipped with joy out of the house.

Nolan gave me a small smile but stopped me before leaving. "Wait, in case I'm at the brewery when you get back." He went into the junk drawer and pulled out a key. He placed it in my hand. "This is your home too."

I gave him a quick kiss and clutched the key in my hand before taking off in my sister's car to the other side of town.

CHAPTER TWELVE

NOLAN

I watched Avery's ass sway behind her as she walked out the door. I didn't care what she said. Pregnancy made her curves look delicious. My jaw was unhinged while I watched her walk away. I was jolted from my staring by the punch my brother landed on my arm.

"Ow!" I exclaimed and fixed a glare at Declan.

"Dude, Gem's right. You're whipped."

I gave him the finger. "I'm trying to take care of my baby mama."

He rolled his eyes. "Yeah, by being a stage five clinger."

"You're just jealous I'm getting laid."

He made a grossed-out face. "Doesn't that hurt the baby?"

I groaned. "Fuck, I did an awful job when I gave you the sex talk."

"No?" he asked.

I shook my head. "No, buddy. Sex doesn't hurt the baby. There's a... ahh... mucous plug."

A look of horror crossed my brother's face. "EWWW!"

I smirked. "It's not gross, Dec. It protects the baby. Which is great because their Mama is insatiable right now."

"Gross."

"Dude, she woke me up for sex last night."

"TMI."

"Seriously, if you got here five minutes earlier, you would have been a major cockblock."

He rolled his eyes at me. "Yeah, we heard you in the shower. Gross, bro!"

I shrugged. I couldn't help it this morning when Avery was feeling self-conscious about how big she was getting. I wanted her to know she was sexy as fuck to me, so of course, I went down on her in the shower. I didn't care that our siblings were downstairs, being the nuisances they both always were. If they hadn't barged over here, we would have had shower sex.

"Should have called before you came over," I said to him.

He shoved me, but I laughed.

"Are you serious about the plan you texted me last night?" he asked.

I nodded.

"You hate Christmas. You only ever put up the tree at my insistence."

The reason I hated Christmas? Our parents died in a car accident after coming home from a Christmas party. Christmas wasn't the 'holly jolly' season for me. Christmas meant pain and being reminded of everything I lost. Talk about ironic. I was going to marry the woman who was Drakesville's unofficial Queen of Christmas.

Avery loved Christmas with her whole heart. She loved the cheesy Hallmark movies, the decorations, and even the carols. I joked she made more Christmas cookies than the town bakery. She loved the holidays, and if she was going to move in here and become my wife, I wanted to bring it to life for her. Even if it gave me painful memories of the worst night of my life. I'd sacrifice that for her. I hadn't exactly told her why I hated Christmas so much.

"Avery loves Christmas," I said.

Declan sighed. "Dude, I know you're allergic to feelings, but you have to tell her how you feel."

"Come on, I think the tree's in the attic," I said to my brother, hoping to distract him from this conversation.

"Don't change the subject!"

I fixed him with a glare. He shook his head and let the argument drop.

We walked up the steps in silence, and I pulled down the stairs to get up to the attic. I followed him up the steps into the cramped space. He searched for the tree while I looked for the decorations.

"I think I found it!" Dec called from the back of the attic. He slid over an oblong box, and I inspected it. Ornaments, but no tree.

"Just the ornaments."

I went down the steps and put the box on the floor.

"Do you think maybe she'll want a real tree?" he called down to me as he stomped around, searching for the fake tree.

"Nah. She uses an artificial one."

"Oh, got it!"

He walked down the steps and dropped the box on the floor. I closed up the attic, and we went into the living room. I inspected the area and tried to figure out where to put the tree.

"In the corner," Dec offered.

"Okay. Yeah," I said in agreement.

My brother and I worked to get the tree set up and started decorating it. Dec looked over at me while he hung a candy cane on a branch. "Maybe you should take the night off," he suggested.

"Why?" I grumbled and started fixing everything he did.

I frowned when I realized Mom used to do that. This holiday was hard on me. When our parents died, I had to do everything to ensure my little brother was taken care of. I didn't resent Dec for it, but it had been a massive undertaking at eighteen.

"Everything's happening so fast. You need to spend time with Avery."

"Why?"

"To figure out the wedding and all the other stuff."

I shrugged. "She wants a courthouse wedding. Don't even think about trying to set up a bachelor party. I don't want it."

"Come on, we could get all the guys and go to a Bulldogs game; you'd love it. Hockey and beer, your two favorite things."

I stroked my beard as I thought about his suggestion. He was right about that, but I couldn't afford to take any time off from the brewery. Especially when I had a baby on the way.

"I'm good. Come outside and help me put up the lights before Avery gets home."

We grabbed our coats and walked outside. Declan untangled the lights from the plastic bag someone had shoved them inside. I grabbed the ladder from the shed and put it against the house. Declan directed me where to hang the lights while he held the ladder. I wasn't sure how long we had been out there, but it felt like it took forever. I didn't care how long it took; I just wanted it to be perfect for Avery.

"I think it looks good," Declan called up to me.

I walked down the ladder, and he ran inside to flip the switch. The house lit up with twinkling white lights, like some fucking winter wonderland. Avery never would have expected me to decorate for Christmas. I wanted to surprise her with it, to make it feel like this was her home, too.

Dec came out of the house and whistled. "Looks good. She's gonna love it."

I frowned and ran a hand down my beard. "I hope so. I want everything to be perfect for her."

Dec nudged me with his elbow. "Take the night off. Go help your baby mama get the rest of her stuff and get situated. The brewery will be fine without you for one night. Okay?"

"I..."

He cut me off by holding up his hand. "Nolan, this is why we have staff. You don't have to work your fingers to the bone like when we first opened. You're the head brewer. You don't have to micromanage every tiny detail of the process. I know you're stressed about money, but it's gonna be okay."

"I want to be good enough for her. And for Peanut."

"Peanut?" he asked with a confused look.

I shrugged. "It's what I call the baby."

My brother beamed at me. "That's so cute."

I punched him in the shoulder. "Shut it!"

He pushed me back. "Get out of here. I'll handle shit at the brewery tonight. Go help your lady."

Declan didn't have a life outside of the brewery, either. He was just as bad as I was. I couldn't remember the last time he even went on a date. I don't think he's had a serious relationship since his high school girlfriend Lila broke his heart when she went to college in California and never came back.

I was about to run back into the house for my car keys when two cars pulled up into the driveway. I planned to go over to Avery's apartment to help so she didn't have to carry all those boxes inside. She shouldn't be lifting anything heavy in her condition. I hadn't realized how long it took us to get the tree up and decorated. Getting the lights up on the house had taken longer than I would have liked, even with my brother's help. I felt like a dick. I should have helped her pack up all her things.

Avery got out of her car with a box in her hand, and I rushed over to help her. She scowled at me. "I can lift a box, Nol," she argued, but the debate died on her lips when she looked up at my brightly lit-up house. "Oh... Oh! You put up Christmas lights?"

Her eyes sparkled as the reflection of the lights hit her just right. The way her entire face lit up in delight struck me in the chest.

"Nolan, did you do this for me?" she asked in surprise.

I grunted in response.

"But you hate Christmas."

I took the box from her and walked into the house. I smiled when I heard her gasp. "Oh, Nolan," Avery whispered.

We stored the boxes in the guest room until we figured out how to merge all of our stuff. She still needed to figure out what to do about her apartment, but she didn't feel like dealing with it today.

Gem and Dec made excuses to leave as soon as possible.

I pretended not to notice the kissy faces they made behind Avery's head. Dicks.

Avery put her hands on her hips and gave me an annoyed look as soon as the door slammed behind our siblings.

"What?" I asked as I rubbed a hand through my beard nervously.

"You know what."

I sat down on the couch and pulled her into my lap. She shifted around but cuddled into me like she fit there.

"What?" I asked again.

She gestured to the room and the decorated tree in the corner. "Nolan. You hate Christmas."

"But *you* love it."

"You didn't have to do this. You do too much for me."

I placed a hand on her baby bump. "Let me, okay? I want to take care of you."

She grumbled and slid off my lap.

"Where are you going?"

"To make dinner."

"Avs, you don't have to."

"I want to. Let me take care of you too."

I nodded and let her cook for me.

I had to admit it was nice of her. She browned some beef in a pan and made tacos. She didn't let me help, even when I offered to dice the tomatoes or grate the cheese. It was quick and easy, but nice. I didn't even know I had this stuff. Being a bachelor usually meant I ate a lot of takeout or pub food at the brewery. It wasn't the best diet, another thing I needed to work on, especially with the baby coming. I wanted to be healthy for my baby, and I had to take better care of myself, for Avery, and our unborn child.

"When are you going to the brewery?" she asked as she cleared the table.

"Why don't you rest, and I'll do the dishes?" I offered instead.

She waved me off. "No, I got it. When do you have to go?"

"I'm gonna take the night off."

Her eyebrows rose high. I never took nights off from the brewery.

"When was the last time you did that?"

I shrugged and rubbed the back of my neck. "When we conceived Peanut."

She shook her head. "That's not true. You worked the booth at the Arts Fest."

She got me there.

I shrugged.

"Do you even know how to relax?"

"Of course, I do!"

She smirked at me. "Do you know how to relax and not obsess over the next beer you want to make?"

I grumbled.

She laughed. "Try to. I have to grade some papers."

"Okay. I think I'll watch the hockey game."

She made a face.

"What?"

"If by relaxing you mean 'get mad at the Bulldogs because they suck' sure!"

I laughed. "I don't know. Noah Kennedy has been on fire lately."

She nodded. "True, but nobody else is doing jack shit out on the ice."

"Except Metzy," we said in unison and laughed that we

were both such goaltender apologists. I loved that this woman could talk hockey as much as the next guy.

I took a beer out of the fridge, and when I turned around, she had slunk off upstairs. I thought she would be up there grading papers for the night, but she came down seconds after I turned the game on. She snuggled up next to me on the couch, with the throw blanket over her and a stack of papers in her lap. I put an arm around her, and we sat together in companionable silence. It felt so natural, like watching hockey while she graded papers was something we did together every night. If this was a glimpse into our future, I wanted it.

She shifted around a couple of times to get comfortable. "You okay?" I asked.

"My back hurts."

I reached over and rubbed her back for her.

"Oh my god. Thank you."

"That's what I'm here for."

She put her papers to the side and shifted to look at me. "Nolan, you're doing too much for me. I love the support, but..."

"But what?"

She squeezed her eyes shut. "I don't want you to sacrifice everything for me."

I cocked an eyebrow at her in confusion.

She gestured to the Christmas tree, fully decorated and lit up in the corner. "I love that you took the effort because I love the holidays, but I don't want to force you into anything. It's why I said no when you first proposed. I didn't want you to think I baby trapped you."

I took her hand and kissed the back of it. "You didn't baby trap me. I know we didn't plan for it, but I want this."

"Why?" she asked. She pulled her hand away as if I had

burned her. "You specifically told me you would never get married again."

"Avs, I failed Kath. I never wanted to fail anyone else ever again. I definitely don't want to fail you."

Her eyes softened, and she leaned forward to give me a small kiss. "Oh, Nolan. You're such a good man. I can't see how you failed her."

"Do you know why we got divorced?"

She shook her head.

"I wanted kids, and she kept pushing me off."

She gave me a confused look and took a beat to respond. "That doesn't mean you failed her, you just wanted different things, and that's okay."

I put a hand on her stomach. "It made me feel like a failure. It really hurt when you told me I didn't want the baby and when you turned down my proposal. I don't want to fail either of you."

"Oh, Nolan. You won't fail us. You've already done so much."

She kissed my cheek and went back to grading papers.

I should have told her then that I loved her. I should have opened my big mouth and told her why I was doing all this stuff for her. I wanted to make her happy. When I first saw her crying in my brewery, Cupid struck an arrow in my heart. But I've never been a man who was good with his words.

I watched the hockey game, which was not enjoyable because our team sucked. The curse of being a Bulldogs fan. Avery was right; this wasn't relaxing.

She was quiet on her end of the couch, so I thought she was busy doing her work until I felt a hand crawling up my thigh.

"Avs?" I asked, but she wasn't looking at me. With one

hand, she graded papers, while the other unzipped my jeans and dove into my boxers.

"Hmm?" she asked, feigning unawareness.

I nearly choked on my beer when her deft hand reached inside and pulled out my cock. Of course, I got hard as soon as her hand was near it. She stroked it and hummed to herself while she read through her papers.

"Avery," I gasped.

She looked at me with fake shock. "What's wrong?"

I glared at her and gestured down to my dick out in the open and her hand pumping up and down my shaft. "Um... care to explain what you're doing?"

She gave me a wicked grin. "Helping you?"

"I don't—" I cut myself off with a moan when she tossed her papers aside and leaned down to lick the bead of moisture off the head.

"Shush, baby. You take care of me so much, let me help you," she said with a purr, like the little vixen she was. She moved onto her knees on the floor in front of me.

"I don't want you to hurt the baby."

She shook her head and bent her head to lick me from root to tip. "I'm good. Now shut up and let me suck your big cock."

"Fuck baby..." I moaned.

She grinned up at me and took me into her mouth. She sucked and bobbed up and down, all the while holding the base of my shaft with her hand.

I ran a hand through her dark brown hair and bunched it up on top of her head, so I could watch her suck me off. "You're a dirty girl, huh?"

She nodded and moaned on my cock, taking my cock as far back as she could. I groaned when she gagged on it and then pulled it out again. She licked along my shaft, getting it really wet again before taking me back down her throat.

I gripped her hair harder. This woman was such a goddess, and I fucking loved it. She pulled me out of her mouth but jacked me off with her hand. "Nolan."

I looked down at her through lust-hooded eyes. "Baby..." I moaned. "Don't stop."

"Fuck my face," she demanded.

"What?"

"Fuck my face and come down my throat. You want to do that, right, baby?" she asked all sweetly while she kissed my thighs and teased me by not putting my cock back into her mouth.

"Fuck yes!" I exclaimed.

She laughed and took me into her mouth again.

I thrust up into her while I gripped her hair. "Gonna come down your throat. You want that?"

She nodded while she moaned.

Fuck, I loved how she moaned when she sucked my cock

"You gonna be a good girl and swallow it all down?" I growled.

She looked up at me while she sucked my cock even harder, like she was proving a point. I groaned at the sight, and then I was coming hard and fast. My cock twitched violently, spilling the warm liquid into her mouth. She sucked and sucked until it was all gone. Then she hopped off and went back to her schoolwork like nothing had happened.

I sat back on the couch, my cock still hanging out while I tried to catch my breath. "Fuck," I sighed.

"What?" Avery asked without looking up from her papers.

I pushed her hair behind her ear and saw her trying to hide her naughty smile. "If you weren't already pregnant..."

"What? What would you do?" she asked, goading me with that grin across her face and the seductive tone in her voice.

"Put a baby in you. Damn, Avs, that was..."

She kissed me, and I tasted myself on her tongue. "Watch the hockey game, baby. I have papers to grade."

"No," I growled.

She bit her lip. She was playing dumb. She knew what she was doing to me. "No?" she asked innocently, with that sweet smile.

I put my beer down. "Get your fine ass over here."

She threw her papers down and jumped into my lap. I kissed her fiercely while I carried her upstairs to our bedroom.

I would do everything in my power to keep this woman happy. The first way to do that was to give her as many orgasms as she wanted. She would get everything she wanted from me and then some.

CHAPTER THIRTEEN

AVERY

When I woke up the following day, I had to blink to remember where I was. There was a warm body beneath me and the sound of a thump-thump-thump against my ear. I slowly opened my eyes and realized I was curled around Nolan like a koala bear in a tree. My leg was wrapped around his bigger one, and my head rested against his heart.

I vaguely remembered falling asleep in Nolan's arms after we fucked for the third time in a row last night. I had to hand it to him; my future husband didn't quit until I was completely satisfied. It surprised me that at his age, he had the stamina, but I wasn't complaining. I was pretty sure we used an entire bottle of lube last night, too. Nolan had been serious about making everything feel good for me. If that was how our marriage would be, he would make me a very happy wife.

I wanted to sleep longer, but I had a lot of work to do today. I had papers to grade, and I needed to call my landlord about the apartment. I hadn't started making any batches of my Christmas cookies yet, and that wasn't like me at all.

With a groan, I slid out of Nolan's arms and got dressed. I changed into leggings and a tank top and looked at my bump in the mirror. I was starting to show, but I kept it hidden underneath my flowing blouses and dresses. I threw on a sweatshirt and tip-toed down the stairs, so Nolan could sleep in.

When Gemma and I packed up my things yesterday, we discussed what I would do with my apartment. I was on a month-to-month lease, so it wasn't like I was stuck paying for a while. Gemma surprised me when she said she would take the apartment if my landlord was cool with it. If my sister moved in, he wouldn't have to find a new tenant. It was a win-win for everyone. Gemma could keep my furniture since it was in better shape than the shitty stuff she had in her apartment in the city. I knew she loved living in the city, so it surprised me she wanted to move back to the 'burbs.

I made coffee and ate a granola bar before I made the call to my landlord.

"Avery, how are you?" Peter asked.

"Hi, Peter. I'm sorry if this is too early," I said into my phone.

"Not at all. What's up?"

"I need to move out."

"Oh. Okay. Everything okay with the place?"

"Oh, it's been great. I love the place, but I'm pregnant, and my fiancé moved me into his house. It's too small for the baby and me."

"Congratulations! We totally understand."

"My little sister Gemma might be interested in the place. Can I give her your number?"

"Of course! That makes it easier for me. Why don't you give me her number, and we'll talk, okay?"

I rattled off my sister's number to him and then hung up. That was done, now to do everything else on my list. It was going to be a long morning.

I didn't feel like grading papers or working on my lesson plans. Instead, I got the mixing bowl out and started making the dough for chocolate chip peanut butter cookies. When Gem and I brought my stuff over yesterday, the first thing we did before she left was unpack my food, more importantly, my cookie ingredients. Nolan putting up lights on his house and decorating a Christmas tree to surprise me meant a lot to me. He knew I loved Christmas, and it was a sweet gesture. I never pressured him, but I knew there was a reason he was such a Grinch. Maybe he would confide in me what that was now that I would be his wife.

The box upstairs had the recipes I used for my Christmas cookies, but I knew them by heart. They had been handed down to my mom from my grandmother, and when I had been old enough, my mom did the same with me. They weren't anything special, but mom always prided herself on taking the time to make her Christmas cookies from scratch. It was important to me to continue the tradition.

I looked down at the growing bump on my belly and thought about how this meant I could pass that on to another generation. Happy tears pricked my eyes that I was finally getting what I wanted.

I mixed butter, peanut butter, white and brown sugar into a bowl and hand-stirred it until my hand felt like it would fall off. This was my favorite recipe to make, but it was also a pain because the peanut butter was so sticky and could be tough to mix. The pain was worth it for the delicious outcome. I added the vanilla extract and milk, stirred it up, then added the salt and flour.

I was dumping in the chocolate chips to finish when my phone buzzed on the counter. I saw Lizzie's name across my phone screen and swore under my breath. I hadn't intentionally kept my pregnancy a secret from her, but I had been blowing her off because of it. At the tree lighting ceremony, I was glad Nolan walked over when he did because she had been bugging me. She hadn't seen me in a while. I felt like a shitty friend, but the first trimester had been awful. I was sick all the time, tired, and annoyed with everyone.

I lifted the phone to my ear and tilted my head to press it against my shoulder while I finished mixing the cookie dough. "Hey!"

"Hey, you! Are you mad at me or something?" she asked.

I sighed. "No."

"Girl, what's up? I need some adult attention right now. Wyatt's taking the kids to his dad's so 'mommy can have some alone time.' I need a Sunday Funday day-drinking session with you."

I sighed again. "I can't."

"Oh, bummer. Raincheck?"

"Hang on a sec," I said and set my phone down.

I finished stirring the cookie dough and covered it with plastic wrap. I put it in the fridge to chill and then washed my hands. I picked my phone back up. "Sorry, you caught me in the middle of making dough. I can hang out, but..."

"But what?"

"I can't drink."

"Oh. Okay. Wait... why?"

I sighed and cringed before I answered. "Because I'm pregnant."

"What?" she shrieked. "Why didn't you tell me?"

I laughed. "Maybe you should come over. I have a lot to tell you."

"Um, yes, you do! I'll bring bagels from the coffee shop."

"Oh my god, I love you. Can you get me a French toast bagel if they have it? With the apple cinnamon raisin cream cheese."

"On it!"

"Wait!" I stopped her before she hung up on me. "Come to Nolan's."

She didn't miss a beat and laughed. "Oh, girl, we have A LOT to talk about. What does the big grump want?"

"Bacon, egg, and cheese on an everything bagel."

She hung up without a second word, and I got back to work on making dough.

I found another bowl and started preparing the dough for snickerdoodles. I went into the pantry, gathered all the ingredients, and set them down on the counter. I searched the cabinets for my hand mixer, but I had no idea where Gemma unpacked it. Had she unpacked it? I could beat the butter and sugars by hand, but my hand was already killing me from making the other dough.

I shot a text off to my sister.

ME: *Where's my hand mixer???*

GEM: *Your what? Why are you texting me soooo early?*

ME: *My hand mixer! The Beater!!*

GEM:...

GEM: *Yeah, I don't know what you're talking about.*

ME: *MY EGG BEATER! You're not getting any Christmas cookies if you don't tell me.*

GEM: *I don't know! Did we forget to pack it?*
ME: *GEM!!!*

Sometimes I forgot how forgetful my sister was. Nolan didn't have a hand mixer. That meant I had to go back to my apartment to ensure I didn't forget anything else. Pregnancy brain was no joke.

A knock on the front door prevented me from tearing my hair out. It also must have alerted Nolan because I heard thunderous footsteps from upstairs. Nolan stood in the kitchen with sweatpants on, no shirt, and a serious case of bedhead.

His scowl turned to concern when he saw me standing in the kitchen, gripping my hair in frustration. He pulled me into his arms. "Baby, what's wrong?" he asked.

Nolan used to only call me 'baby' during sex. Maybe it was just my hormones, but hearing him call me that now made my heart flip over in my chest.

"I can't find my hand mixer. And Lizzie's at the door," I said in between tears.

He pulled away with an unsure look, but then he walked over to the front door and let Lizzie inside. I sprinted up the stairs and went into the guest room. I started tearing up the boxes we brought up here yesterday, but my hand mixer was nowhere in sight. Eventually, Nolan came to get me. He had fixed his hair and put on a shirt.

"Avs, come on, why don't you eat something first?" he suggested and kneeled on the carpet next to me. The tears continued to fall.

"I can't make snickerdoodles if I don't have my hand mixer!" I cried.

I could tell he was trying not to laugh. This shouldn't be such a big deal that I was crying over not being able to find a kitchen appliance. He gently wiped my tears away. "Let's eat the bagels Lizzie brought over, and then we can figure it out, okay? I'll even go to the apartment for you."

"Okay," I blubbered.

He gave me a reassuring smile.

"I'm being ridiculous right now, aren't I?"

He cringed, but Nolan was a smart man and didn't answer that. Instead, he put a hand on my bump. "You need to eat something."

"I ate a granola bar."

"You need more, okay?"

I nodded and wiped my eyes. "I'm sorry."

"It's okay."

"Are you mad I invited Lizzie to your house this morning? I didn't tell her about the pregnancy, and I keep on making excuses on why we can't hang out."

He put his hands on my shoulders. "Avery, listen to me. This is your house, too. We're gonna get married and raise our kid here. I don't mind. Got it?"

I nodded.

He groaned as he got up, and I bit my tongue before making an old man joke. He helped me off the floor, and we walked down the stairs and back into the kitchen together. Lizzie was unloading the bagel sandwiches onto plates at the table. She gave me a smile when she saw me.

I went over to her and hugged her. Her mom instincts must have told her I needed that. When I pulled away, she studied me. "Aw, you look so cute pregnant!"

I grumbled.

She laughed. "Oh, girl, you need to eat."

I went over to the table and sat down next to Nolan. I took the first bite of my bagel and moaned. "Oh my god, I was kind of hungry."

Nolan grinned at me, and Lizzie laughed.

"I can't believe you didn't tell me!" she exclaimed.

Nolan put a hand on my stomach. "We wanted to wait until we made it through the first trimester."

I put my hand over his, and Lizzie gasped. "Oh my god! Are you getting married too?"

We nodded.

"Fucking finally."

"What?" I asked while I shoved more carbs into my mouth.

Lizzie rolled her eyes. "It was pretty obvious you two were meant for each other."

Nolan grunted next to me and finished his bagel. "Where are your keys?" he asked.

"On the hook," I said through a mouthful of bagel.

He kissed my temple. "I'll be back. I'll find your mixer. Text me if you forgot anything else."

I nodded, but as soon as the door slammed on his way out, Lizzie fixed me with a glare. "Spill!"

I swallowed my last bite. I gestured to my stomach. "Surprise? I'm pregnant?"

She rolled her eyes. "Yes, I can see that, but tell me everything. How did the thing with Nolan happen?"

I squinted at her. "Like when we conceived the baby?"

"Was that the first time?"

I shook my head.

"You're such a liar!"

I scowled at her. "What do you mean?"

"Every time I said something about him, you got flustered. How long have you been fucking?"

"Occasionally."

"How long?"

"Two years," I said in a small voice and squeezed my eyes shut.

"TWO YEARS?" she bellowed. "You're such a LIAR!"

I opened my eyes, but she smiled at me.

"Girl!" she yelled at me again.

"What?" I grumbled and finished my bagel.

She grabbed my hand and inspected my ring. "Wow, this is so unique."

"It was his mother's."

Her mouth was agape. "Nolan proposed with his mom's ring? Wow. I think that man really loves you."

I shook my head and got up to put the dishes away. "No. He just wants to do the right thing. He thinks he has to because of the baby."

Lizzie looked around and eyed the Christmas tree in the living room. "Avs, I love you, but you're wrong."

I ignored her as I loaded the dishwasher. "Any chance you want to help me make cookies today?"

Her eyes lit up. "Really? Can you teach me how to bake? I feel like the worst mom ever that I can't do that stuff with my kids."

I waved her off. "Lizzie, you're such a good mom. I'm afraid I don't know what I'm doing with this baby."

She got up from the table and hugged me. "It's gonna be fine. I didn't think I had any maternal instincts... you're gonna be scared, and it's gonna suck, but it's also gonna be great."

I leaned into her hug. "I'm sorry I didn't tell you."

"I understand."

"Everything's happening so fast," I admitted while I took the dough I made this morning out of the fridge and walked it over to the table. I preheated the oven and found the baking sheets. "Here, grease this pan, and I'll do this one," I instructed as I laid them on the table and handed her the butter wrappings I saved from this morning.

"Okay, what are we doing?" she asked as we spread the butter, wrapping facedown, on the metal baking sheets to grease them up.

"We're going to shape them into balls and then flatten them," I said.

I demonstrated by rolling a ball of dough onto the sheet and flattening it with the bottom of a glass. I handed her a glass so she could try. I watched her do one and nodded my approval.

We worked together and chatted until she finally asked, "How did he propose?"

I grimaced.

"What?"

"Well, I turned him down at first."

"What changed?" she asked.

"My sister told me he wanted to give me what I've always wanted. A home and a family, and that I should take the risk."

"So then you said yes?"

I nodded. "That was on Friday, and we just got my stuff from my apartment yesterday."

"Okay, I see why you felt like it was too soon. Although... you love him, don't you?"

"Lizzie, you don't understand, I've been in love with Nolan, probably from the moment we met, but I knew it would never come to anything."

"Why would you think that?"

"When we first hooked up, he made it clear it was a one-time thing. Then it kept happening. He always said he was never getting married again. But..." I trailed off as I thought about all that Nolan had done for me so far. My mind was still thinking about yesterday morning when I heard him talking to my pregnant belly.

"But what?"

"Yesterday, when I woke up, I heard him talking to the baby."

"Cute! Wyatt did that all the time when I was pregnant."

I smiled. "Yeah, but he was saying how he felt like he wasn't worthy of me. But he wasn't telling me that. He thought I was asleep."

"You need to talk to each other. Nolan's never been a man of many words, so you need to prod him a bit."

"I'm scared to ask. My heart can't take it if he doesn't feel the same way. But..."

"But what?"

I pointed to the Christmas tree in the other room. "Nolan hates Christmas, but he decorated his house for me."

Lizzie laughed. "I think that's his way of expressing his feelings. He didn't *have* to go all out for Christmas, but he did because he knows how much it means to you. He loves you and probably always has."

I mulled over her words. I wanted to believe her. My big, hopeless romantic heart wanted to believe that Nolan felt the same way I did. But if he did, why hadn't he ever told me? I agreed to marry him because I thought maybe we could find love in each other. I wanted the future he promised me so badly, but I was too chicken to tell him how I really felt.

CHAPTER FOURTEEN

NOLAN

*A*very freaking out about not being able to find her mixer wasn't normal. It had to be pregnancy hormones, something I was becoming very familiar with handling. If that made her happy, I didn't have a problem driving to the other side of town to get her mixer. I wondered if she had forgotten anything else, but she hadn't texted me. She warned me she was struggling with 'pregnancy brain,' whatever that was.

It confused me when I keyed into Avery's old apartment and noticed the lights were on. I stomped up the steps and came face-to-face with a screaming Gemma.

"NOLAN!" she screeched at me while brandishing a wooden spoon. "What are you doing here?"

I tried not to laugh at the thin slip of a girl trying to defend herself against a guy my size. "Sorry, Gem, I came to find Avery's mixer. What are you doing here?"

"Moving in!" she said and gestured to a couple of boxes scattered in the kitchen.

"Gem, by yourself?"

She gave me a stern look. "Yes. Don't worry, I started last night, and it's mostly just my books and clothes right now."

I ran a frustrated hand through my beard. The Jensen women sure were stubborn. A thought occurred to me as I stared at Gemma. "Does Avery know you started moving in?"

Gemma shook her head. "No, but I figured it was fine since she already paid this month."

I sighed. "Gem, did you even talk to the landlord?"

She waved me off. "Not yet, but it's fine."

I highly doubted that, but it wasn't like I was going to tell Gemma what to do. There was no stopping her when she put her mind to something. Avery would be so annoyed when I told her Gemma had already started moving in without talking to the landlord first.

"You should have talked to the landlord," I said to Gemma.

She rolled her eyes at me. "Nol, it's fine!"

"Well, you should have at least waited so I could ask Dec and the other guys to help," I said with a grumble.

"Relax, grumpy bear, I have it handled."

I grunted at her in response and looked through the cabinets in the kitchen. I found the mixer underneath the sink. Gem was unpacking boxes of books onto the bookshelf when I stepped back into the living room.

"You sure you're okay?" I asked.

She waved me off and flipped her hair over her shoulder. "I'm good, Nol. Actually, this move was simple because Avery said I could keep all the furniture since she won't need it at your place."

I glanced around. "What about the stuff at your place on South Street?"

She shook her head. "I live in a tiny studio and sleep on a futon. I'm going to take it over to my dad's at some point. My lease isn't up for a bit."

"Call me when you do, okay? I'll come do it."

"Nol, you're such a softie. I'm fine."

I rubbed my beard again. "It's the right thing to do, Gem. We're family."

She smiled at me. "Have you told my sister that you love her yet?"

Time shifted as her words hit me. Was I so obvious to everyone?

"What?" I choked out.

She stood up and gave me a knowing grin. "That's why you asked her to marry you, right? Because you love her. Not just because of the baby."

I nodded.

"Then tell her."

"I don't know how. I don't deserve someone like your sister. I think she feels like she baby-trapped me, but I think it's the opposite. I baby-trapped her."

Gem's eyes softened at that, and she put a reassuring hand on my arm. "You didn't. I think the baby's pushing you two where you need to be. It's fate."

I rolled my eyes at that. Gem was kind of into all that woo-woo shit. I didn't believe in fate. Okay, that was a lie. I believed in fate; I just thought it was an asshole. Was it fate to lose my family and have to raise my younger brother? Was it fate that my ex-wife never wanted kids? Fate could eat a bag of dicks as far as I was concerned.

"Did your sister leave anything else here?" I asked instead, changing the subject.

Gemma frowned but pointed to the box on the coffee table. I shoved the mixer inside and hefted the box into my arms.

"Nolan?"

"Yeah, kiddo?"

She blanched. "Gah! Stop it with the kiddo shit."

I liked to tease Gemma since she was so much younger than me. "What's up?"

"Don't be mad at me."

I raised an eyebrow. "About what?"

She bit her lip and ran a hand across her tattooed arm. That was a telltale sign she was nervous. "I let it slip to Dad that Avery's pregnant."

"Okay... wait, what?"

She gave me a guilty look. "I thought he knew. She didn't want to tell him at Thanksgiving."

"Why not?"

She gave me an annoyed look. "Because she wanted to invite you to Thanksgiving dinner, but you were a crotchety asshole to her."

I sighed. Avery had asked me about Thanksgiving at our Doctor's appointment right before the holiday, and I had been an enormous dick to her. I didn't know she was trying to ask me to come to her dad's.

"I was a dick."

"Colossal one. I thought she told him now that you're getting married. I'm sorry, I thought he knew."

"Avs and I will deal with it."

"I'm sorry."

"Gem, it's okay. He would find out soon, anyway. Shit, should I have asked for his blessing?"

She laughed. "Hell no! My sister would have definitely said no again if you did that."

"Thanks for the heads up. I better get this to your sister before I head to the brewery."

"I'll see you later for my shift," she said and went back to unpacking her things.

Without another word, I walked down the steps and drove back to my house. When I walked into the house, it smelled like a bakery. Avery and Lizzie were sitting at the kitchen table, laughing over a plate of cookies. I set the box down on the table and pulled out the appliance.

I held it up. "This is what you wanted, right?" I asked.

"Oh, thank you!" Avery said and jumped up to hug me tightly. Her baby bump pressed against my stomach as I wrapped my arms around her.

"Did you know Gemma already started moving into your apartment?" I asked while resting my hands on Avery's stomach. It still wowed me that our baby was growing inside there.

Avery looked confused. "No... I think my landlord needed to talk to her first..."

We shared an exasperated look.

Avery sighed. "She just up and started moving in, didn't she?"

I nodded. "You know, Gem. She already had boxes and everything."

Avery shook her head. "She wasn't supposed to just move in! I guess it doesn't matter; this month is already paid for."

"That sounds like Gemma," Lizzie cut in. "She waits for no one."

I nodded in agreement; that definitely was Gemma. Sometimes, she could be a flake, but no one could stop her when she set her mind to something.

Lizzie got up from her chair. "Hey, you two, I'm gonna get out of your hair."

I shook my head. "No, you stay. I gotta head out to the brewery, anyway."

She shook her head and put her coat on. "Nah, Wyatt and the kids should be home soon, so I better go. I'm happy for you two. Am I getting invited to the wedding?"

Avery shook her head. "We're gonna go to the court-house. You understand."

Lizzie nodded. Wyatt came from a big family, and neither of them wanted a big fuss. They ended up going to Vegas and got married by Elvis. It suited them. I let go of Avery and let her hug her friend goodbye.

"Do I get a cookie?" I joked when Lizzie left.

Avery laughed and handed me two. "Sure big guy, you deserve two." She leaned up on her tiptoes to give me a quick kiss... or attempted to. Avery was so tiny that I had to bend down to press my lips against hers. "Thanks for dealing with my moodiness this morning."

I patted my stomach. "I can't have all these cookies in the house."

"They're not all for you!" she teased.

I crammed the cookie in my mouth and chewed around it while I watched her ease herself back into the chair. "How do you feel?" I muttered through bits of cookie.

"Do you want to use your words this time?" she asked in her teacher's voice. That shouldn't be sexy to me, but it was. I had always been hot for my smart English teachers.

I swallowed and asked again, "How are you feeling?"

"Tired," she said. "But okay. Are you gonna head over to the brewery?"

I nodded. "Unless you need me here?"

She shook her head. "No, Nol. You gotta go to work. I

have papers to grade and a lesson plan to create, anyway. Will you be home for dinner?"

"Dinner?" I asked, confused.

She rolled her eyes at me. "Yeah, you know that thing you eat before you go to bed?"

"You don't have to make me dinner."

"I gotta eat anyway. If you'll be home, let me know, and I'll have it ready for you. If not, I'll leave you a plate in the fridge."

Kath and I never did dinners together, mainly because we were never on the same schedule. It was weird that Avery wanted to do that for me.

"It's not a big deal," she reassured me.

Instead of saying 'okay, sure' like a normal person, I blurted out, "Why haven't you told your dad about the baby?"

She sighed. "Yeah, I got an earful about that right before you got home."

"Why haven't you told him?" I asked again.

Her brow creased, and I knew I was bugging her. "Nolan, can we talk about this later? You gotta get to the brewery. I'm not keeping you from your work. Go."

I didn't know how she did it, but she forced me to make my way out the door and down the block to the brewery. I hung my coat up in the office and put on my apron as Declan walked in.

My brother gave me a toothy grin. "Well, look who showed up."

"Not gonna completely ditch my work," I snarled at him.

He raised his hands in surrender. "Sorry, dude. What's got your panties in a twist?"

I rubbed my beard. "Nothing. I got beer to brew so we can stay in the black."

My brother nodded. "Bro, we're doing well. Winter's good for us. You brew that holiday beer everyone loves."

"We had to dump that last batch. That cost us a lot," I reminded him.

"I didn't forget, but we can make it up."

"Dec, I have a baby on the way."

"Dude, I know! What does that have to do with us being in the black?"

I sighed. "I'm worried."

My brother sat in his desk chair and steepled his hands in front of his face. "Dude, sit down."

I huffed but slumped into the chair in front of his desk.

"Spill."

I sighed. "Avery has a teacher's salary."

"Yeah?"

I gestured to the room we were sitting in. "We're not exactly swimming in money. I need to provide for my baby. To provide for Avery."

"I think you're suffering from stupid man syndrome, and you need to get your head out of your ass."

"Man, fuck you!"

My little brother laughed. "Too easy, man."

"Asshole!"

"I think you need to relax. Yeah, we're not swimming in dough, and Avery doesn't make a lot of money on her teacher salary, but you both love what you do. You're both gonna do everything you can to make sure your baby's taken care of. And she will be."

"She? We don't know the gender yet."

"Gemma has a feeling."

I rolled my eyes.

My brother laughed. "I love Gemma like a sister, but she's something else sometimes. Are you good now?"

I shook my head. "Avery didn't tell her dad."

"Tell him what?"

"About the baby. Gemma let it slip."

My brother winced. "Well... that sucks, but I'm sure she had her reasons. You have to talk to her, not grunt and do things for her like she understands what that means."

I sighed. I felt like I was getting this from both Gemma and my brother today. What gives?

I stood up from the chair. "I gotta go check on the hops."

"Would it kill you to talk about your feelings?" my brother yelled after me as I walked out of the office.

I pretended I didn't hear him and kept walking.

CHAPTER FIFTEEN

AVERY

"*H*ey, what are you doing up?" Nolan asked.

I was still awake and sitting up in our bed when he came home from the brewery. I smiled and watched him strip off his shirt and get out of his jeans. I dropped the pen I was using, and my eyes trailed down his chest.

"Avs?" he asked.

"Huh?" I asked and shook myself out of my daze. His brown eyes twinkled with amusement. He totally caught me being hot for his bod.

"My eyes are up here."

"That's not what I'm interested in right now," I muttered.

He chuckled and got into bed beside me. "Is that why you're still up?"

I glanced at the clock; I hadn't realized it was eleven o'clock already. Since it was a school night, I should get to bed soon.

I shook my head. "Nope, I still need to finish grading these papers."

"Oh, you're not awake hoping to get a ride of this?" he teased and gestured to his body.

I laughed and shook my head.

"You sure?" he asked with a naughty grin.

I bit my lip and shook my head again. I was lying. I was so horny for my baby daddy, but I was also exhausted and needed to get to bed. "I gotta finish this."

He took the pen and papers out of my hand and put them on the bedside table next to me. "Avs, you gotta get your rest."

"I know, but I have a lot to do."

He placed a hand on my growing stomach. "I know, but the stress isn't good for the baby. Let's go to sleep."

I yawned and nodded. "Okay. Did you eat? I left you a plate in the fridge."

He nodded as he lay on his back and rested his head against his pillow. "Yeah. Thanks, baby. That was really nice."

Warmth filled my body when he called me 'baby.' Some women didn't like that, but I loved it. It made me feel like I was really his, and forget my fears that our upcoming marriage was only a convenience because of the baby.

I waved him off and went into the bathroom to brush my teeth. It was nothing to make him dinner. I didn't mind doing it since I had to make dinner for myself, anyway. I was a caregiver, and I liked taking care of Nolan. Making him dinner was the least I could do for him when he did so much more for me.

I slid back into bed and melted into him when he wrapped his arms around me.

"Avs?" he asked.

"Yeah?"

"Why didn't you tell your dad about the baby?"

I sighed. I didn't want to get into this with him. I didn't want to explain that I was scared of miscarrying like my mother did. Or that I was thirty-five and scared to tell my dad I got 'oops pregnant.'

"Do you know why my sister and I are so far apart in age?" I asked.

"No."

"My mom miscarried in between us. I wanted to make sure this was real. That we wouldn't lose Peanut."

He reached a hand up and lightly caressed my face. "Oh, baby, why didn't you tell me?"

I shook my head. "I'm sorry."

His thumb stroked against my cheek, and his calloused manly hands comforted me as the tears fell. This pregnancy was turning me into a weepy mess.

He wiped the tears away. "I promise you, nothing's gonna happen to Peanut."

"What if it does?" I cried.

He pressed a kiss to my lips to silence me, and it worked. Feeling his lips on mine, the way he fit against me, comforted me better than he would ever know.

He pulled away and stroked my face again. "Hey, it's gonna be okay. I promise you. Now get some sleep."

I nodded. "Okay. Nolan?"

"Yeah, baby?"

I couldn't help the smile spreading across my face at him calling me that again. "We should have my dad over for dinner."

"Okay. Tell me when and I'll make sure I'm home."

"Okay. I'll call him tomorrow."

He pressed a soft kiss to my forehead and leaned me

onto my side. I closed my eyes to the feeling of his chest pressed against me and his hand protectively on my stomach.

When I woke up the next morning, I was confused because Nolan wasn't in bed next to me. I was cuddled up in the blankets, and I didn't want to leave the comfort of the bed, but I had to get to school. I smelled something good cooking downstairs. I tip-toed down the steps and found my fiancé making breakfast. My fiancé, who came home late last night, was awake and making me breakfast.

"Aw, Avs, don't do that!" Nolan said while he looked over his shoulder at me.

I hefted myself into one of the kitchen chairs. "Do what?" I asked, trying to keep the tears from falling.

"Cry over my bad cooking," he joked.

That put a smile on my face. "Sorry, hormones."

He came over to me and kissed me on the top of my head while he slid eggs and toast on the plate in front of me. "No morning sickness anymore, right?"

I shook my head. Today officially marked the second trimester, and I had woken up feeling energetic. "I think it passed. Just horny and hungry."

He laughed. "Well, that's what I'm here for."

I dove into breakfast but watched the clock to make sure I wasn't late for school. When I lived across the street, being late was never a problem. Now that I was living on the other side of town, I needed to add extra time to my commute so I wasn't late. Nolan poured me coffee, and I savored it, as it was the only way I would get through trying to teach Shakespeare to my kids today.

Nolan took my plate away when I finished and started loading the dishwasher.

"You didn't have to make me breakfast, but thanks."

"I wanted to make sure you ate before you left. You're gonna drive to school, right?"

I hadn't thought about it; it wasn't a far walk over to the school. That was the benefit of living in such a small town. Pregnancy was tiresome, though, and the idea of walking over there didn't appeal to me, especially while bogged down with my bag.

"Yeah, I'm not walking. I better start getting ready."

I kissed him on the cheek and went upstairs to take a quick shower. When I was getting dressed, I realized I had a problem. One, I still hadn't unpacked all my clothes. And two, I needed to get maternity wear. I was practically falling out of my bra, and my dress pants didn't fit anymore.

That's how Nolan found me, sitting on the bed crying because I had popped the button off of my favorite pair of pin-striped dress pants.

He kneeled in front of me and took my face in his hands. He was such a champ for dealing with my constant crying. "Hey, what's going on?"

"I can't fit into my pants!" I fumed.

He placed his big hand on my stomach. "Avery, first, I love your curves. Second, you're growing our child inside you."

"I feel so unattractive right now, and I'm not even that big yet!" I said with a sob.

"Hey, I think you're sexy as hell, okay? You carrying our baby? That's sexy. What if you wore one of your dresses to work instead?"

I wiped my face with the back of my hand. "Okay," I blubbered.

"You know you have me to lean on, okay? I'm here."

"I know."

"Do you? Because it feels like you want all the weight on your shoulders right now."

I shook my head. "No, I know. Sorry, you're dealing with a lot of crying pregnant lady lately."

He brushed my hair out of my face. "S'okay, baby."

I leaned into his touch. "Thanks. I better find a dress that works. I have to talk to the Principal about my maternity leave plans."

He kissed my forehead and went to get a shower. I found one of my flowy dresses and threw on leggings since it was winter in Pennsylvania. I was looking in the full-length mirror, inspecting the baby bump, when Nolan got out of the shower.

"See, there's my sexy mama," he said with a big grin on his face.

I gave him an annoyed look. "I can't tell if I look pregnant or like I ate too many cookies yesterday."

"I know I did," he teased.

"Don't eat them all."

"Don't make them so good."

I smiled. "My mom taught me how to make everything from scratch. I'm glad I can pass that on to Peanut. Gemma sure as hell didn't care to learn."

His face softened at that. "Is that why you love Christmas so much? It reminds you of your mom?"

I nodded and looked in the mirror while holding my stomach. Nolan got dressed and came up behind me. He wrapped his arms around me and put his bigger hands on top of mine. I loved the protective nature of his touch. I hoped Peanut felt the love he poured out to them every time he touched my belly.

"Mom made Christmas exciting. I loved making all the cookies with her. I want to keep up that tradition," I said to him.

"Peanut will have that."

"Nolan?"

"Hmm?"

"Why do you hate Christmas?"

He pulled away and sighed. "It's not that I hate it, it's just..." he slumped down on the bed, and the look of hurt on his face surprised me.

I didn't mean to hurt him with that question. I had asked him before, and he always shrugged me off. I never wanted to press, but if he was going to be my husband, I wanted to know why he hated Christmas.

I sat on the bed next to him. "It's okay. You don't have to tell me."

He ran a hand through his bushy beard. "Do you know how my parents died?"

I shook my head.

Gemma and I didn't grow up in Drakesville. Our dad was from here, but we grew up a couple of towns away. I didn't know that much about the town until I got the teaching job at the high school. Nolan and Declan didn't like to talk about their parents' death. All I knew was that they died when Nolan was eighteen, and he took on the job of raising his brother, who had only been twelve.

"They died in a car crash coming home from a Christmas party."

Oh.

Oh, that made so much sense now. The holiday reminded him of everything he lost and how he had to figure out how to take care of his little brother at only eighteen. I felt like a jerk for teasing him about being such a Grinch.

"Oh, Nolan, I'm sorry," I said.

"It's in the past," he said with a grunt.

I reached a hand up and brushed his hair behind his ear. "I still miss my mom. It's okay to still grieve for them."

"It's fine," he insisted and pulled away from me. "You better get to work, yeah?"

"Nolan."

"Avs, can you drop it? I don't want to talk about it anymore."

I nodded.

I knew he didn't like to talk about his feelings, and I didn't want to push him, but I was worried. Why would he put up the Christmas tree and lights on his house if it was all a reminder of the worst day of his life? I didn't want him to be in pain because he knew how much I loved the holiday.

He rubbed a hand down his face. "Baby, I'm..."

"It's fine. I gotta get to work," I said sharply and gathered up my things.

Big lie, it wasn't fine. I wanted Nolan to open up to me, but it hurt how dismissive he was. I knew this was a sour subject, but I wished he wasn't so closed off.

He didn't stop me from leaving, so I knew the conversation was over. I couldn't help but feel guilty about the downtrodden look on his face, though. Maybe I'd get him to open up to me, but it definitely wouldn't be today.

I didn't have time to prod him, anyway. I had to make it to school early to talk to Principal Mathews. Helen was the only one at school who knew I was pregnant. I had kind of made a spectacle at the brewery when I told Nolan I'd marry him. Nolan liked to remind me we lived in a gossipy small town, so odds were the entire school knew I was pregnant by now. Maybe even the whole town.

I dropped my things off in my classroom, peed for the millionth time that day already, and walked over to the main office. Claudia, the secretary, smiled at me. "Hi, Avery, he's waiting for you."

"Thanks."

"Congratulations!" she called after me as I walked into the office.

Welp, I guess my secret was out.

"Avery!" Grayson Mathews greeted me and gestured to the seat in front of him.

I gave him a tight smile and took the seat. "I guess you know why I'm here."

"News travels fast in a small town."

I groaned. "How did you find out?"

"Oh, Felix is my cousin. And I ran into Gemma at the coffee shop this morning."

I sighed. Gossipy small town indeed. I didn't think I needed to tell my sister to keep it on the down-low. I would be having some words with her later. I was still mad at her for spilling the beans with our dad.

He laughed. "When are you due?"

"Not until June. I might duck out early depending on when the baby comes."

"What about leave? Will you use any of your personal time?"

The school I taught at didn't give paid maternity leave. It was bullshit. If I didn't love what I did, I'd probably look for a different career.

"Probably for whenever I end up going out on leave, but I plan to be back in the fall as usual."

"Okay, that sounds good."

"I'll need to take a couple of mornings off. We're going to get married, so I need to apply for the marriage license and then get married."

"Oh. I didn't realize you were engaged."

"Not gonna lie. This pregnancy was a surprise, but the dad and I have known each other for a while, and we're getting married."

He furrowed his brow. "Oh. Who are you getting married to?"

"Nolan MacGregor."

"Mac? Really?"

I hated that old nickname. Nolan would never be 'Mac' to me.

"What does that mean?"

He shook his head. "Nothing."

"No, explain it to me."

"Kath said he was a robot."

I furrowed my brow in confusion. "Your wife? What does she have to do with it?"

"They used to be married."

I felt like the floor dropped out from underneath me. I had no idea that my boss' wife was Nolan's ex. My heart broke for Nolan, though, because Grayson and his wife had a kid, and he was one of my students. She had a kid with Grayson when all those years she told Nolan he didn't deserve that. I could never tell him about this; it would absolutely break him.

"I better get to homeroom before the little demons tear it apart," I finally said.

"Avery, I'm sorry."

"For what?"

He leaned back in his chair. "I feel like I offended you."

I curled my hands into fists at my sides and hoped he

didn't see. I clenched my teeth and tried to think carefully about my next words. "I'd appreciate you not talking bad about my fiancé. He's the father of my child and a good man. Kath didn't deserve him.'

I sped out of the office before I said something even worse, like something that could get me fired. I was probably going to get a reprimand for that outburst.

A protectiveness had snarled up inside me when he said Nolan was a robot. Yes, the man had a problem talking about his feelings. I dealt with that just this morning, but he was a good man. He didn't deserve the hurt the world had put him through. He deserved love and happiness, and maybe Peanut and I could give him that.

NOLAN

I wiped the sweat off my brow as Allen and one of our other brewers, Ryan, worked on bottling more of our holiday beer.

"Did you check the levels on the tank for the next batch?" I asked Ryan.

Ryan was new to brewing. He had started as a bartender when we opened up the taproom. I worked with him at a different brewery before Declan and I started our own operation. He was a quick study, which was why I hired him as our new cellarman.

"On it, boss," Ryan said with a smile across his golden-brown face as he went to check.

I was still worried about the loss of revenue from when we had to dump that bad batch. It was why I was putting in the extra hours to produce as much beer as possible.

"Ryan's a quick study," Allen said with a nod.

I grunted in response and got back to work.

"You're chatty today," he teased.

I didn't respond and moved on to bottling the rest of the beer we were working on. I'd been at the brewery all day, working hard on our production and researching what beer to make next. That pumpkin beer had been an experiment, but people liked it. It brought in beer drinkers that didn't like IPAs. As a craft brewery, we needed to be more versatile. Craft beer drinkers would always come for the hoppy IPAs and Pale Ales, but I wanted us to reach *all* beer drinkers.

Allen gave me a concerned look.

"What?" I snapped.

"You need to relax."

I sighed and stroked my beard. "I'm worried about the tank calibration fucking up production."

Only partially a lie. Avery and I didn't leave things on good terms this morning. She prodded me to talk about my parents, and I got snippy with her. I needed to apologize when I went home tonight. She was going to be my wife. I shouldn't dismiss her like that. I'd felt shitty about it all day.

He eyed me cautiously. "Nolan, we're gonna be okay. Just because you're the brewmaster doesn't mean you need to micromanage every little detail."

"I know. I…"

I couldn't finish the thought because my brother came into the tank room. "Do you have your phone on you?" he asked.

"No. Why?"

"Avery's been trying to get a hold of you."

My heart jumped up into my throat, and I raced into the office where my phone was charging. I hit her number in my contact list, my heart pounding, thinking something happened to her and the baby.

"Hey, there you are," she said cheerfully. "I figured you

didn't have your phone on you when you were in the middle of production."

"What's wrong? Is Peanut okay?" I rushed out. When Declan said Avery had been trying to get a hold of me, my mind immediately went to the worst thing. Maybe I was just wired for phone calls spelling bad news.

"Oh, nothing's wrong. I'm sorry, did I make you think it was an emergency? I told Declan to have you call me back when you got a chance, not this second."

I sighed and slumped down in the chair across from Declan's desk. I ran a hand through my hair and sighed. She was fine. The baby was fine.

I checked my watch; it was almost five, and Avery was probably home by now. Or maybe she was still at school? We had only been living together since this weekend, so I didn't know her work schedule yet.

"What's going on?" I asked.

"Do you think you could be home for dinner tonight? My dad ambushed me, and he wants to come over and meet you."

"I think I can be home. You need me to stop at the store?"

"I'm there now, but thanks for the offer. Sorry if I worried you."

"S'okay, baby," I said in relief. "Let me finish up my current task, and I'll meet you at home."

I hung up and ran a hand through my hair again. I hadn't been expecting to meet Avery's dad so soon. I looked up and saw my brother standing in the office doorway with a smug look on his face.

"What?" I barked out.

"You called her baby," he said in a teasing tone.

"Yeah?"

He smirked.

I stood up and punched him in the arm. "Don't do that to me again."

He rubbed his arm. "Ow, what the fuck!"

"You made me think something was wrong with the baby!"

He shook his head at me. "Man, you're so high-strung. What did she want?"

"Her dad's coming over for dinner, and she wants me home."

"Go on. Ryan and Allen can handle the bottling. Go be with your baby mama."

I took off my apron and put on my coat. "Are you sure?" I asked.

Declan pushed me out of his office. "Please go. Your stress is annoying everyone."

I glared at him, but left in a rush to get home. Avery wasn't home yet when I got there, so I put the Christmas lights on while cleaning up the kitchen. I took a shower and was trimming my beard when I heard her coming into the house.

I walked downstairs and lifted the grocery bags out of her hands when I reached the kitchen. "Hey, give me that."

"Nolan, I can carry the groceries in the house."

"Sit your cute butt down and rest while I unload them."

She smiled at me and did as she was told, slumping down into a kitchen chair and rubbing her stomach. She looked exhausted, and that worried me, but the Doctor said that was normal. I went outside to bring in the rest of the groceries.

"C'mere," she practically growled at me when I finished unloading everything.

I smirked at her and crossed the room toward her. She

lifted her hands to my face and pulled me down into a heated kiss. I smiled into it, but pulled away before it went further.

"I'm sorry about this morning. I was a dick," I said.

She held my face in her hands. "It's okay. I know I pushed a nerve. Just know, I'm here, okay?"

I nodded.

She brought me down for another brain-melting kiss, and I felt my cock harden against my thigh. She rubbed a hand over my crotch, and I had to pull away from the kiss as much as it pained me.

"Baby, you better stop if your dad's coming over," I warned.

She leaned into my chest and smiled up at me. "Sorry, I'm horny for that big dick."

"Christ, Avery," I swore.

She laughed and stood up. "Sorry, it's the hormones!"

I watched her ass sway as she walked over to the counter and started getting out the pots and pans we needed to make dinner. Damn, did she look good in my kitchen. And it did nothing to quell the raging boner in my pants.

She gave me an exasperated look when she caught me staring at her with my mouth hanging open. "Nolan, I can feel you burning a hole in my ass with your eyes. Don't distract me while I need to make dinner."

"Let me help. What are we making?"

"Chicken parm, it's my dad's favorite. But fair warning, it's gonna get messy since we need to bread the chicken."

I rolled up the sleeves of my plaid button-down. "Tell me what to do, Teach."

She laughed. "Okay, let's get to work. Hey, do you have any of that Holiday Hops beer?"

I frowned. "You can't have any."

"For my dad," she explained. "He loves that beer."

"Yup. I got some in the fridge."

She made a face. "So gross!"

"It's a bestseller!" I argued.

"Too hoppy."

"Says you," I teased.

"You could always make another Christmas beer."

"Like what?" I asked.

The thought had crossed my mind, especially since the pumpkin beer had sold well. I hadn't been ready to make another holiday beer this year, but we could consider it for next year. I always liked to have new seasonal beers in the pipeline alongside our core beers.

"Well, you know I like a wheat beer or a stout," she said.

"Porter would be good for winter too."

She pointed at me. "True. You'll figure it out. Enough chit-chat, big guy, let's get to work."

We worked together in the kitchen, and I realized how nice it was. It was a welcome occasion to cook beside her and ask about her day. I was hit with a sense of déjà vu of my parents in this kitchen cooking together.

A memory flashed in my mind of a Thanksgiving when I was a kid. Mom was making the turkey while Dad peeled potatoes at the counter next to her. He played that awful jazz music and twirled her around in the kitchen. My parents had been so in love. I always wanted that kind of marriage.

A hand on my shoulder pulled me from the memory. "Hey, where did you go?" Avery asked.

I smiled at her and put a hand on her growing stomach. "Just lost in thought."

It looked like she wanted to say something, but then the

doorbell rang, and the moment slipped away. Avery pulled away from me and wiped her hands on a hand towel. I heard her greeting someone at the door and then footsteps toward the kitchen.

Avery's dad was lanky and tall, with a head of hair that had gone completely white.

"Dad, this is Nolan," Avery introduced me.

I put out a hand to him, and he shook it. "Good to meet you, sir."

He laughed and pulled his hand away. "Sir? Come on, kid, we're family now. You can call me Sal. Or Dad."

"Sure, Sal. You want a beer?"

He smirked at his daughter. "I like this man already, sweetheart."

She rolled her eyes and went back to finishing the rest of dinner. I walked over to the fridge and pulled out two beers. I popped the tops and pulled glasses out of the cabinet. I poured the beers into the glasses and brought them over to the table.

"Oh glasses, you're fancy," he joked and took a sip. "Oh, that's a good beer."

"I told you!" I said to Avery.

"Still gross!" she teased back as she carried the casserole dish of the chicken parm over to the table.

I got up and brought the pasta pot over to the table to help her. Her dad smiled at us from over his beer glass, and the three of us filled our plates for dinner.

"How are you feeling, Avery?" Sal broke the silence.

She chewed thoughtfully. "Okay, I guess. I'm past the morning sickness, just tired."

Her dad nodded. "That's normal. Why didn't you tell me?"

I squeezed her hand under the table in comfort.

She chewed her food in thought and let the question hang in the air. "I was scared of telling you and then miscarrying. I wanted to wait. Apparently, Gemma didn't get that memo."

"I understand, sweetheart. It would have been nice to hear it from you, though."

"Dad," Avery started. "I was gonna tell you, I just wasn't ready yet."

"You felt sick at Thanksgiving, didn't you?"

Avery nodded.

He narrowed his eyes at Avery. "Is that why I found all that Drakesville Lager in the garage the next day? I thought that was weird because I thought for sure I picked up some beer for you to drink with the meal."

Avery cringed. "Yeah. I was scared to tell you all, and Gemma was helping cover for me."

"Ah, sweetheart, you should have told us."

"I didn't want to be a disappointment."

Her dad frowned, and Avery covertly brushed her fingers under her eye. I hated that she was such a ball of nerves and tears all the time. Her dad's eyes widened when the light reflected off the ring on her hand.

He looked at me, and I nodded at his unspoken question. "We're getting married too," I said.

"Oh! That's wonderful news. Avs, sweetheart, why are you crying?"

"I'm sorry," she blubbered. "I feel like I let you down."

"How?" he asked.

"Because I got 'oops pregnant,' and I'm having a shotgun wedding," she cried.

Her dad and I shared a look. He put a hand over hers. "Avery, I don't care how you got pregnant. This baby might be a surprise, but babies are a blessing. I can't wait to meet my first grandchild. Lord knows your sister's not giving me any."

She laughed. "She said the fifth of never."

"No more crying. Let's eat!" Sal said with a laugh and dug into his chicken. "Aw, sweetheart, you made my favorite!"

I cut into my food and tasted it. Avery was such a superb cook. I had 'helped' with dinner tonight, but mostly I just did what she told me to.

"Nolan helped," she admitted sheepishly.

Her dad smiled. "He did? That was nice of him. You're gonna name the baby after me, right?"

She laughed again, and the tension in the air dissipated. "Dad! What if we have a girl? I can't name her Salvatore!"

Her dad drank more of his beer and squinted at her in thought. "I don't know, Salvatrice has a nice ring."

"Dad!" Avery laughed and shook her head at him.

He laughed and looked over at me. "Nolan, you and your brother own MacGregor Brothers Brewing Company, right?"

"Yes, sir."

Sal nudged Avery. "Sweetheart, where'd you find this formal guy?"

A small smile formed across her lips. "He's usually not like this. He was nervous about meeting you."

"She's not wrong," I agreed and took another sip of my beer.

Sal pointed at himself. "Me? Am I intimidating?"

No, he didn't look intimidating at all. But I knocked up his daughter, so I assumed he would hate me.

I shook my head.

"Dad, stop interrogating him. Nolan's a good man. We've been friends for a while," Avery said.

"Let me see the ring," he insisted.

Avery held out her hand, and her dad examined it. "Pretty and unique."

"It was my mother's," I said and drank more of my beer, hoping to swallow the lump in my throat.

The older man gave me a sympathetic smile. "I'm sure she would have loved Avery. Did you have to get it resized?"

"No, it fit her perfectly."

Avery pulled her hand away and put it on her stomach.

Alarm bells went off in my head. "You okay?"

She nodded. "I thought I felt the baby, but I think I imagined it. It's still too early."

"You'll get there," her dad reassured her.

"You're really not mad?" she asked her dad.

"Avery, you're a grown-ass woman. Why would I get mad? Do you have any of those Christmas cookies?"

She glared at him. "I knew you had an ulterior motive for coming here! After dinner."

After dinner, I gave Sal a refill on his beer, and I told Avery to take a load off while I cleaned up in the kitchen. Dinner had gone better than I expected. I thought her dad would hate me, but he was a chill guy. Maybe the fact I moved her into my house and we were getting married did it. In his eyes, I was doing the right thing by making an honest woman out of her.

I put the leftovers away and scrubbed the pans. In the living room, I heard the low murmuring of Avery and her dad talking about the hockey game. It turned out her dad was a huge Bulldogs fan, so we got to talking about if the team could make the playoffs this year. They hadn't won the cup since the eighties, though. It was frustrating to be a Bulldogs fan. It made sense that Avery was such a big hockey fan now; she got it from her dad.

I dried off my hands and walked into the living room to find Sal in the armchair and Avery curled up asleep on the couch. I sat down on the other end of the couch next to Avery. I took a swig of my now lukewarm beer and made a disgusted face.

Sal chuckled. "Too warm?"

"Didn't drink it fast enough."

He eyed me warily. "Does my daughter know how much you love her?"

I studied the bottom of my bottle. Was I that obvious to literally everyone but the woman in question?

He gave me a hard look. "You didn't ask her to marry you because you thought it was the right thing to do, right, son?"

I nodded and then shook my head. "No, she doesn't know, but yeah, I didn't ask because I felt like I had to. I wanted to."

He pointed at the sleeping form of his daughter. "She needs to know that."

I picked at the label on my beer. "I was married before, and it didn't work out."

"What happened?"

"I wanted kids. She didn't. I don't know if Avery told you about my parents—"

He cut me off. "I'm from Drakesville. I knew your parents back in high school. I'm sorry for your loss."

I nodded and stroked my beard. "I had to take care of my little brother. We don't have any other family. Kath and I got married young, but I always felt like I didn't deserve another shot at love or a family."

"That's the dumbest thing I've ever heard. Tell my daughter you love her. I know you'll make her happy, but you have to tell her that."

I couldn't respond because Avery stirred on the other side of the couch. She sat up and looked around in confusion. She blinked at me and then turned to look at her dad. "Oh, dad, I'm sorry. Growing a baby is tiresome."

Sal smiled at his daughter, but his eyes told me I needed to think about what he said. I wasn't a man of many words. Finding the words to tell her how I felt was hard for me. What if she was only marrying me because she felt like this was her only chance at the life she wanted? What if she was settling for me?

Avery looked at her dad and me. "What are you two talking about?"

"I was asking Nolan when you're having the wedding," he lied.

"Oh, we haven't discussed it, but I want a simple courthouse wedding before I turn into a whale."

Her dad laughed.

She hefted herself off the couch. "Dad, let me make you up a box of cookies to take home."

Her dad smiled at her as she walked away. He left soon after, and we sat on the couch together, watching the Bulldogs lose, until Avery said she couldn't keep her eyes open any longer.

When we crawled into bed, an idea popped into my head.

"Avery?"

"Yeah?"

"How do you feel about getting married at the brewery?" I asked.

She leaned on her side and gave me a confused look. "But how?"

"Well, we don't have to get married by a minister in PA.

We can apply for a self uniting license with our marriage license."

"How do you know all this?" she asked as she ran a hand through my beard. I think she noticed I trimmed it up tonight because I wanted to make a good impression on her dad.

I grumbled under my breath.

"Use your words," she joked.

I kissed her hand. "I've been researching our options. I don't want a religious ceremony, and the law is confusing about people who get ordained online."

"Me neither. I kind of like that idea."

"Yeah?"

She nodded. "Gemma got ordained online a few years ago, but maybe we could have her preside over it?"

"Yeah, I would really like that."

I wondered if she liked the idea because the brewery was where we began. If her date hadn't stiffed her with the check, she wouldn't be lying in bed with me wearing my mother's ring and carrying my baby.

"When?" she asked.

"You want to do it soon, right?"

She nodded.

"What about Christmas?"

Her face fell, and she put both her hands on my face. "Oh, Nolan, no."

"No?" I asked and furrowed my brow. "But you love Christmas."

She sighed. "I love Christmas. I love it so much, but you hate it. I'm sorry I pushed you to talk about it this morning. I'm sorry it reminds you of all you lost."

"Then maybe we should do it, so I'll have a reason to love it again."

"Again?"

"I wasn't always a Grinch."

"Nolan, we don't have to get married so soon. Christmas is only in a couple of weeks."

"Let's do it before Peanut gets here. Take the morning off tomorrow, and we'll go get the paperwork started so we can get married in time."

She seemed to think about it for a little bit.

"Come on, Avs. You love Christmas. Let me give you a Christmas wedding."

"Oh, Nolan..." she sighed, but in happiness, and then she kissed me.

We savored each other until our mouths got greedy and our tongues waged war on each other. The sheets tangled around our legs, and my head somehow ended up underneath my pillow while she straddled me.

I smirked up at her when we pulled away from each other and laughed. "I thought you couldn't keep your eyes open?"

She ground down on my boner. "Not too tired to ride this dick."

"Oh. Is that so?"

She nodded. "Uh-huh."

"C'mere you," I growled and pulled her down for another kiss.

It wasn't long before she was riding my dick and screaming out my name. I couldn't wait to make this woman my wife and have her be my forever.

CHAPTER SEVENTEEN

AVERY

"What about this one?" Gemma asked. She held up another dress for me to look at.

It had been about a week since I moved in with Nolan and agreed to marry him. We went to get our marriage license earlier this week, and I was surprised we got it back yesterday already. I was worried they would give us a hard time about the self uniting license since we weren't Quakers, but it was a breeze.

We decided to get married on Christmas Day, up in the loft space of the brewery, with Declan and Gemma as our witnesses. It would be a small ceremony with our siblings, my dad, and some of the staff from the brewery. Lizzie and Wyatt were still unsure if they could come because Christmas morning was chaos with their kids.

Since we were on a time crunch, Gemma dragged me out to look for a wedding dress today. I felt like she had taken me everywhere. We started at a bridal shop, then she took me to her favorite consignment shop, and now we were at the King of Prussia Mall. I was cranky and tired, and I wanted to crawl back into bed and sleep all day.

"Gem, can we go?" I begged.

My little sister rolled her eyes at me. "Come on, Avs, you need to find a dress for your wedding."

I glared at her. "I will get married in a hockey jersey at this point. I don't even care. Nolan might like that. I'll even wear a TJ Desjardins one; he's Nolan's favorite player."

Gemma flipped her fading pink hair over her shoulder and rolled her eyes at me. "You're so annoying. Okay, wait." She pulled out her phone, scrolled on something, and then shoved it in my face. "What about this?"

I peered at the screen. On her phone was the image of a vintage-style white-ivory dress with half sleeves and an A-line skirt that hit at the knees. It was perfect. It was nice enough for a wedding dress, but not too fancy for my mini-malistic style.

"Oh. Do you think that would come in time?" I asked.

Christmas was two weekends from now, so our wedding was fast approaching, and I was already worried we wouldn't be ready for everything. Especially since my sister had taken over planning it.

"Do you want it?"

"Yeah, Gem, it's perfect."

She gave me a cheeky grin. "Okay, good, because I ordered it like ten minutes ago, and I paid more for rush shipping to get it here on time."

"Gem!" I screeched and clenched my jaw. "Then why are you torturing me?"

She stuck out her tongue. "Because it's fun, and because I wanted to spend time with you. I feel like I don't get to see you now that you're shacking up with your baby daddy."

I frowned at that. I hadn't realized I had been

neglecting my sister. Sometimes, she could be needy, so I think today was just an excuse to get in some quality sister time.

I hugged her. "I'm sorry if you felt neglected."

She leaned into the hug. "I'm just teasing. I'm so happy for you and Nolan. You're the sunshine to his grumpy bear nature. He needs you."

I let go of the hug, and we walked out of the dress department. I eyed my sister suspiciously when she led me over to the lingerie department. "Do you need more bras?" I asked.

She shook her head and grinned. "No, for your wedding night."

I sighed.

I had put little thought into our wedding night. Our wedding was going to be small. I didn't need to make a big production about wedding night sex. It wasn't like Nolan and I hadn't been having sex. We had been having it a lot. A LOT. So much that I was wearing him out. Last night, he said he was too tired. What man ever said that?

"Gem, you didn't have to buy my dress," I said to her. "And I don't need lingerie for my wedding night."

She waved me off. "I wanted to do it. You won't do a registry or take my money if I write you a check. You can count it as a wedding gift."

She walked over to the black lace teddies on the rack and fingered the lace. I moved down the aisles to look at the babydoll sets. I didn't like to wear teddies, but a babydoll set would be nice. It would look flattering over my baby bump. Even though Nolan kept reassuring me, I looked sexy pregnant. I sure as hell didn't feel sexy.

Gemma noticed me looking at the black lace babydoll in thought. "What does Nolan like?"

"Me with no clothes on," I joked.

She tipped back her head and laughed. "Well, he is a man."

I stepped over to the next aisle and came face-to-face with a red lacy babydoll set with a matching g-string thong. He loved red, and it was perfect for a Christmas wedding.

"He really loves red," I said.

She raised a perfectly sculpted eyebrow. "Really? That's interesting."

I frowned. "Why?"

She shrugged. "I thought all guys liked black lace. Some like white for that virginal shit. Nolan likes red, though. Huh."

I fingered the material. "I think it's perfect."

She nudged me. "Then get it and surprise your husband."

I put the clothing in my arms. Behind it, I saw another set that looked like a halter top with red lace cups, but the rest of the material was sheer black.

"Oh, pretty, get that one too!"

I bit my lip. "Should I?"

"Girl, yes!"

"I don't know if he'll like it..."

"He's a man. Men love seeing us in sexy outfits just for them. Hey! Where are you going for your honeymoon?"

I cocked my head at my sister. "We're not."

She gave me a quizzical look. "What do you mean?"

"Well... I'm pregnant, so..."

"So, what? You should still take some time to be together. You have time off during the holidays."

I shrugged.

I put the lingerie in my arms and went to purchase both sets. It was exciting to have a surprise for Nolan. He would love them, even though he would want to rip them off immediately.

We walked out of the store and to my sister's car to make the trek back to Drakesville. I always worried about her when she was living in South Philly and commuting. I was glad she moved into my old apartment. Now that she had moved to town and our places were within walking distance of each other, I hoped we'd see each other more often.

"You want to get dinner?" I asked.

"Yeah, I'm off tonight, so let's get dinner. But not at the brewery."

"What about the Mediterranean place near the town square?" I offered.

"Near the bakery?" she asked.

"Um, yeah, on the cross street near the firehouse."

"Oh! I've always wanted to try that place."

"Let's do it!"

I needed food. I had been out with my sister all damn day trying to find a dress for the wedding. I didn't think I needed to wear something nice, but Gemma insisted.

On the drive back to town, she convinced me that a flower crown would look cute instead of a veil. She would make one up to look Christmassy with red and white roses and fir or evergreen as the crown. I told her it sounded like a Christmas wreath, and then she got all excited about making me look like a Christmas Bride. I didn't care, but she enjoyed planning stuff like this, so I was going to appease her on this one.

We parked in the town square and walked over to the restaurant. We ordered, and I ate half the hummus while we waited for our food. Gemma stared at me like I had three heads.

"Shut up!" I said. "I'm pregnant, and you made me go shopping today."

"Sis, I want to ask you something, and I don't know how to," she admitted after taking a long sip of her water.

I cocked an eyebrow at her. "What's up?"

"Are you and Nolan good?"

I plastered on a fake smile. "We're great."

She sighed. "Did he tell you how he feels?"

"Um..."

"Oh, Avs," she sighed and gave me a sad smile. I didn't like the pitying look she gave me.

Our food came, and I shoved my falafel wrap into my mouth so I didn't have to answer her next question.

When I came up for air, my sister looked at me sadly, but then she straightened up her spine. "Okay, do you know about the five love languages?"

"No. What's that?" I asked around a mouthful of pita bread.

"I think Nolan's love language is acts of service. Dec said he would rather get his hand stuck in a bear trap than talk about his feelings."

I didn't think Dec was being hyperbolic. That was the god's honest truth.

"What do you mean by acts of service?"

"Nolan moved you into his house, shifted his entire life for you, and then he decorated his Grinch lair to look like Santa's workshop. That was him showing his love for you."

"You think?" I asked.

She nodded enthusiastically. "You, on the other hand, need him to tell you he loves you. You need the words of affirmation."

I chewed thoughtfully at her words.

Gemma gave me a cocky grin. "I'm right, aren't I?"

"Yes," I muttered.

"Who's idea was it to have a Christmas wedding?" she asked, even though she already knew the answer.

"His."

She gave me a smirk, and I wanted to smack it off of her pretty face. She must have noticed the torment across my face because the smile disappeared in an instant, and she rushed over to my side. She took the napkin in front of me and dabbed at my eyes as she hugged me close.

"Oh, Avs, I'm sorry. I didn't mean to make you cry."

I took the napkin out of her hand and dabbed at my eyes. "Why doesn't he love me?"

My sister squeezed me in her arms and stroked my hair. "He does! He just doesn't know how to tell you. Why else would he do all these things for you?"

"I want to be loved, Gem," I cried.

"You are," she said and squeezed me for extra measure. "I love you. You're my favorite sister."

I glared at her and pinched her side. "Your only sister, you jerk. I'm sorry, it's pregnancy hormones."

She squeezed me tighter. "I know, but trust me, Nolan would move mountains for you if he could. He just doesn't know how to tell you that. You might need to make the first move."

No way. That was too scary. What if I told him how much I loved him, and he told me he didn't feel the same way?

Instead of voicing my concerns to my sister, I plastered on a fake smile. She went back to her side of the table while I wiped my tears away. I changed the subject, and she exhaustedly told me all the brewery gossip.

"Hey, I know!" Gemma exclaimed as she pulled into Nolan's driveway after we left the restaurant.

Nolan's car was here, but the house was dark, meaning he was at the brewery. One reason the MacGregor brothers bought the brewery in the first place was that it was within walking distance of their house. It was one thing I loved about living here. Everything was within walking distance.

"You know what?" I asked.

"You should go up to the cabin."

"In the Poconos? For what?" I asked with a frown.

"Your honeymoon!" she said with an exaggerated sigh.

I gave my sister an amused look. That had come out of nowhere, but it wasn't a bad idea. Getting away from everything and relaxing would be nice. I could lie in bed and read, and maybe I could finally tell Nolan how I felt.

"It would be fun! You guys could get away from everything and have some quiet nights in front of the fire. Nolan could keep you warm at night." She gently nudged my arm with her elbow.

"I'll think about it," I muttered.

It wasn't the worst idea. It wouldn't be expensive to take a couple of vacation days, but Nolan didn't like to take time off from the brewery. I didn't know why I was entertaining this idea.

I hugged my sister goodbye tightly. "I'm sorry I ruined dinner by crying into my falafel."

She laughed into my hair. "I love you, okay? Talk to Nolan. You need a break from everything. Going up to the cabin would be good for both of you."

I had no intention of talking to him about it, but he brought it up when he slid into bed later that night.

I stirred next to him. "Hmm?"

"Sorry," he whispered as he curled around me and placed a hand on my belly.

I closed my eyes to go back to sleep, but he stopped me.

"Avs?"

"Yeah?"

"We should go on a honeymoon."

I slid my eyes open. "Did my sister get to you?"

He shook his head and rubbed his beard. "No, unless she and my brother are co-conspirators..." he trailed off, and we groaned in unison. "Never mind, they are."

"So nosy!" I exclaimed. "My dad has a cabin up in the Poconos."

"Yeah? What would we do up there?"

"Nothing, and it would be glorious. You could go skiing if you want, and I'll read."

He chuckled, and I felt the vibration in my chest. His hand swept across my face, and he pushed my hair behind my ear. His thumb lingered on my cheek in a way that made me melt at his touch. "Is that what you want, baby?"

I nodded. "We're so busy all the time, you're always at the brewery, I have school, and... it would be nice to spend quality time together before the baby comes. It would be nice to get away and have a honeymoon."

He gave me a quick kiss. "Okay, let's get married on Christmas morning, and then we'll head up to the cabin. I want to spend time with you too. I'm sorry if you felt like I was neglecting you."

I shook my head. "It's not that, it's just... our lives will get busy once the baby's here. And you need a vacation. When was the last time you took one?"

He grumbled.

I poked him in the stomach. "When, Nolan?"

"The day you moved in. Before that... I can't remember."

"Okay, then we'll get married, and we'll spend Christmas up in the mountains. It'll be perfect."

In the dark of the bedroom, I saw a smile spread across his face. "Avery?"

"Yeah?"

"I can't wait to marry you."

His words wrapped around me like a warm hug. "It's gonna be the best Christmas," I agreed.

He gave me one final kiss goodnight and wrapped his arm around me. I lay on my back and put my hand over his. The way he cradled me protectively in his arms made me feel safe and secure. It made me feel like maybe we could find love together. One day.

CHAPTER EIGHTEEN

NOLAN

"You ready?" Declan asked as I stood in front of the mirror in my bedroom and adjusted my tie.

I knew Avery didn't give a shit about what I wore to our wedding. I could've shown up in jeans and a button-down shirt, and she would've been happy. Or my Desjardins hockey jersey. She probably would have laughed about that because he was her favorite hockey player, too. I wouldn't have done that because I wanted to look good for her on our wedding day. Hence the suit and tie. Gemma tried to convince me to get a tux, but I didn't think that was necessary.

"Almost," I muttered.

Declan peered at me. "Dude, you look fine. Did Gemma seriously make Avery sleep at her place last night?"

I laughed.

Yes, my sister-in-law insisted Avery sleep at her old apartment, so I didn't see her in her wedding dress. Avery rolled her eyes about it but appeased her sister. Gem was eccentric, but she was ours. Truthfully, I think Gemma wanted to have Christmas Eve with her sister. I hadn't realized until Avery moved in how close the sisters were. I saw Gemma way more than I was used to now.

Avery and I hadn't exchanged Christmas gifts yet, because we wanted to do that when we got to the cabin. I was excited to go up to the cabin and get away from everything for a couple of days. I hadn't been on a real vacation since before my parents died.

"Gem is seriously weird," Declan laughed.

I smirked at him. "I know, but she's family."

"Are you nervous?"

I nodded. "A little."

He clapped me on the shoulder. "It's gonna be fine. You two are meant for each other, and now it will be official."

I gulped. I still hadn't told Avery how I felt about her. I was a chicken. I was afraid she only agreed to this marriage because I was her last resort. I was terrified that she couldn't ever feel for me what I felt for her.

I put on my suit jacket and motioned to my brother that it was time to go. I didn't want to be late for my wedding. We walked over to the brewery, and inside, the lights were already on, but dimmed. There were white fairy lights wrapped around the stairs leading up to the loft space. We never used that space, and Declan had been harping on me to figure out a use for it. It was perfect for my wedding, though. It let me get married to the woman I loved in the place I held most dear.

There was soft instrumental music coming from the loft. When we reached the top of the stairs, I found Gemma with freshly dyed hot pink hair, wearing a sparkly black dress, standing in front of a Christmas tree. That definitely wasn't here last night. When did she have time to do all this?

I raised an eyebrow at her, and she gave me a coy smile.

We didn't have many guests at the wedding. Allen, Helen, Wyatt, and Lizzie were also here. It was small and intimate and exactly what we wanted.

"Get over here," Gemma ordered.

I took my place in front of her. Although we were technically 'marrying ourselves,' Gemma was presiding over the wedding. At the end, Gemma and Declan would sign off as witnesses so our uniting marriage would be legal.

Gemma changed the music, and I heard footsteps coming up the steps. We all turned to see Avery coming up the stairs with her arm linked with her dad's. She wore a white dress that came to her knees and did nothing to hide her growing baby bump. She looked sexy as hell. Her dark hair was curled at the ends, and instead of a veil, she wore a flower crown with red and white flowers. It kinda looked like a Christmas wreath, but it looked perfect on her. She looked like the Queen of Christmas, and she had never been more beautiful to me.

Marrying her on Christmas had been the best idea ever.

Her dad kissed her cheek and whispered something in her ear. She smiled at him and then walked over to me. The smile never left her face when she clasped hands with me. The sight of her made my chest constrict. I wanted her to smile at me like that every day for the rest of our lives.

One thing was for sure, I was never getting married again. Avery would be my forever, and I wouldn't make the same mistakes I did with my first marriage. I wouldn't fail her like I had Kath.

Gemma cleared her throat. "Friends and family! As you know, my older sister had to be unconventional and get married at a brewery." Gemma paused at the laughter from our friends. "Today, I'm standing before them, but not as their officiant. These two knuckleheads are marrying themselves."

Avery glared, and Gemma stuck her tongue out in response.

Avery cleared her throat and looked up at me. "I, Avery Jensen, take you to be my husband."

I squeezed her hand. "I, Nolan MacGregor, take you to be my wife."

"Nolan, I promise to be there for you in sickness and health, for richer, for poorer. And when the Bulldogs are losing badly," she said with a laugh.

That made me laugh too. I honestly think one reason we became friends was our mutual love for our terrible hockey team.

"I promise we'll have a good life together. I swear I won't let you eat too many of my cookies, but I'll always save you the best ones. I promise to be your shoulder to lean on and your ear to listen."

I put my hands on her belly as I spoke my own vows. "Avery, you're one of my favorite people. Some people might say I'm less of a grouch when you're around. I know we didn't plan for Peanut, but I can't wait to meet them and start our life together. But please stop letting me eat all your cookies. If it's the last thing I do, I'm gonna be a good husband to you and the best daddy to Peanut I can be."

Her eyes got shiny, and she wiped them discreetly while Gemma handed her the ring.

"I give you this ring as a sign of my determination for a happy and successful marriage," Avery said while she slipped the ring onto my left hand.

We had picked up our wedding bands together last

week. I went with a wooden ring with black ceramic. Avery said it looked like a keg, and it was perfect for me. Who was I to argue with my wife? I convinced her to pick something nice for herself. At first, she went for a simple plain band, but I persuaded her to get the band with tiny diamonds across the top. She deserved something as beautiful as she was, especially when I wanted to make sure she never took it off.

I took her ring in my hand. I looked deep into her eyes as I said the words and slipped the ring on her finger. "I give you this ring as a sign of my determination for a happy and successful marriage."

I turned toward our small audience. "We're married!"

Avery smiled at me, and I bent my head to capture her lips with mine. When I kissed my wife, everything shifted away. The only thing I paid attention to was the woman in my arms. The woman I never wanted to let go of. Avery was the light I needed in my life, and even though we didn't plan for the baby, I finally felt like my life was clicking into place.

"Okay!" Gemma beamed. "Before you two get on the road, we have brunch for you."

Avery furrowed her brow and gave me an annoyed look. I shrugged. I was just as clueless as she was.

"You guys," Avery cried. "You didn't have to do brunch for us."

"We wanted to," Declan said and waved her off. "Don't worry, I'm giving our staff overtime."

"What do you mean?" I asked with a scowl.

We ran numbers the other day, and we were barely in the black. My brother kept telling me to worry about the beer, and he'd worry about the business side, but sometimes I wondered if I should be more involved.

"Don't worry about it," he said with a glare.

We would talk about that later.

There were tables in the back set up next to each other, and I led Avery to one. I told her to take a seat while I made plates for us. When I came back over to her, she was sitting with Wyatt and Lizzie, and her face was stained with tears.

"Baby, what's wrong?" I asked as I put down our plates and sat beside her. I wiped the tears from her eyes, careful not to mess up her makeup.

"Happy tears," Lizzie explained while she shifted her baby in her arms.

"I thought you couldn't come," I nodded to Wyatt.

He shrugged as he cut up food for his son sitting next to him. He ruffled his son's hair. "This one got up before the sun."

Avery was still in tears. "It means so much that you came."

Lizzie squeezed her hand. "Your wedding was beautiful. It was perfect for you two."

Avery turned to me. "Everything has been absolutely perfect."

"Hey, c'mere."

She gave me a funny look, and I pointed to my lips. She smiled and gave me a quick kiss. "This was perfect. You're perfect," she said, and she was glowing.

It wasn't just a pregnancy glow. I'd never seen her this happy before, and I wanted to put that smile on her face every single day. I knew she thought this was a marriage of convenience, that we only got married because she was carrying my child, but I wanted so much more with her. I just had to figure out how to show her that.

"Aw," Lizzie cried. "You're so cute. I can't stand it."

I smiled at her as I took a sip of my coffee and ate some eggs.

Avery's dad came over after we finished eating and handed me the keys to the cabin. "Here, you two," he said with a smile.

Avery hugged her dad. "Thanks, dad. Are you sure it's a good idea to go up to the cabin in winter?"

He nodded. "It's all good. I went up the other day to make sure everything was prepared. Weather should be good for you; just be careful."

Avery scoffed. "Dad, Nolan has been driving like a grandmother since I got pregnant. I'm sure it's gonna take us like five hours to get up there."

I glared at her. "That's not true."

She raised her brows but said nothing.

Sal laughed. "Welcome to the family, Nolan. This is what you signed up for."

I smiled and put my hand on Avery's belly. "I'm not going anywhere."

Avery beamed at that.

Gemma raced over to us. "Hey, can you two come back over to the tree so I can get some pictures?"

I grumbled.

Gemma gave me an annoyed look. "Come on, boss man, it's not for me; it's for the brewery."

I frowned. "What do you mean?"

She nodded her head at Declan, who was talking to Allen. "You know I help with social media, right? We're gonna post about the wedding and advertise this space for parties and events. It will bring more money in."

I stroked my beard. It was an idea Declan had been trying to get me to focus on, but I was too busy trying to up our production output.

Avery laced her hand through mine and got up out of her seat. Gemma instructed us to make a couple of poses, one of us kissing, one with our hands on Avery's baby bump, and then a normal one of us standing next to each other.

"Smile, boss man!" Gemma teased behind her phone.

Avery smoothed down my beard. "Smile for me, please, baby?" she cooed.

Avery could make me do anything when she asked in that sweet voice. She knew it, too. I smiled for the camera, and soon the smile wasn't fake because that was Avery's effect on me. She was my light in the dark, even if she didn't know it yet.

"Okay, perfect," Gemma said to us, and then she walked over to show my brother, who nodded his head.

Avery tilted my head down and met me in a quick kiss. "Thank you."

"For what?"

"Appeasing my sister. Now let's get out of here so we can do absolutely nothing together for an entire week."

"Merry Christmas, baby."

She smiled and kissed me again. "Just so you know, I intend on watching the cheesiest Christmas movies up at the cabin."

"Can't wait," I said, and I wasn't being sarcastic.

I was amped to be cuddled up with my pregnant wife and away from our nosy siblings. Honestly? The idea of doing absolutely nothing and just being with her had an enormous appeal. Even if she made me watch cringe-worthy cheesy Christmas movies. If I got to spend my Christmas honeymoon with my beautiful wife, I'd do anything she wanted.

CHAPTER NINETEEN

AVERY

"Can I get out of the car now? I really have to pee," I called to Nolan from the car. My husband grumbled from the porch with a shovel in hand.

Of course, it snowed on the drive up to the cabin, and it took us longer than expected to get here. Part of that was because I had to pee every twenty minutes. We left Drakesville early enough that we still had some daylight. When we finally pulled up into the drive, Nolan insisted on shoveling it and the porch, so I didn't fall. Falling while pregnant was a tremendous risk, so I wasn't mad at him for being so protective. I just had to pee.

I peered up at the two-story log cabin where I had spent my summers, and nostalgia hit me. I hadn't been up here in a while. I don't think I'd ever been up here during the winter, but it looked beautiful. The lake was iced over, and there was snow on the ground, giving it that winter wonderland feeling. It was a picturesque Christmas honeymoon, and it was absolute perfection.

The best part was watching my husband being all Mountain Man while shoveling snow before letting me get out of the car. I stared down at the shiny rings on my finger. I couldn't believe we had gotten married.

After what seemed like forever, he rested the shovel against the cabin wall and walked down the steps toward the car. He opened the passenger door and helped me get out. I yelped when he lifted me in his arms, bridal style, and carried me inside.

"Nolan!" I shrieked.

"What? Aren't you supposed to do that when you get married?" he asked with a laugh as he gingerly set me down on the couch.

Nolan looked around at the stone fireplace and the granite countertops in the kitchen. Dad put a lot of work into the cabin over the years. It had been my grandparents before they passed it on to Dad. Gem and I spent many summers up here on the lake. Maybe we could vacation here when the baby was older. There were three rooms upstairs, so there was enough room for us, my dad, and even Gemma. I really liked the idea of doing family vacations here again.

"Wow, this is much nicer than I expected. I was expecting it to be a one-room log cabin."

"Nope, there are three bedrooms upstairs. Dad fixed it up and did a bunch of upgrades over the years. Do you want help bringing in all the stuff?" I asked.

He shook his head. "Nope. You sit your beautiful ass down and let me do everything."

"Nolan!"

He gave me a stern look. "I don't want you to fall and hurt the baby. Let me, okay?"

I sighed and toed off my high heels. I was still in my

wedding dress, but I had tossed the floral crown in the back-seat of the car an hour ago. We had stopped at a store for supplies, and it wasn't until the cashier gave me a funny look that I realized I was still wearing it. I let Nolan bring our things into the house while I walked around, turning on the water and heat and making sure nothing was amiss. I took a much-needed bathroom break and then went to check on everything else.

I peeked into the fridge and was surprised to find it stocked. Until I saw the note on the counter in my sister's handwriting.

Avery & Nolan,

Enjoy your honeymoon in the Poconos. I stocked the fridge, so you don't have to worry about anything while you are boring people who do nothing!

Love,

Gemma

I shook my head at my sister's antics, but a smile played across my lips. Gemma was a bit much, but she only did it because she loved me.

I climbed the stairs and went into the big bedroom that used to be my parents. I laughed when I saw the rose petals lying on the bed. Dad said he checked in on the place, but Gemma must have come with him. No way my dad did that.

I turned at the sound of Nolan's laughter. "Gem's doing?"

"Who else?"

He set our suitcases on the bed, and I unpacked our clothes into the dresser while he brought in everything else. When I walked back down the stairs, I saw Nolan had started a fire.

I sat on the couch and noticed the Christmas gifts on

the coffee table. Nolan finished what he was doing and finally took off his boots. He sat on the couch next to me. He looked exhausted, so I reached out a hand and massaged his neck.

"Oh, that feels nice," he moaned as I kneaded the tight muscles in his neck.

"Thank you."

"No way was I letting my pregnant wife carry all our bags in," he grumbled at me.

I squeezed his neck teasingly. "You're so difficult sometimes."

He grunted, but then he handed me one of the bigger gifts. "Hey, we didn't do our Christmas gifts yet."

I took the gift from his hands.

I opened the box he handed me and was surprised to find he gifted me a year of a book subscription box. Inside was a new adult fantasy book, a lovely aromatherapy candle, quote cards, and a book hook to use as a bookmark.

"Oh, this is so cool! Open yours!" I said excitedly.

He pulled the heavy package I wrapped for him into his lap. "What is this?"

"You'll see," I said as I read the back of the book that came in the box.

That was thoughtful of him. And cool, because if he had asked me if I wanted a particular book, I would have shown him my impossibly long wishlist.

He tore open the package to reveal the craft beer of the month club subscription I bought him. Funny that we both went with subscription boxes for things we loved.

"Oh, this would be great for research," he said and smiled at me.

"I didn't know if that would be good for you or not."

He kissed me. "It's perfect. Oh, I got you something else."

He handed me a smaller package. I had a feeling it was jewelry, and I hoped he didn't spend a lot on it. I wasn't into fancy jewelry, and our wedding bands had cost a lot. With him owning his own business and me on a teacher's salary, we didn't have a lot of money between us. I didn't want him to spend a lot on me.

I smiled when I saw the bangle bracelet inside the tiny box with a couple of charms depicting a mushroom, a rabbit, a teacup, and the Cheshire cat. "Oh! It's Alice in Wonderland! That's my favorite."

"I know."

"Oh, Nolan," I cooed. "Wait, there's one more for you."

He opened the other box and looked at the engraving on the beer glass. His fingers traced across the words '#1 Dad.' It was kind of cheesy, but he looked a little choked up about it. "Oh, Avs."

"What?" I laughed. "I know. It's cheesy."

"I love it," he whispered. He set the glass down on the table and put a hand on my belly. "I can't wait to meet Peanut. I know we didn't plan for this, for the baby and this marriage, but I promise you I'm gonna make you happy."

Tears welled up in my eyes. I put a hand over his, and I smiled at seeing the wedding bands on our fingers. Nolan was giving me everything I wanted, but I still didn't know if I had his love, too.

I put the bracelet on my wrist and kissed him. "I have a surprise for you."

"Yeah?" he asked, and his whiskey-colored eyes got dark with desire.

I nodded. "It *is* our wedding night."

He arched his eyebrow at me. "Hmm... it's not quite

nighttime yet."

I glared at him and gestured across my body. "You want a piece of this or not?"

He laughed. "Of course I do. Lead the way."

He followed me upstairs into the big bedroom, and I pushed him onto the bed, sending rose petals flying. "Stay there. I'll be right back."

He arched an eyebrow while he shrugged off his tie. His suit jacket had gotten tossed in the backseat of his car on the ride here.

I went into the dresser and fished out the red lingerie, but hid it in front of me as I shuffled to the bathroom. In the bathroom, I realized I should have asked him to unzip me, but after some maneuvering, I got the dress off and put on the babydoll set. I took a deep breath and touched up my make-up in the mirror. I was nervous. I had never worn something like this before. He liked me in my red bra and panty sets, but I never wore legit lingerie for him.

I opened the door and leaned against the frame. Nolan looked up at the noise. He was leaning against the headboard of the bed, his tie off and the top button of his dress shirt undone.

"Whoa."

"You like it?" I asked nervously and bit my lip.

"Do I like it?" he repeated as his eyes trailed up and down me.

"No?" I teased.

"Baby," he moaned.

"What?"

"Get your ass over here," he growled.

I smiled and walked over to the bed. He crooked a finger at me, and I crawled into the bed and straddled him. He slid his hands across the red lace cups of the top and roamed down my stomach. He played with the ends of the material while I hungrily pressed my lips to his.

I opened to him, letting him have the control he always wanted. His hands wandered underneath the skirt of my lingerie until he was gripping my ass. He pulled away from the kiss, his eyes ablaze with desire. "You know I love red."

I nodded, and I dipped my head down to kiss his neck. I felt his cock harden underneath me, and I ground against him while I unbuttoned his dress shirt. I pulled the shirt out of his pants, and he helped me get it off of him. I ran my hands down his big hairy chest and kissed down his torso until I was undoing his belt and unzipping his pants.

He ran a hand through my hair. "What are you doing down there?"

I gave him a cheeky grin, and he helped me get rid of his pants and boxers. I took his cock in my hand. I stroked slowly while I leaned down and licked along the shaft. His hand was in my hair by the time I sucked the head of his cock into my mouth. I bobbed up and down on his shaft, rubbing my hand on it and then coming back up to lick and suck around the head.

I looked up at him and saw his head tipped back, his eyes closed in pleasure. His brown eyes snapped open. "I'm gonna come if you keep doing that."

I pulled his cock out of my mouth and licked the length of it. "Then come."

"Not there tonight," he said. He flipped me onto my back and hovered over me.

His eyes roamed down my frame. "You look so fucking sexy. Can we take this off now?"

I nodded enthusiastically.

He helped me up, and I unhooked the back of my lingerie while he helped me pull it over my head. He took his time kissing me on my lips, my neck, and then down the valley of my swollen breasts. He hefted one breast in his hand and swirled his tongue around my nipple, and then he repeated the action with the other one. He gave me a sly smile as he moved further down to take off my skimpy underwear.

He spread my legs and kissed one thigh, then the other. "I want to taste you before I'm inside you. You want that?"

"Uh-huh."

He nipped at my thigh. "Be a good girl, and say the words."

"I want you to eat my pussy like it's your last meal."

"That's a good girl," he cooed.

He grinned as he dipped his head low and flicked his tongue over my clit. I moaned at the sensation as he lapped at my center.

"Baby," I moaned and gripped the sheets when he pressed two fingers inside me.

He made noises of enjoyment as he tasted me and slid his thick digits in and out. He stroked slowly and savored every last inch of me until I didn't recognize the cries coming from my lips.

"That's a good girl. Let me hear that moan," he growled. "I want you to scream my fucking name."

I clenched his hair in my hands and pressed my hips up to meet his mouth. He devoured me whole, making a meal out of me with his talented tongue. I let him get his fill of me while I arched up into him and came all over his face.

"Please," I begged.

He lifted his head, and I moaned at the sexy sight of his beard dripping with my cum. "Please, what?"

"Get inside me."

"No. You gotta come all over my face first."

"I already did. Please, baby, I need you."

"Not enough. I need my beard soaked with your cum."

I moaned. That was so sexy.

He grinned and dipped his head back down. He slid his magical tongue across my seam until he pulled my clit in for another long suck. When he spread me wide and curled his fingers up inside me, I was done for. I moaned his name as another orgasm wracked my body. I held his head in my hands and gripped his hair tight while I came with a scream loud enough to wake the dead.

I let go of his hair and smoothed it down with a sheepish look. He looked up at me with a wicked grin and nipped at my thigh. "Good girl."

"Nolan," I groaned.

"What?" he asked innocently while he made his way up my body.

I stroked a hand across his cum-stained beard. "Need you, now."

"Be a good girl and wait."

I whined.

He gave me that cheeky grin again and leaned over to wipe his beard off with a tissue from the bedside table. He sat up against the headboard and crooked a finger at me. "C'mere."

I jumped at his command. I swung a leg over his thick thigh and slid down onto his cock. His hands roamed down my body while I put my hands on his wide-set shoulders and rode him. He squeezed my ass and gave me a little slap while I ground down on him.

"I like married fucking," he murmured into my ear as he kissed my neck.

I laughed and gasped as his thumb pressed against my clit. "Me too. I like being married to you."

He thrust up from below, and I let him take control. "I like being married to you, too.'

"I like being Mrs. MacGregor."

"I love that you took my name, that you're mine," he growled.

He arched up into me again, hitting me so hard he sent my tits bouncing.

"I'm yours, baby," I moaned as I tipped my head back and gave in to the pleasure once again.

"Avery," he moaned as we moved together in unison.

I clenched his shoulders tight as he hit me deep. His upwards thrusts were erratic, like he couldn't get enough of me.

"So good," I cried out as another orgasm wracked through my entire body.

"I love you," he moaned into my ear, and then he roared out his release.

I didn't process what he said until I was sprawled out across his chest in recovery. He kissed the top of my head and stroked my hair. I lay there quietly, lost in my thoughts. Did he mean what he said? Surely not. You didn't tell someone you loved them seconds before you orgasmed. That was just heat of the moment sex talk.

"You hungry?" he asked.

I nodded, but my mind was still racing at what he said. He hadn't repeated it, so maybe I just imagined it. I was too scared to ask him about it.

"Your dad said he has a grill out back. I'll fire it up and make burgers. You want that?"

I nodded into his chest.

He tilted my face up to him. "You okay, baby?"

I nodded, but instead of answering, I kissed him and let him take care of me for the rest of the night.

CHAPTER TWENTY

NOLAN

$\mathcal{A}$very got weird last night after I told her I loved her. Maybe she didn't believe me since I said it during sex. The nagging part of my brain kept screaming at me she didn't feel the same. That she only agreed to marry me because we were having a baby together. It was trying to convince me she settled for me.

When I woke up alone, the doubt crept in even more.

I walked downstairs to find my pregnant wife snuggled up in a blanket on the couch with a cup of coffee. She had the book I bought her for Christmas in her lap. She looked so cozy and cute, and she was mine. She was wearing the ring that told everyone she was mine for life, and I had to make sure she knew that.

She craned her head up at my approach. "Hey, sleepyhead," she teased.

I rubbed a hand through my beard and smoothed down my bedhead. "What time is it?"

She glanced at her watch. "Just about noon."

"Shit, Avs, I never sleep in that late."

She smiled when I bent down and gave her a quick kiss. "I know, but you needed the rest. Might as well get our sleep now before Peanut gets here."

"Avs, you're ice cold," I said and rubbed my hands across her arms.

She shrugged. "I'm okay. I put the heat on, but yeah, it gets drafty in the cabin."

I pulled away from her and ran back up the stairs.

"Where are you going?" She called up to me.

"Getting dressed!" I yelled down at her. I pulled on my jeans, an undershirt, and a long-sleeved plaid shirt.

"Why?"

I stomped down the steps, went to the front door, and pulled on my boots. "I'm gonna go chop some more wood for the fireplace."

She stared at me with her mouth agape.

"What?" I asked as I shrugged on my jacket.

"You're gonna go outside and chop wood for me?"

I furrowed my brow at the giddy look on her face. "Yes? Is that a problem?"

She laughed and shook her head. "Nope."

"Avs, why are you being weird?"

She laughed again, and the look she gave me cut into me. She looked at me the way she would before straddling me or taking my cock in her mouth. What the hell?

"It's like all my fantasies come true."

I gave her a confused look. "Huh. How's that?"

She gestured to me. "It's the beard and the red plaid and the fact you're about to chop wood to keep me all nice and toasty."

"I don't understand."

"You look like a total sexy mountain man!" she exclaimed.

"Oh, is that your fantasy? You like the lumberjack look?" I teased.

"Go chop me wood, husband," she teased back and returned to reading her book.

I grabbed the maul I left next to the wood rack and walked outside. I went over to the stump next to the big tree and put a log on top of it. I put on my safety goggles and started splitting the wood.

I didn't want to run out of wood while we were here. Avery said there was heat in the cabin, but I think she enjoyed sitting in front of the fire. I liked taking care of her and providing for her and the baby. My inner caveman told me I was supposed to, that I had to sacrifice everything for her.

I split wood until my muscles were aching from overuse, and I was sweating from the exertion. I piled the wood pieces into my arms and went back inside. I put all the chopped pieces into the wood rack next to the front door.

"I think we're good," Avery tried to reassure me from the kitchen where she was cracking eggs into a mixing bowl.

I leaned against the wall and tried to catch my breath. "I don't want to run out. What if it snows again and all the wood gets wet?"

She rolled her eyes at me and walked over to the thermostat, pushing a couple of buttons. "Then we'll turn up the heat."

"I'll be back," I muttered. I didn't miss her rolling her eyes at me.

I was outside for so long that my muscles screamed in agony. I made a couple of trips to bring all the wood inside, but I was satisfied with my work. I shed off my jacket and stomped off my boots while I got the fire going.

"Come eat," Avery called to me as she put a plate of food and a cup of coffee down on the table.

I poked at the wood and made sure the fire was stoked before I walked into the kitchen. I rolled up the sleeves of my shirt and washed up in the sink.

Avery eased herself into a chair at the table. "Don't make a pregnant lady wait. I'm going to eat everything."

I chuckled and took the seat across from her. I surveyed the plate of eggs, bacon, toast, and a large stack of French toast in front of us. "You must be starving," I teased as I started on the French toast.

She shrugged with a mouthful of food.

"You should have woken me up earlier."

She shook her head. "We're on vacation; you need to relax."

I grunted at that. I guess she had a point.

We ate in peaceful silence, both of us too hungry to talk. I slurped down my coffee while I eyed her from across the table. Her dark hair fell into her face, and the light hit it just right that her auburn highlights shone through. My wife was gorgeous, and all I could think about was how I wanted this with her forever. She smiled at me from across the table, and all my worries melted away on the spot. She and Peanut were the only things I would care about for the rest of my life. But I still hadn't worked up the courage to ask her about last night.

It had taken everything out of me to tell her how I felt. I wasn't good at talking about my feelings, but she hadn't said a single word after I told her I loved her. Not a single thing. I didn't expect her to say it back, but her not acknowledging what I said cut me to the core.

A dark thought crawled into my brain, whispering that she said nothing because she didn't feel the same way. That she only agreed to my proposal and married me in some misguided idea that she was never gonna find someone better.

I scowled and bitterly drank my coffee; my mood soured at the thought.

I cleared the plates when we finished eating and did the dishes while she went back to the couch to snuggle up and read.

"Do you realize you hum while you clean up?" she called after me.

I frowned. "I do?"

"You do."

"No, I don't."

"Okay, grumpy bear, you don't," she teased.

"My mom used to hum when she cleaned," I blurted.

I didn't know why I said that. I never liked to talk about my parents; it hurt too much. Telling Avery the reason I hated Christmas felt like someone had a knife at my throat.

I wiped my hands on a hand towel and joined her on the couch.

"You want to talk about her?" she asked and gave my hand a little squeeze.

I shook my head.

She pulled away, and the hurt look on her face stung me a little. She wasn't trying to pry, but I didn't like to talk about my parents.

Kath said I'd rather chew off my arm than express any emotion. Maybe it wasn't just the kid stuff that caused our marriage to fail. Maybe it was me. When I saw the downcast look on Avery's face, I knew I wasn't being fair to her.

"Hey," I whispered. "Tell me what's wrong."

"I wish you would talk to me. You're my husband, but it's like you're keeping me three arms' lengths away."

I traced the curve of her cheek and pushed her hair out of her face. "I'm not. I'm here.'

"Anytime I bring up anything serious, you push me away. If you can't talk to me about the important things, I'm not sure this can last."

A lump formed in my throat as her words washed over me. I didn't want that. I wanted us to last. I didn't understand why she said that when I told her how I felt last night, and she said nothing in return.

"I wish you would tell me what you mean," I growled and rubbed a hand down my face.

She narrowed her eyes at me. "What does *that* mean?"

"Well, you say you want me to talk to you about the important stuff, but when I told you how I felt, you ignored it and got quiet for the rest of the night."

Her gaze clouded as she stared at me. "What are you talking about?"

"Last night when I told you I loved you!"

She reared back at that, but then she put her book down on the coffee table. "Do you mean when you said, 'I love you,' and then came inside me? I didn't think you meant it."

"Why wouldn't I mean it?" I snapped.

Why was she being so difficult? Of course, I fucking meant that. I wouldn't have said it if I hadn't.

"Because it was a heat of the moment thing!" she exclaimed and glared at me. "It's not like I'm what you want. I know you only married me because you wanted to do the right thing. You don't have to lie to me!"

She shoved the blanket off her lap and sat up on the couch.

"Why do you think it's not true?" I asked through gritted teeth.

She stared into the flames of the fire but wouldn't look at me. "When we first hooked up, you told me you weren't the type of man who fell in love. And it's not like we've been exclusive."

Ouch. That was like a knife to my gut. My heart ached in my chest at hearing the words I knew were true. I had been exclusive to her, not on purpose. Still, once Avery dug her way into my heart, I never imagined being with anyone else.

"Avery, I didn't think I would ever find someone I could open my heart to again. And it's not like you ever told me you wanted more. You constantly went on dates, and when they were losers, you used me for sex."

She turned to me, her eyes shiny with tears, and I felt like the world's biggest asshole. "I said that to reassure you because you told me that was all you could ever give me! You said you were there for a 'good time, not a long time.' I was only one of the many women you took to your bed. I know I didn't matter to you."

What the fuck? How could she not see that everything I did was because I loved her? Why did she think she didn't matter to me? She was the only person who would matter to me for the rest of my life.

"Baby..." I said, but she shook her head as more tears fell from her eyes. The ache in my chest tightened at seeing her cry. At the fact *I* made her cry.

"I think we should get an annulment. This marriage isn't gonna work out," she blubbered.

My heart plummeted into my stomach at her words. I was trying so desperately to find the words again, to make her understand she was my world. I couldn't do that if she wanted an annulment. This wasn't how I expected our marriage to begin.

"What?" I asked and stared at her, my thoughts swirling around in my head in utter confusion.

"I'm never gonna be good enough for you," she sobbed.

I tugged on her wrist. "C'mere, let's talk about this."

She shook her head. "There's nothing to talk about. You don't love me. That's why I said 'no' when you first asked me to marry you. You're a good man, Nolan, and I thought maybe Peanut and I could win you over. I want so badly to have a family, and I thought we could have something real together, but I can't be married to someone who will never love me in return."

Before I could stop her, she rushed up the stairs. I watched her go in silence as I mulled over her words. I held my head in my hands as I contemplated the argument. I never wanted to hurt her or for the tears in her eyes to be from something I had done.

I pinched the bridge of my nose, and that's when something finally clicked about what she said during the argument.

I can't be married to someone who will never love me in return.

Oh, fuck!

She loved me, but I was such a closed-off asshole that I never saw it. Never thought for a second that Avery could ever love me the way I loved her.

I sighed and ran a hand through my hair as I thought about what to say to fix this. I had to do something now before she walked away from our marriage. Before she walked away from me.

I got up from the couch and climbed the steps. What I saw in the bedroom made my heart squeeze in my chest.

My pregnant wife was crying her eyes out on the bed because she thought I didn't love her. In truth, I loved her with all my heart, but I was allergic to talking about my feelings.

I sat on the bed next to her and reached out to stroke her hair. "Avery? Listen to me, okay?"

She nodded, wiping the tears from her eyes.

"You know why I said I didn't want to get attached?" I asked and tilted her chin up so she'd look at me.

She shook her head and wiped her eyes.

"Because Kath took my heart, ripped it out of my chest, and fed it to me. I didn't want to go through that again. Then I met you."

She gave me a suspicious look. "You made me think..."

I sighed. "Because you went on all those dates."

"Nolan, I haven't slept with anyone since I met you."

I furrowed my brow. "Really?"

She nodded. "I'm so in love with you it hurts sometimes, and I thought you just said you loved me because of the sex. It hurt because I knew you didn't mean it."

I bent my head to her, pressing our foreheads together. "Can I tell you a secret?"

She nodded.

"I haven't slept with anyone else since I met you either."

She looked up at me with wide eyes. "Really?"

"I never thought I was good enough for you."

"But you're a good man. You're loyal to your friends, you're protective of your family, and you'll always take care of Peanut and me. No matter what."

I cupped her face and wiped away more stray tears. I hated that her face was splotchy, and her eyes were red from all her tears. Especially since I was the one who caused her that pain. "I love you," I said.

She searched my eyes for the truth, and I stared back at her, hoping she saw I was baring my soul to her. "Do you really mean it? It's not just because of the baby?"

"No, Avery, I love you. And I'm gonna love Peanut just as much, but I love *you*. You're my light in the dark. Everything's better when you're near."

"Nolan..." she sighed.

"I love you with all my heart."

"I love you too, you big grouch."

I caressed her cheek. "You make me want to be a better man. I'm not good at expressing my feelings."

She rolled her eyes. "No, really?"

"I'll try for you. I'm sorry I shut down when it comes to my parents. It's the blackest day of my life. I don't want to remember it."

Her face softened, and she cradled my face in her hands. "I'm sorry. I pushed too hard. Tell me when you're ready."

"I don't want our marriage to end here today," I said. I held up my left hand and then joined it with her own. "You see these rings? This means you're my forever."

"I want to be your forever. Can we blame my outburst on pregnancy hormones?"

I laughed. "Sure."

Her smile was a thousand-watt. "See, you're good at this whole husband thing already. You already know when I'm right."

I glared at her, and she laughed. That sound was music to my ears after what we just went through. "You really didn't think I was telling the truth?"

She shook her head. "But I do now. Tell me again."

"I love you," I said again and gave her a soft, slow kiss, putting all the passion I could muster into it.

Her eyes were still closed when I pulled away from her. Although her face was stained with tears, my wife was still a vision, and I couldn't believe she was mine. Today proved that if I wanted to keep it that way, I had to fight for her. Had to fight tooth and nail to let her know she was my queen. She was the light in my dark world, and I never wanted to make her cry like that ever again.

"I love you," I said to her again. "I love you with all my heart, and I'm sorry I didn't tell you that before I knocked you up. I should have told you two years ago."

She beamed and wrapped her arms around the back of my neck. "I love you too. I never thought I'd hear those words from you. Tell me again, please?"

"I love you," I said again, giving her a kiss in between each word.

When I pulled away, she beamed and got a cocky little grin on her face. "You want to show me how much?"

I started unbuttoning my plaid shirt, and she bit her lip in anticipation. "Oh, you want me to bring your lumberjack fantasy to life, huh?"

She nodded. "Yeah, you've spent ALL morning chopping me wood. Let me make you feel better, baby."

I threw my shirt to the floor. "I'll show you some wood."

"Yes, please!" she squealed with delight.

I certainly did, and then some.

CHAPTER TWENTY-ONE

AVERY

Nolan stroked my belly while I lay on my back, naked in bed. Having that fight today sucked, but it was necessary to get everything out in the open.

"Wait..." I trailed off as the realization came to me.

"What's up?"

I glared at him. "We were basically dating, and I still went on all those horrible dates?"

He chuckled beside me, the vibration of his chest shaking the bed. "Hey, I didn't know either! Always worked out for me. You really never slept with any of them?"

I stuck out my tongue. "God, no, none of them ever made it past the first date. The dating game is rough."

He kissed down my body and placed a gentle kiss on my belly. "You hear that, Peanut? If it wasn't for you, mommy and daddy might have never figured it out."

I smiled at him. I loved when he talked to my belly. Peanut was going to be showered with so much love between the two of us, I was practically vibrating with happiness over it.

He groaned when he lay on his back again.

"What's wrong?"

"I think I overdid it with the wood today."

"Baby!" I scolded.

He shrugged. "I didn't know if it would snow again. I wanted to be prepared."

I smoothed down his beard and ran a hand through his hair. "See, I love how you like to provide for me. Maybe you should soak in the tub."

He gave me a funny look.

"What? It's a nice tub," I tried to convince him. "We could get in together, and you could make my boobs shiny."

He cocked an eyebrow. "Okay, I'm listening."

I laughed. "Men!"

I got out of bed and stretched. I went into the bathroom, started the water, and tested it to ensure it wasn't too hot. Hot baths weren't good for pregnant women, but it should be okay as long as I kept it to a certain temperature. Honestly, I think Nolan needed it more than me. I checked the temperature and got into the tub, sighing in relief at the feeling on my back.

Nolan stood in the bathroom's doorway, so I crooked a finger at him. He climbed into the tub and sat across from me. "I think I'm too big for this."

I laughed. "You're fine."

I let him make my boobs nice and shiny while I massaged his neck and shoulders. I fingered the grey hair at his temples. "Did I give you more of these today?" I teased.

He glared. "I'm not that much older than you."

I kissed him and turned around, so I was sitting in between his legs. Was I smiling because I felt him getting hard against my back? One hundred percent. He wrapped his hands around my waist to rest on my stomach, and he kissed my neck.

"You're right. This feels nice. I don't know how to relax," he said into my ear.

"No kidding!" I teased. "I'm sorry about starting the fight."

"We need to be better at communicating. I'm sorry, I'll try to be better *for you.*"

I leaned my head back, and he kissed me. "Love you."

He smiled down at me. "Love you too. I understand why you wanted to come up here. It's nice to get away and not have to worry about anything for a couple of days."

"And sex!"

He kissed my neck again. "You're insatiable."

"I can feel your dick poking me in the back. I don't see you complaining."

He laughed into my skin. "Definitely not."

I lay back into him, and he stroked my hair while I closed my eyes.

"I don't know how to relax because since my parents died, all I've done is make sure my brother was taken care of," Nolan admitted after a couple of minutes passed. "I have to be the provider for the people I love."

I turned in his arms and looked into his whiskey-colored eyes. He frowned like it pained him to talk about his doubts. "Nol, you did such an outstanding job with Declan. You guys are doing great with the brewery. I know you can't help but worry, but all the burden isn't on your shoulders."

He sighed.

"Look at me," I demanded.

He looked up at me, and the doubt on his face crushed

me. I wanted to take the burden off his shoulders. Isn't that what I told him in our wedding vows?

I held his face in my hands. "We're a team. You don't shoulder the burden to provide for the baby and me. We're a family, and whatever happens, we'll get through it together."

"I know."

"Do you? Because you know I'm not quitting my job after the baby comes."

He nodded.

"You're not alone," I reassured him and put a hand on his heart. "I'm here. We're doing this together, okay grumpy mountain man?"

He smirked at me, and I beamed at the fact that I got him to switch his mood immediately. He tilted his head up and kissed me. "I told you, you're my light."

"You know, when my sister told me I should marry you, she said you're always a grouch when I'm not around. That's true, isn't it?"

He nodded. "You make me want to be a better man, but I'm not sure I can."

"You can, you will," I said firmly. "You're gonna be such a good dad."

"I've already got the dad bod," he joked with a shrug.

I trailed a finger down his chest. "I love your dad bod."

He furrowed his brow in confusion.

"You really don't see how women look at you at the brewery?"

He looked unconvinced, but then shrugged. "I only ever had eyes for you."

My face hurt from how big my smile got at his words. "You were what I always wanted, but I never thought you saw a future with me."

He frowned. "I can't believe we had feelings for each other this whole time."

"I know! We could have had like three kids already if you told me how you felt."

He raised his eyebrow. "Three kids?"

I placated him with a kiss. "Kidding! Let's have this one first and see. I wished we told each other how we felt sooner; it would have lessened our pain."

"Me too. I promise you, we're not wasting any more time."

"Good," I said, giving him another small kiss.

I got out of the tub and wrapped a towel around myself.

Nolan cocked an eyebrow at me. "Where are you going?"

"I can't be in the water too long; it's not good for the baby. But stay and relax. You need it," I said.

I brushed my hair out and blow-dried it. I spied him in the mirror, leaning his head back against the tub and closing his eyes. My husband was wound so tight, and being up here in the cabin with absolutely no plans was precisely what he needed. I hadn't realized how stressed he was about the baby coming. I didn't want him to think he had to do everything.

I put a hand on my belly.

"You're so gorgeous," his gruff voice startled me.

I peeked in the mirror and saw him standing behind me with a towel wrapped around his waist. He pushed my hair off my shoulder and pressed a delicate kiss on my skin. When he touched me and kissed me like that, it sent tingles down my spine. He made me come undone just at his feather-light caresses.

Okay, it could also be my horny pregnant brain.

He chuckled into my ear. "You're so horned up."

"I can't help it!"

He wrapped his arms around my waist. "I don't deserve a sexy woman like you."

I twisted in his arms and shook my head. "You do, Nolan. You're my sexy lumberjack, and don't you forget it."

"Oh, you want some more of this wood?" he teased and pressed said 'wood' into my back.

"Maybe..." I trailed off, my lips curling up into a smile.

"Yeah, you do," he growled and spun me around in his arms.

I laughed when he lifted me up and carried me back into the bedroom. I was glad my sister persuaded me to take this honeymoon. I would enjoy every minute here with my sexy lumberjack.

I heard Nolan's footsteps come down the stairs as I lay on the couch, reading my book and waiting for my pie to come out of the oven. Coming to the cabin always made me want to bake. It reminded me of all the summers we came up here, and my mom tried out all these weird pie recipes. She always made things fun.

After Nolan and I had another round of sex upstairs, I told him to take a nap. It surprised me when he listened, but he overdid it by chopping wood today. I didn't want him to overdo things because he wanted to take care of me.

Nolan came into the living room and sat down on the couch beside me. He put my feet in his lap, and I moaned when he started rubbing them. I liked that I never had to ask him to do that. He just knew I needed it and wanted to take care of me.

"Are you already done with that book?" he asked.

I shrugged. "Almost, I'm a fast reader."

He sniffed the air. "What's that smell?"

"The pie," I said as I turned the page in my book.

He seemed to take the hint that reading meant 'do not bother me,' but I liked him next to me. His presence was calming. I had restarted the fire, but the oven also made the cabin feel warmer. It made everything nice and toasty underneath my blanket.

The timer on my phone dinged, and instead of getting up myself, Nolan pushed my legs off his lap and went to go check it for me. "Looks done to me!"

"How do you know?"

"My mom baked a lot. I know how to tell if a pie is done or not."

That was the first thing he ever told me about her. It occurred to me I didn't even know his mother's name. I wasn't about to push him on it, though. I set my book down, but then Nolan came back into the living room. He checked on the fire and sat down next to me. He continued to rub my feet.

He gave me a sly grin as his hands kneaded my feet in all the right spots. He was so good at taking care of me. I closed my eyes and lay back on the couch. This was the best honeymoon. It might have been rocky at first, but I was having some of the best sex of my life, and this man was doing everything to tend to my needs.

"She would have loved you," Nolan whispered.

"Hmm?" I asked and slid open one eyelid.

"My mom. She would have loved you."

"You think so? All things considered?"

He nodded. "Mom was a schoolteacher too. You would have had that in common."

"What did she teach?" I asked.

If he was finally opening up to me, I wanted to encourage him but not push him. Who knew that getting teenagers to open up would prepare me for getting my emotionally inept husband to open up?

He grinned at me. "English."

I laughed.

"Don't take this the wrong way..." he trailed off.

"What?"

"You're a lot alike."

I wasn't sure how I was supposed to take that. "How so?"

"Well, baking, teaching. You had that in common. But she was kind, and she always put everyone's feelings before her."

My brow creased at his comment. "How is that like me?"

He gave me an annoyed look. "You worry about your sister. You sometimes put her needs before yours. Even though you're pregnant and have your own stuff going on, when Gemma needs you, you go to her."

"You think I coddle her."

He shook his head. "Not that. You want to make sure she's happy before yourself. And you worry about your dad being lonely too, but he seems fine."

I frowned.

"It's not a bad thing. It's one thing I love about you."

I beamed at that. Hearing him repeat it made me giddy. I wanted to get up and dance a little jig. Nolan MacGregor loved me. I never thought I would hear those words out of his mouth.

"What was your mom's name?" I asked.

"Norah. Why?"

"Norah..." I trailed off. "Norah MacGregor."

He stared at me for a second while I rubbed my belly in thought. I really liked the sound of Norah MacGregor.

Nolan put a hand next to mine on my stomach, and I smiled up at him. I loved how protective he was of the baby and me. I knew he was going to be the best daddy to Peanut.

"I really like the name Norah," I said and rolled around the name in my head.

Nolan cocked an eyebrow at me. "Okay..."

I could tell it wasn't clicking with him what I was getting at. We hadn't talked about names at all yet. I wanted to think about it some more, but the name had a really nice ring to it.

My stomach rumbled, breaking through the quiet in the cabin. We both laughed. I shrugged. "I guess I'm still hungry."

Nolan stood up from the couch. "Let's go get you some pie, huh?"

"Yay! I'm craving some right now," I said and jumped up from my spot.

He laughed as we walked into the kitchen together. I got plates out, and he cut into the pie. We ate at the table, and Nolan furrowed his brow as he ate.

"What's wrong?" I asked.

"This tastes familiar. Like... it tastes like my childhood."

"Of course it does."

He frowned. "What do you mean?"

"Your brother gave me the recipe. He said it was your mother's favorite."

His brown eyes got shiny at that.

"Nolan?"

"Really?" he whispered.

"Yeah?" I asked and chewed on my slice. It was fantastic. It was nothing too fancy or original, but I think I understood why he said it reminded him of his childhood. I hoped I did his mom's recipe justice.

"She used to make it for my birthday."

Oh.

Oh fuck, did I mess up here?

"I'm sorry."

He jerked his head up. "For what?"

I gestured to the pie in front of him. "Reminding you of your dead mother. Shit, I messed up."

He put a hand on my wrist. "No, baby. It's good. It's so good."

Now I was confused.

"Good?"

He nodded. "I haven't had this in a long time. I told you, you're my light. Anything about my parents reminds me of the darkest days of my life, but when you're involved, you keep the shadows at bay."

"I still feel like I fucked up by making this today."

He pulled my hands to his chest, and I felt his heartbeat. "You didn't fuck up. Never," he reassured me and kissed my hand.

"Nolan?"

"Yeah?"

"If we have a girl, can we name her Norah?"

He stared at me for a moment. "Really?" he croaked out, and he did that 'tough man' thing where he pretended he didn't cry. He did the same thing when I gave him that cheesy beer glass. Nolan was a big, grumpy bear who clearly needed to work on his communication skills, but it was so cute to see him fight back the emotions.

I nodded. "Yeah. I really like that name."

"You wouldn't want to name her after your mom?"

I made a face. "I'm not naming my baby 'Mary,' that's so boring."

"How about Norah Mary MacGregor?"

Now it was my turn to fight back the tears. "I—my mom would have loved that," I croaked out. "I miss her so much some days. She would be over the moon if she knew."

Nolan reached and squeezed my hand. "If we have a girl, we can name her after both of our moms. And we'll tell her all about them."

The burly man beside me smiled, but tears leaked from his eyelids, and I wiped them away. I never thought I would see Nolan MacGregor shed tears over the idea of naming his daughter after his mother. He continued to surprise me.

"Nolan?"

"Yeah, baby?"

"Will you tell me more about her? About your dad too?"

"Okay," he whispered.

It surprised me when he opened up to me and told me about his parents. Once he started, he couldn't stop. I never thought Nolan would gush out every feeling he ever had when we came up to the cabin for our honeymoon. It was the best idea Gemma ever had. I owed her big time.

CHAPTER TWENTY-TWO

NOLAN

"Well, look who it is!" my brother teased me as I walked into the brewery for the first time in a week. I couldn't remember the last time I had been away that long. Probably never.

I couldn't even muster the energy to flip him the bird; that's how sated Avery kept me up in the Poconos last week. I hadn't realized how much pressure had been weighing me down until she told me we were a team. Relaxing at the cabin had been exactly what I needed.

All the sex helped, too. We had so much sex on our honeymoon, maybe too much. We did it on the couch in front of the fire, all over the main bedroom, and even in the kitchen one night. Sometimes Avery wanted to 'play lumberjack,' which I obliged. Who knew she was into role-playing? Not me, but I didn't hate it. Not one bit.

It was the best Christmas I had since my parents died. Probably in my entire life. She really was the Queen of

Christmas. She brought the magic of the holiday back to life for me.

I took my jacket off and hung it up behind the door in the office. I took a seat across from my brother, who was behind his desk, staring at his computer screen.

"How are sales looking?" I asked.

"You worry about the beer, okay? I got this," he reassured me.

I narrowed my eyes. "Declan..."

He waved me away. "We're fine. Actually... I don't want Gemma to tend bar for us anymore."

"What?" I snapped.

"Geez, not like that. Gemma's a great bartender, but she's a whiz at our social media. You know she went to school for marketing?"

I shook my head.

I didn't even know Gemma had a degree. I didn't have a degree. How could I when I had to make sure my brother was taken care of after our parents died? It's how I got into the beer business. I took the first job at the local bar in town, waiting tables until the bar was short-staffed one night, and I learned how to bartend. Eventually, one of the local brewers and I got to chatting about my interest in home-brew. I left the bar a couple of weeks later to go flip kegs until I was the brewmaster's assistant. Now I was doing it all on my own, without a fancy degree, but with a lot of experience under my belt.

"What do you think she should do instead?" I asked.

"She should handle all our social, maybe even our entire marketing plan."

"What did she say?"

Declan sighed. "Hard pass."

"Really? But she already handles all the social media accounts, and that's not part of her job."

He nodded. "I don't get it. We could pay her better money."

I shrugged. "Gem's a people person. She enjoys being up front and helping people. She loves being a bartender."

My brother nodded. "I know, but I wished she realized her potential. You know we posted the photos of your wedding and lined up a bunch of events in the new year. Gem's ideas are good. I don't get it."

I shrugged. "If she doesn't want it, she doesn't want it. I gotta go check on production. I want to work on a new summer beer."

Declan gave me a confused look. "Besides Radle My Cage?"

I nodded. "Yeah, the lemon radler is great for summer, but something different. People liked that pumpkin beer."

"So a chick beer?"

I scowled. "No. A beer that non-beer drinkers might be interested in. A beer that will get people who don't like pale ales into the door."

Declan leaned back in his chair and stroked his clean-shaven jaw. "It's not a bad idea."

"I know! That's why I make the beer around here."

I turned to walk out the door, but he stopped me. "Nolan?"

"Hmm?"

"You look really happy."

"I am," I said with a toothy grin, and then I walked back into the tank room.

I got to work, and it was a relief that nothing had gotten fucked up while I was on my honeymoon. Allen had my back, and I trusted the brewers on our payroll that they knew what they were doing. It was why I hired them in the first place. I had shouldered the burden of worry for so long that I didn't know how to stop. Even when it came to my business.

I worked and researched for so long that it was getting rowdy in the bar when I walked out onto the floor again. It was New Year's Eve, so the place was packed. I even saw Declan standing at the host stand as our regular hostess was rushing around trying to bus tables. I peered over at the bar and saw Felix, Gemma, and Asher busting ass to serve our customers.

I hung up my work apron in the office and called Avery.

"Hey, you," she said into the phone.

I smiled at her voice in my ear. I hadn't heard from her all day, and I missed her. God, was I whipped or what?

"Hey, baby," I sighed.

"What's wrong?"

"The bar's packed tonight."

"Yeah? It's New Year's."

I ran a hand through my hair in frustration. "I think I'm gonna stay and help."

"Okay."

"Are you mad?"

"No. Why would I be mad? It's not like I had big plans to go out drinking."

I laughed. "I know, but I don't know when I'll get in."

"S'okay, baby. I'm probably gonna pass out soon, anyway."

"I don't deserve you."

"Hush, yes you do, and I deserve you. Nolan?"

I closed my eyes as I listened to her sweet, melodic voice in my ear. "Yeah, baby?"

"I love you."

My chest ached at hearing those words from her. I couldn't believe we had been afraid to tell each other how we felt. I never wanted to fight like we did that day at the cabin. I etched its memory into my brain to remember that I needed to tell her how I felt from time to time. To never let her wonder in the dark if she was my world or not. Because she was. Avery was my light, my life, and my everything.

"I love you too," I whispered. "I'll try not to wake you when I come in."

"Okay, baby," she said, and then I heard her yawn.

I hung up the phone, and when I looked up, I saw Gemma standing in the doorway with a plate of food. I cocked an eyebrow at her, and she put the plate in front of me.

She put a hand on her hip. "You're staying, aren't you?"

I sighed. "Can't help it. You look swamped."

She nodded and bit her lip like she wanted to say something else. "Thanks. It's chaotic out there. Avs said to make sure you ate dinner."

I furrowed my brow at my sister-in-law. "How? We were just on the phone?"

The younger woman tipped back her dyed pink head and laughed. "Oh, Nolan, you're cute! Women know how to multitask."

I took a bite of the sandwich she brought in and muttered thanks. I felt Gemma's eyes on me and noticed she hadn't walked away.

"What?" I asked sharply.

She had a mischievous smile on her face. "Did I eavesdrop on you saying those three little words?"

"Since when is my marriage your business?" I grumbled.

She laughed again and took the seat across from me. She

stole a fry from off my plate. "Since you knocked up my sister. Did I hear right?"

"Yeah."

"I heard about the fight."

I grunted as I chewed my food.

She rolled her eyes. "I don't know how my sister puts up with you. So broody!"

"I have a big dick," I muttered under my breath, hoping she didn't hear me.

When I looked up, Gemma's mouth was flopping open like a fish. It took a lot to render Gemma Jensen speechless.

"Holy shit, Nolan!" Gemma exclaimed and cackled. "My sister really made you come out of your shell."

I glared at her. "Don't you have drinks to pour?"

She gave me a sarcastic salute. "Aye, boss man!" But we were both smiling when she went back out onto the floor.

It was going to be a long night. I wanted to go home and crawl into bed with my pregnant wife, but I couldn't leave my guys hanging.

I ate quickly and went out on the floor to help Felix, Asher, and Gemma behind the bar. Since it was a holiday, it was a busy night. Good for business, bad for my marriage.

"Hey, stranger!" a familiar voice greeted me as I set a beer down for another patron.

I looked up and came face-to-face with my ex-wife.

"Hey, Kath. What can I get you?" I asked.

Kath had cut her white-blonde hair to chin-length, and she wore plastic-framed glasses. She frowned. "I want to apologize."

"For what?"

She eyed my left hand. "I heard you got married."

I leaned my arms on the bar. "You want to say sorry for that?"

She shook her head and looked back at the dark-haired, lanky guy at the table behind her. Grayson. We all went to high school together, and she had married him a couple of years ago.

"My husband was rude to your wife," she said.

I frowned.

"Oh, Grayson's the principal at the school."

While I knitted my brows at her, her face softened, and her mouth formed a tiny 'O.'

"She didn't tell you."

I shook my head. "Nope. You want a drink or not?"

"Um... do you have a recommendation? I'm not into IPAs."

"You'd probably like the Drakesville Lager," I suggested.

"Okay, sure."

"Hey, what type of beers do you usually go for?"

"Why?"

"Research," I explained while I pulled a glass out and filled it with a Drakesville Lager from the tap.

I slid the glass over to her, and she handed me her credit card. I rang her card through the machine and returned to the bar with the slip for her to sign.

She gingerly sipped on the beer I gave her. "I like this. I like a wheat or hefeweizen beer."

I nodded and stroked my beard. A hefeweizen would be a nice summer beer. I hadn't made one of those in a while.

"What did your husband say to Avery?" I asked.

"That you were an emotionless robot," she said, and then cringed.

"Oh."

"Sorry, but your wife kind of gave him the business

about that, anyway. He felt like an ass, as he should. He doesn't know you."

I laughed. Avery was a little quiet and kind to most people. Still, if anyone ever said anything bad about someone she loved, she was protective. Warmth spread across my chest at her being protective of me when someone said something rude about me. Even if it was partly true.

Kath nodded at something on the wall behind me. I turned around and saw a photo from the wedding where Avery and I were kissing each other, and my hands were on her pregnant belly. I couldn't help the smile that spread across my face.

"You look really happy," Kath said and gave me a small smile.

I turned back around. "I am."

"I'm glad you're getting the family you deserve. I'm sorry I could never give that to you."

I shrugged. "Kath, we weren't meant to be."

"I know, but I'm sorry that I hurt you. Our divorce hurt me, too. Don't carry around the hurt with your new wife, okay?"

"Hey, how is your stepson doing? He still wants to open a bar?" I asked, swiftly changing the subject.

She waved her hand at me and made a face. "That was a passing phase. You know, Avery's his favorite teacher. He wants to go to school for English, but we haven't told his dad yet."

I laughed.

A year ago, Kath reached out to me because her stepson said he didn't want to go to school, but instead, he was going to open a bar. Kath had sent him to shadow me. I didn't sugar-coat it for the kid. My job was hard work, and being a small business owner was nothing to sneeze at, either. Most days, I worried Declan and I couldn't keep the business afloat. That was even before Avery got pregnant. It was a constant worry when you owned your own business.

"It was good to see you, Kath."

"You too. I'm happy for you and Avery."

"Thanks."

"You're gonna be a wonderful dad. Just make sure you tell your wife how you feel once in a while."

I frowned. "Yeah, yeah, I get it."

She left a tip on the bar and walked back over to her husband. Gemma sidled up beside me. "Who was that?" she asked.

"My ex-wife," I said plainly, while I cleared away the glasses and took the next customer's order.

Gemma frowned, but she took another customer's order, so she didn't get to say whatever she was thinking.

I ended up leaving the brewery a little before midnight, but I was dog-tired. Declan said I didn't need to stay, but it was my business too, and I felt bad for leaving when we were so swamped.

The light was on upstairs when I walked into the house. It surprised me that Avery was still up; she sounded so tired when we had been on the phone. I walked up the steps and into our bedroom and was taken aback at the sight of Avery sitting up in our bed wearing sexy lingerie. It wasn't the same red number she had worn on our honeymoon. The cups of the bra part on this one were red, but the rest of the material was sheer black all the way down. She looked sexy as hell.

"Um, hi?" I asked, giving her a quizzical look.

She crooked a finger at me. "C'mere you."

I sat on the bed next to her and took off my boots. I

sighed as she brought her hands up to my neck and rubbed my tight muscles. "Oh, that feels nice."

She kissed my neck as her small hands kneaded my shoulders and moved down my back. "I knew you needed it. You've been at the brewery all day."

I sighed. "Sorry."

"S'okay baby, the brewery's your life's work, just let me take care of you when you get home."

I turned in her embrace, and she kissed me slowly. Her lips on mine were soft and gentle, like she was teasing the stress out of my body. Things had shifted between us since we had that fight at the cabin that almost ended our marriage. I would make damn sure she was mine forever. Avery was my end game, and I was never getting married again.

I pulled away from her kiss and pressed my forehead against hers. "Love you."

She smiled. "Love you too."

I gestured to her outfit. "You didn't have to wait up for me wearing this."

She brought my hands up to her swollen breasts. "I wanted to. You want to ring in the new year, right?"

I groaned. "Fuck, baby..."

She smirked at me. "Yes, please."

"You're a naughty girl."

She shook her head and bit her lip seductively. "No, I think I'm a good girl."

I laughed. "You want to be a good girl and ride this dick?"

She nodded enthusiastically, and soon we were tumbling down into the pleasure of each other again and again. Fucking my wife into the New Year? I think it would be a new tradition.

CHAPTER TWENTY-THREE

AVERY

I glared at Nolan for the tenth time this morning. It was the second week of January, and we were finding out the gender of our baby. It was safe to say he was nervous.

His knee shook next to me as we sat in the waiting room, waiting for my name to be called. I put a hand on his knee. "Stop," I hissed.

The woman across from me gave me a wry smile. "First baby?" she asked.

"How could you tell?" I joked.

She nodded to my husband. "Dad looks nervous."

"Sorry," Nolan muttered.

I shared an amused look with the other woman and slipped my hand into Nolan's. He relaxed at that. I didn't realize until I moved in with Nolan how high-strung he could be. He carried the weight of the world on his shoulders when he didn't have to. I tried to take that burden from him, to show him we were a team, but the old man was stubborn.

He kissed my temple. "Sorry," he whispered in my ear.

"S'okay."

"I really want to find out what we're having."

I couldn't answer because the nurse finally called us back. We went into the room together. Nolan sat in the chair next to the examination table while the nurse checked my vitals and asked me how I was feeling. We waited a bit until the ultrasound tech came in.

"How are you feeling?" she asked.

"Tired, but good," I said.

"Okay, if you lift your shirt, I'm going to pour the gel on, and you can get a look at the baby," she said.

I did as she asked, and Nolan held my hand as we looked at the grainy screen where we saw the tiny being growing inside me. We had the sonogram from my first appointment on the fridge, but this was different. It was like Peanut was finally real to us.

I looked over at Nolan and noticed he was doing the whole stiff upper lip thing, but his eyes were shiny. My heart wanted to burst out of my chest at the way he felt for our baby. Peanut made this big, stoic man come out of his shell.

A whooshing sound came over the machine.

"That's the baby's heartbeat," the tech said. "Do you want to know the sex?"

"Yes!" Nolan and I said in unison.

She laughed and moved the wand on my stomach for a bit. "It's a girl."

"Oh," I sighed. "A girl."

"We're having a baby girl," Nolan whispered, almost under his breath.

I squeezed his hand. "Nolan."

He smiled at me, and this time I knew he was crying. Oh wow, I didn't think I would ever see that from him.

The ultrasound tech smiled at me. She wiped the gel off my stomach and put the machine away. "Congrats, you two."

When she left, Nolan stood up and bent down to kiss my stomach. "Hi, Peanut. I can't believe we get to meet you soon. I love you so much."

"We can name her after your mom."

He pressed another kiss to my belly. "After both our moms. I'm so glad we're doing this, that we're gonna be a family."

I stroked his hair. "I love you, and I'm glad it took an accidental pregnancy for us to figure it out, but get up because I need to get back to work."

He smiled up at me but did as I asked. He helped me off the examination table, and we walked out of the doctor's office, hands clasped and giddy grins across our faces. Nolan drove me back to the high school. I had scheduled the appointment over my prep and lunch period, so I didn't have to take time.

"Stop worrying," I said to him when he parked outside the school.

He ran a hand through his beard. "Sorry."

"Hey, we're in this together, okay?"

He nodded. "I was just thinking about what color to paint the nursery."

"Not pink. I told you, I want something gender-neutral."

He pulled a handful of paint swatches out of the pocket of his flannel shirt. "Pick one!"

I laughed. "You aren't serious, right?"

He shrugged. "I want to get started on it, so we're not fretting before Peanut gets here."

I rubbed my belly. "Norah," I whispered.

"She's always gonna be Peanut to me."

My heart sang at that. He would be an awesome dad, and I loved him because of it. I peered at the paint swatches. "Go with a pale yellow or green."

He smiled and kissed me hard. "I love you."

"I love you too, but I need to get back to school."

"I'll see you later tonight?"

I shook my head. "I'm having dinner with Gemma. I'm kinda worried about her. She's being needy right now."

He smiled at me and brushed my hair behind my ear. "That's what I love about you."

"What?"

"You put everyone else's needs before yourself."

I glanced at the clock. "I gotta go. Don't stress about the nursery, okay? We'll do it together."

He nodded, and I kissed him one last time before getting out of the car. Only to come face-to-face with my students loitering outside the building. They definitely should be in class right now.

"Oooh, Miss J, is that your boyfriend?" one of them teased me.

"No! That's my husband," I teased back. "Don't you have to be in class?"

"Gym class," they said.

I crossed my arms over my chest. "Uh-huh, so shouldn't you be running on the track? Not out here loitering."

"Yes, Miss J," they groaned in unison.

I gestured behind me. "Go on. Get back to class before Coach Kyle has something to say about it."

They groaned but did as I told them to and walked back

around the building. I shook my head as I walked into the building and to my classroom. The bell was about to ring for the next period, and I really needed to pee. It felt like I always had to pee lately. Norah seemed to love sitting on my bladder.

I was washing my hands in the bathroom when Helen walked in. She smiled at me. "Hey, how did it go?" she asked.

I gave her a big smile. "Awesome. Baby's perfect, and Nolan's already planning on painting the nursery as we speak."

She squeezed my shoulder. "I wanted to ask you, you guys are good, right?"

"Why wouldn't we be?"

She sighed. "Well, your wedding vows..."

I cocked an eyebrow at her. "What?"

"Your vows felt very stilted. You didn't talk about how much you loved each other, and I know you do."

I sighed. "Yeah, we hashed that out on our honeymoon."

Her face transformed from concerned to happy, and a smile spread across her dark complexion. "Oh, good! I was worried you only got married because of the baby."

"Well, Nolan's not very good at expressing his feelings."

She snorted. "I hear that. Is that a brewer thing? Because Allen, I love him to death, but sometimes it's like pulling teeth to get him to tell me anything."

I nodded in sympathy. "Hmm. Maybe."

She surprised me by pulling me into a hug. "I'm glad for you. You deserve happiness; you both do."

I hugged her back and laughed as my bump brushed up against her flat stomach. "Sorry, I'm getting bigger by the minute. I better get to my classroom before those animals tear it apart."

She laughed. "I hear that!"

I dried my hands under the dryer and walked back to my classroom just as the bell rang. I had some stragglers come in after the late bell, but I was too happy to reprimand them. I had a hard time focusing during the rest of the school day.

After the last bell rang, I did prep work and graded more papers. Tyler Mathews' paper was the last I looked at, for a reason.

I jerked at a knock on my classroom door. I looked up and was surprised to see the teenager in question standing in my doorway, looking nervous.

I gestured to him. "Come in."

He ran a hand through his short-cropped brown hair as he walked over to my desk. "Hey, Miss Jensen, you got a minute?"

"Sure, Tyler. What's up?"

He paced in front of me for a few seconds, making me dizzy.

"Tyler, will you sit? You're making me sick."

He gave me a sheepish look and took the seat in the chair next to my desk. "Sorry, is that bad for the baby?"

I shrugged. "No clue, but you're making me nauseous."

"Sorry."

"What's going on?"

Tyler was a decent student, but I had noticed an uptick in his grades lately. Helen had him last year and said he was a good kid, but he lacked focus.

"Why did you want to be an English teacher?" he asked.

I shrugged. "I love reading mostly, and I love inspiring the young people in my life. I know reading a bunch of dead

Brits probably isn't the most exciting, but that's the curriculum."

He nodded. "I really like your class."

"Oh."

"You're my favorite teacher."

"Really?"

He nodded. "You don't treat us like little kids; you try to make us understand the stuff in terms of our own world. I like that."

"Okay..." I trailed off. I wasn't sure where he was going with this.

"I'm thinking about getting a degree in English."

"Oh!" I said and quirked my eyebrows up at him. That was the last thing I expected him to say to me.

He sighed at my surprised expression. "I came to ask you for a letter of recommendation, but I think I need advice."

I scribbled something into my planner to remind myself to write the letter for him. Tyler was a good kid, and I'd seen his growth. I'd make sure to write him a good letter. I was more concerned that he wanted advice from me.

"What do you need advice with?" I asked.

He grimaced. "Talking to my dad. He won't want me to get a degree in English."

I chose my words carefully because I wasn't sure that tracked with Grayson for me. After all, he was in education, but that might also be why he didn't want Tyler to get a degree in English. There wasn't a lot of money in public education.

"Okay... do you want to teach?"

He shrugged.

"Listen, Tyler, I think you're an outstanding student, and I noticed a difference in your performance lately. If you want to pursue that, I think it's a good idea, but you still have another year of high school left. You don't have to decide right away."

He nodded. "Yeah, that's what my girlfriend said."

I smiled. I noticed his grades had improved when he started dating my star pupil, Abigail. Their relationship had been teacher's lounge gossip, but I thought they were cute together.

"And tell your parents what you're thinking."

He frowned. "I change my mind a lot. They think I don't have focus."

I nodded. "Okay... I get that, but you're also sixteen. You don't need to know what you want to do with your life right this second. It's ridiculous that we tell students they need to decide their entire life at your age. Take your time and figure out what you want to do."

"Thanks, Miss J."

"Sure. That's what I'm here for."

He eyed me. "Do we have to call you Mrs. MacGregor now?"

I sighed. I didn't know that word had gotten around about who my baby daddy was. The kids knew I got married because they asked me about my holiday break plans, and I told them I was getting married on Christmas Day. I finally told them about the baby when one asked why I always put my hand on my stomach. I had to remind them it wasn't polite to make comments on anyone's body.

"My parents told me," he explained.

"Ah."

"Also, we live in a small-ass town."

I laughed. "True. I am gonna change my name, but I haven't done it yet."

"Why?" he asked. "Isn't that some patriarchal bullshit?"

I had a feeling that was something his girlfriend said to him.

"Maybe, but I like my husband's name. It's a strong Scottish name, and I want our daughter to have the same last name as me."

"You're having a daughter?"

I inwardly cursed. I wasn't supposed to tell people that yet, and I told two people already. "We just found out today."

"That's great, Miss J. You look like you're glowing."

"We'll see by the end of the school year how I feel when I'm as big as a house. Did you need anything else?" I asked.

He shook his head. "No. Thanks for the advice. I'm not sure what I want to do. But thanks."

"Sometimes, you just need someone to listen."

He walked off, and I decided there was no way I was getting any more work done today. I packed all my stuff up, and I walked across the street to my old apartment. My sister must have forgotten I was coming for dinner because she wasn't answering the door. I called her a couple of times, and she didn't answer.

I loved my sister, but sometimes she could be forgetful. How hard was it to call or text me you needed to cancel? I swear, who raised her? Because it wasn't me or dad who taught her to be that way.

I walked down the steps, and when I got onto the sidewalk, I remembered I hadn't driven to school today. Gemma was supposed to drive me home after dinner.

I sighed, walking it was then. I walked down the street toward the brewery. I didn't feel like making dinner tonight, especially if Nolan would be at the brewery all night. Might as well have dinner there and catch a glimpse of my hot brewmaster husband.

When I walked inside, the hostess, April, took pity on me and found me a table right away. I definitely got special treatment since I was married to one of the owners. I spied my husband talking intensely to Allen in the tank room. Did it make me hot that he was so competent at his work? Yes, it did. Someone who was good at what they did and took their work seriously? Hell to the yes!

"Hey, stranger," my brother-in-law, Declan, greeted as he placed a water down on the table. "Nol didn't say you were coming for dinner."

"I was supposed to have dinner with my sister."

He cocked an eyebrow. "Did she bail on you?"

"Yup."

We shook our heads in unison. We all loved Gemma, but knew she could be flaky.

"I hear I'm getting a niece," Declan said.

"You are!" I said with a smile.

"That's great!" he exclaimed with a smile that matched my own, etched across his face.

"How has Nol been today?" I asked.

"Actually, in a really good mood," Declan said, and his brow wrinkled as he stared at me. "I guess that's because of you and the baby, though. Allen asked him if he was sick."

A big belly laugh erupted out of me. Nolan had a reputation for being so grumpy, but it made me all warm inside that the baby and I put him in such a good mood. I rubbed a hand across my stomach as I thought about the little girl growing inside that we would name in memory of both of our mothers.

"You're the only person who can pull him from his shitty moods," Declan said.

I gave him a perplexed look. "Thank you?"

He laughed. "It's a good thing, Avs. You're good for

each other, I'm glad… I'm just glad my grouch of a brother found someone who tolerates him. Now tell me what you want for dinner, and I'll make sure the cooks take care of it real good."

I picked up the menu April laid down on the table. I scanned it briefly, not really looking because I knew it by heart at this point. I didn't realize when I married the brewmaster just how much I would eat here.

I handed the menu back to Declan. "Just get me the grilled cheese, please."

"On it!" he said, taking the menu with him and walking off back into the kitchen.

I was scrolling on my phone when I felt a presence sit down at the table across from me. My smile cracked my face when I saw my husband on the other side. He gave me a confused look. "Did Gemma bail on you?"

"Yup!"

A scowl crossed his face immediately.

I pointed a finger at him. "Stay out of it. It's between her and me."

He grunted his go-to response when he didn't want to argue with me.

"I'm too tired to make dinner, so I came here instead."

"Did you order yet?"

I nodded.

He flagged down April and asked her to help put in his order. A server that I didn't recognize brought him over a beer immediately.

He asked a couple of times if it bothered me if he drank while I was pregnant, but it didn't. He was a brewmaster; he needed to taste his beer. It would have been a ridiculous request for me to make. It was nice that he asked, though.

"What are you doing?" I asked him.

"Having dinner with my beautiful wife. How was work?"

"Fine. Are you gonna be here all night?"

He shrugged. "Maybe. We're a little behind on production."

I frowned. "Oh."

"That's why I'm taking my break now."

We ate dinner together, and I listened to him vent about the problems with production and working on the new hefeweizen beer he wanted to release during the summer. My sister never called me back, which annoyed me. It bothered me way more than I was letting Nolan know.

On the way out, I made a pit stop at the bathroom before walking home, but when I came out, I was in tears.

CHAPTER TWENTY-FOUR

NOLAN

I looked up when I saw Avery coming back from the bathroom. I wanted to go home with her, but I had a lot of work to do tonight. All that faded away when I saw her in tears.

I jumped up in concern. "What's wrong?"

She shook her head.

"Avs, what is it?"

"I think... something's wrong."

"What do you mean?"

She grimaced and wrung her hands. "There was some blood."

I felt the color drain from my face, and my brain fired off red flashing warning signs. I swallowed hard. "How much?"

She shrugged. "Just a little spotting. Maybe it's nothing to worry about?"

"Okay, let's go."

"What?"

I helped her put on her jacket, but she was in a daze. I felt an ache in my chest when I looked at her tear-stained face. "We're going to the hospital to make sure it's nothing, okay?"

"Okay," she muttered.

I cupped her face. "It's gonna be okay."

"What if it's not?" she blubbered.

I wiped her tears away with the back of my thumbs. "Stay here. I'm going to go get the car. Okay?"

"We only live a block away; we can walk."

I shook my head firmly. "No, baby, I don't want to risk it." I gestured to the table we had been sitting at. "Sit, and I'll text you when I bring the car around back."

Her tears were flowing as she gingerly sat back down.

I kissed her quickly. "It's going to be okay."

She looked like she was in shock. I put on a brave face for her, but inside I was screaming in agony. I had to be strong for her, even though I was scared shitless. She was my light, and I wasn't letting her die out because of her fear.

I ran back into the office, and Declan gave me an annoyed look at the outburst. He was wearing his glasses, which meant he was deep in expense reporting. He said staring at spreadsheets in his contacts hurt too much. His expression morphed into concern when he saw my face.

"Something's wrong with the baby," I blurted, and I clenched my hands into fists. "I gotta take Avery to the hospital."

"Go!" Declan said to me. "You don't have to tell me anything. Make sure your family is okay."

"I..."

"Dude, go! Make sure Avs and my niece are fine!"

I walked out of the brewery, but I would be lying if I said I walked home. I ran. Like my life depended on it, but it wasn't my life I was worried about. I let myself take a quick breath and tried to calm down when I walked up to my driveway and into my car. I needed to be calm for Avery. I needed to be the hand she held tonight. I needed to be her rock.

I put my key in the ignition and drove the short drive to the back parking lot of the brewery. I shot off a text to Avery, and she came out the back door in a flash. I threw it in park and jumped out to help her into the passenger seat. As soon as she was settled, I got back into the driver's seat and drove off to the hospital.

Avery was too quiet, but I focused on the road while she tried to call someone.

"Gemma, I need you! Answer your fucking phone!" she swore into the phone and then punched the end button.

I put a hand on her thigh. "It's gonna be okay."

"No, it's not!" she cried.

"Avs, you gotta calm down. It could be nothing."

"How the fuck would you know?" she snapped. "It's not happening to you."

I clenched my jaw and bit my tongue so I didn't say anything I would regret later. She wasn't mad at me; she was just taking her frustration out on me. I had to let it roll off my back. I was more concerned with getting her to the hospital and making sure she was okay. The hospital was a ten-minute drive, so we got there quickly. She was still freaking out when we got to the ER.

"Avs, it's gonna be okay. Let me help get you signed in, okay?"

She nodded and wiped her eyes with the back of her hand. "What if we lose her?"

"Let's not think about that yet, okay?"

I walked up to the front desk and smiled at the older woman behind it. "Hi."

"How can I help you?" the nurse asked.

I thumbed over my shoulder at Avery. "My wife's pregnant, and she had some bleeding."

She thrust a clipboard at me, and I took it back to Avery. She tore it from my hands and furiously started filling it out.

"Avs."

"It's fine," she snapped.

"Baby..."

"Nolan, fuck off."

I held up my hands in frustration and let her do what she needed to do. I didn't want to lose our baby. We were just at the doctor's today, and they said everything was fine. We listened to her heartbeat again and everything. Why was this happening now?

Avery handed in the clipboard, and we sat, waiting for somebody to come talk to us. She was texting angrily, and I had a feeling who it was aimed at. I was walking on eggshells over here.

"Nol?" I heard a familiar voice ask.

I looked up and saw Kath standing in front of us wearing her hospital scrubs and giving us a concerned look.

I knew my ex-wife worked at the hospital, but I didn't think about running into her tonight. I cared more about making sure my wife and unborn child were okay.

"Hey, Kath," I sighed.

Kath's eyes slid over to Avery, whose face was set in a hard line. "What's going on?"

"Kath, you've met my wife Avery before, right?"

Kath nodded. "Nice to see you again. What's going on?"

Avery put a protective hand on her belly.

Kath's eyes widened in recognition, and I nodded. She

looked back at the nurse's station. "Let me see who's on call tonight. I'm just coming in for my shift. Hang tight."

She left as soon as she had appeared.

"I didn't know you were still friendly with her," Avery spat. I didn't recognize the venom in my wife's voice.

"Our divorce was amicable. You knew that," I reminded her.

"You said she broke your heart."

"She did, but I broke her heart, too. She's trying to help us."

Avery nodded, but I could see the dark thoughts clouding her head. I tried to lace her hand through mine, but she pulled away. She was shrinking away from me, and I didn't understand why.

I pulled out my phone and texted Gemma.

ME: *You need to get to the hospital now.*

Five minutes went by, and she still hadn't responded to me. I texted my brother instead.

ME: *Is Gem at the brewery?*

I saw the dots typing, and then a text popped up from him.

DEC: *No. Why?*

ME: *Nevermind.*

DEC: *Are Avery and the baby okay?*

ME: *Don't know yet.*

I didn't know where Gemma was, and it really pissed me off. Avery constantly dropped everything for the girl because she was a dutiful sister. Why couldn't Gemma bother to return the favor? I loved Gemma, but sometimes her flightiness was too much. Especially right now, when my wife was hurting, and all she wanted was to be comforted by her sister.

It stung a bit that Avery didn't want that comfort from

me. I was her husband. She was supposed to lean on me at times like this.

I slid my phone back into my pocket and leaned my elbows on my knees. Avery still wasn't talking to me, and I wasn't sure what to do. I wanted to be her shoulder to lean on, but she wasn't letting me.

"Are you in pain?" I asked.

She shook her head.

"Maybe..."

"Are you the doctor?" she snapped.

I sighed and shook my head.

We waited in silence for another half hour before they finally called us back. I went with her and sat in the chair next to the examination table, feeling like a fool, while she talked to the nurse about what happened. I felt like there was nothing I could do to help the woman I loved. If we lost the baby, I didn't know what I was going to do. I loved Avery, and I knew Peanut hadn't been planned, but I wanted our baby. I wanted a family with her. I wanted to give her the happily ever after she had been chasing for as long as I knew her.

We waited for the doctor, and Avery retold him everything she told the nurse.

"We're gonna run some tests. But if you aren't in pain, I don't think this is a cause for concern. Sometimes a little spotting is nothing to be worried about," the doctor told us.

"We were just at the doctor today," I said.

"Did you have a pelvic exam?"

Avery shook her head.

"When was the last time you had sex?"

Avery's cheeks went red.

"This morning," I grumbled.

The doctor tried to hide his smile, but from Avery's scowl, she saw it. "Could have been from that."

When he left, we were plunged into silence again.

"I'm sorry," she whispered.

"It's okay," I said and squeezed her hand.

"I'm taking my anger out on you. I'm mad at myself."

"Why?"

She wiped away a stray tear. "It's my fault."

"Hey, the doctor thinks it might be nothing. It was just a little spotting, right?"

She nodded.

"Just a little bit?"

She nodded again. "Did I freak out over nothing?"

I shrugged. "I'd rather it be nothing and know my girls are okay. No matter what, it will never be your fault."

Her eyes welled up with tears again. "I want my sister."

"I know, baby."

"Why am I always expected to run to her for every problem she has, but the one time I needed her, she couldn't be bothered?"

"I'm here, okay? Lean on me."

She stared up at me, her eyes brimming with tears again. My heart wrenched at how much pain she was in, especially since I didn't know how to take that all away. "Nolan... I'm scared."

I kissed her forehead. "I know."

"I don't want to lose you."

I furrowed my brow at that. Before I could ask her what she meant, the doctor returned, and they started doing more tests.

It was a long night, and eventually, they let us go home. They didn't think anything was wrong with the baby. They even did another ultrasound, and she looked fine. The doctor thought it was a fluke. It could happen sometimes, but they told us to monitor it.

It was the scariest night of my life. I didn't want to think about the possibility that we could have lost the baby. Avery was afraid of a miscarriage because of her mom's history. I got that. It was why we waited to tell her dad for a while.

Gemma never got back to me, which seriously pissed me off. I could tell it defeated Avery; she really wanted her sister to comfort her.

When we got home, I hopped into bed with her and stroked her hair while she cried into my chest.

"It's okay. We didn't lose her. It's going to be okay," I reassured her.

She sniffled into my t-shirt. "I can't lose her."

I sighed.

She looked up at me. "I can't."

"Avery, you know I love you, right? It would crush me if we lost Peanut. But if something happened, we would get through it together, okay?"

She shook her head. "No. It would end us."

I tilted her chin up at me. "What are you talking about?"

Her eyes blazed in anger. "I saw how you looked at her."

"Who?"

"Your fucking ex-wife!"

I cocked an eyebrow at her. "What does Kath have to do with you and me?"

"You only married me because you got me pregnant. I know you still love her."

I blinked at her. Where the fuck did she get that from?

She stared back at me, and the hurt on her face felt like a knife to my chest.

"You really think that?" I asked.

She nodded.

"What makes you think I still love my ex-wife?" I snapped. "The one who I told you broke my heart, and she's why I can't discuss my feelings? What makes you think I only married you because of the baby? Haven't I fucking proved myself enough?"

I got out of bed in a huff.

"Where are you going?"

I shook my head. "I can't do this right now. We're both upset. Tonight was traumatic. I know you're hurting at the idea we could have lost the baby, but don't take it out on me and try to invent shit that doesn't exist."

I grabbed my pillow from off of my side of the bed.

"What are you doing?" she asked.

"Going to sleep on the couch. I'm not fighting with you tonight."

"But it's true. If I lost the baby, our marriage would be over."

I scrubbed a hand down my face. "I don't know how to tell you how fucking wrong you are. I love you, and I know you're going through some shit right now, but don't tell me how I'm supposed to feel or tell me I don't love you."

I didn't wait for her to say anything else and trudged down the stairs. Maybe it was immature of me, but I didn't see the use of us getting into another knock-down fight. I didn't understand why she thought if she lost the baby, that meant the two of us were over. I thought we had gone over all this shit already.

It pissed me off.

At Avery for thinking I couldn't be enough for her. At Gemma for not showing up when Avery needed her. At Kath for existing and putting dark thoughts into Avery's head. Even though Kath did nothing wrong. I was pretty sure we got seen so quickly because of Kath. We should thank her, not have her force a wedge in-between us.

I lay on the couch and put my pillow over my head, and screamed into it. I shoved it behind my head and stared up at the ceiling. This was totally fucked.

My phone beeped on the coffee table, and I swiped at it. I growled when I saw a text from Gemma.

GEMMA: *Sorry! My phone died. What's going on?*

ME: *Fucking forget it.*

GEMMA: *Nolan! What's wrong? Is it something with the baby?*

ME: *Ask your fucking sister.*

I shut off my phone and rubbed my beard in frustration.

How could things get so messed up in the span of a few hours? I thought Avery and I were happy. I thought we were finally on the same page. If she thought I still had feelings for Kath, I didn't know what to think. I had loved Avery secretly for years and never felt like I was good enough for her, and now she was proving it.

I looked up at the sound of the creaky bottom step of our staircase and saw Avery standing over the couch.

"What?" I snapped.

"Come back to bed."

"No."

"Please, Nolan."

"Why? So we can get into another useless fucking fight where you tell me I'm not good enough for you? So you can ask me for another divorce?"

She sighed and put a hand on her stomach. "I'm sorry. I want to say this is my hormones making me an asshole, but it's my own insecurities coming to the surface. I don't want a divorce." She held up her left hand, showing me the wedding band and my mother's emerald ring on her finger.

"You put these rings on my finger, and I don't want to take them off, ever. I'm sorry for being a dick tonight. I never wanted you to feel like you weren't enough for me. You're my everything."

"Obviously not if you think so little of me," I muttered.

"I'm sorry. Can you blame me for thinking that you wouldn't want to marry me if I wasn't carrying your baby?"

I sat up on the couch. "Why do you think that?"

She bit her lip. "Your ex is gorgeous, and I'm not."

"What the fuck does that mean? You're gorgeous as hell. You're my fucking wife, not her! Whatever my ex looks like has nothing to do with how much I love you. I don't want another divorce."

"I don't want a divorce either!" she shrieked at me.

"Then why the fuck are we fighting right now?" I yelled back.

She reared back at my raised voice, and I rubbed a hand down my face. I thought of my next words carefully. I wasn't sure why she was so convinced I would leave if she lost the baby. Maybe the baby pushed me to finally act on my feelings for her, but they had been there all along. I sat back in silence, never telling her how I felt for years, and I wasn't about to lose her because she thought I still loved my ex. I stopped loving Kath a long time ago, way before Avery was ever in the picture.

When I looked at her again, I felt a pain in my chest at seeing her face still stained from all the tears she shed tonight. "Come back to bed, please," she begged. "I'm sorry. I'm so scared of losing Norah, of losing you. I need my husband beside me tonight. Please, Nolan?"

"Fine," I muttered.

I followed her back up the steps and into our bedroom. I got into bed with her and put a protective hand on her belly.

I was just as scared as she was of losing Norah, but even if god forbid something happened to the baby, that didn't mean I would leave Avery.

I held my wife until she fell asleep, but I knew this was far from over. I made so many mistakes in my first marriage; I didn't want history to repeat itself with Avery. I wasn't sure how I could convince her I loved her, with or without the baby. I just knew I had to try. I wasn't losing Avery. And I wasn't getting another divorce.

CHAPTER TWENTY-FIVE

AVERY

*I*t had been a week since Nolan and I had that fight after we thought we would lose Norah. We weren't exactly on speaking terms right now, and it was totally my fault. I let my insecurities and fear of losing the baby ruin the good thing we had, and now our marriage was in shambles.

What did I do instead of trying to fix it? Hideout at my dad's house watching the hockey game with him.

"You okay?" Dad asked.

"Metzy looks off tonight, right?" I asked instead, trying to redirect his attention back to the game.

"Avery..." my dad said in a warning tone.

It wasn't weird for my sister or me to come over and watch the Bulldogs game with my dad, but since I had been so busy with baby stuff lately, my dad thought it was odd when I showed up unannounced tonight. He immediately thought something was wrong, but I had been brushing him off all night.

"No," I admitted and took a sip of my water.

"What's wrong?"

I sighed. "I thought I lost the baby."

My dad sat up straighter. "What do you mean? Why didn't you tell me?"

"I had some spotting and freaked out about it, but everything's fine."

"How did Nolan take the stuff with the baby?"

I frowned.

"Avery..."

I sighed. I still felt like such an asshole about that night. I apologized, but things still weren't right with us, and I didn't know how to fix it. Nolan said he felt like he wasn't good enough for me, but it was the opposite. He was too good for me. I wasn't worthy of his love, not after everything I put him through.

"We got into a huge fight and haven't been talking," I admitted.

"You can't let that shit stew. If you want to make your marriage work, you gotta talk to each other. How long has it been?"

"A week," I muttered and looked down at the floor.

"Avery," my dad sighed and ran a hand across his jaw. "I love you, sweetheart, but I gotta be honest with you. The reason none of your other relationships worked is that you always run at the first sign of trouble."

I opened my mouth to protest, but he held up a hand for me to stop.

"It's true. When your high school boyfriend went to a different college, you broke up with him even though you could have tried the long-distance thing. The guy you dated right after college who lived an hour away? You didn't make it work because you didn't want to."

I narrowed my eyes at him. "What are you trying to say?"

"I love you, and I want you to be happy, but don't run from Nolan because thinking you lost the baby scared you."

I shook my head in disbelief. "No, if I lost the baby, we'd get a divorce."

"Why?"

"We only got married because of the baby."

Dad gave me a hard stare. The kind he used to give me when I was younger and did something foolish. "Why do you think that?" he asked.

"Because he's still in love with his ex-wife!"

Dad stared at me for a couple of seconds before he replied. "How do you know that?"

"Because she's gorgeous!"

"Sweetheart, you're his wife. They don't belong to each other anymore. You know what I said to him when I first met him, and you fell asleep on the couch?"

I shook my head.

"I asked him if you knew he loved you. He loved you then, Avery. He doesn't love her anymore. He loves you. Don't run away from him because you're afraid. If you lose the baby, he's going to be the shoulder you cry on. He'll be your rock."

Dad took a swig of his beer and turned back to the hockey game. I let his words settle on me.

My pregnancy had my emotions all over the place, so maybe I had imagined Nolan was still in love with his ex-wife. If Dad saw that Nolan loved me the first night they met, could I have been wrong? When he looked at Kath, was that the same way he looked at me? Had tensions been so high that I just saw what I wanted to see?

When I thought back to it, Nolan hadn't looked at Kath

in any particular way. If anything, he looked terrified. He put on a brave face for me while I was fretting about losing our baby, and when I saw his ex-wife, the lizard part of my brain made a connection that wasn't there. Then I picked a fight with him and made him think he wasn't worthy of me. When the opposite was true. Since the moment I met Nolan, I knew there was something special about him. Nolan gave me everything I ever wanted, but instead of giving him the love he deserved in return, I let my insecurities get the better of me.

God, I was such an asshole. My dad was right. I was trying to run away from my problems.

A sob bubbled up from inside me, and I pressed a hand against my mouth as I realized just how much I fucked up with Nolan.

Dad looked up in alarm, and his face fell when he looked at me. "Oh, sweetheart."

"I don't want to lose either of them. I can't lose Nolan. He's my everything," I sobbed out and let the tears flow.

Dad handed me a box of tissues, and I blotted my eyes with a tissue.

I didn't want to admit it, but my dad was right. I literally ran to my daddy when things got too hard with my husband. I didn't want to face the hard stuff, so I had been giving my husband the cold shoulder instead. How could Nolan ever love me with the way I treated him?

I wiped my tears away, and my dad looked like he was going to say something else, but my phone beeped in my purse and distracted me. I took it out and saw a text from Nolan.

NOLAN: *Are you going to be home for dinner?*

ME: *No, I'm at my dad's watching the game. Do you want me to come home?*

NOLAN: *No.*

I cringed at his one-word answer. That was not good. I needed to fix this. I couldn't let Nolan go back inside himself and keep his feelings from me. I couldn't push him away because the idea of losing Norah scared me to death to the point I accused him of being in love with his ex-wife.

I put my phone back into my purse and stared blankly at the TV screen as I thought about how to fix my marriage. I wasn't sure I knew where to start.

"I think I need to go home soon," I said.

"Okay, sweetheart. Hey! Did you find out what you're having?"

I nodded and put a hand on my stomach. "A girl."

"You got a name?"

"We're gonna name her Norah Mary MacGregor."

Dad pinned me with a curious look. "Norah Mary..."

"To honor both of our moms."

The corners of Dad's eyes crinkled, and he looked like he was about to get choked up. "Your mother would have loved that."

"I wish she were here."

"Me too. She would have been so proud of you. Of both you and your sister."

The front door banged open, and Gemma barged into the house like she knew we were talking about her. She stomped the snow off her boots and took them off at the door.

"Speak of the devil!" Dad joked.

Gemma rolled her eyes as she brushed snow out of her hair and took off her jacket. She slumped on the couch next to me and looked at the TV screen.

"What's up with Metzy tonight?" she asked. "He can't cover a goal to save his life."

"What are you doing here?" I asked.

She and Dad shared a look.

"Well, I went to your house, but Nolan said you were here. He was grouchier than normal. Are you guys okay?"

I shook my head and willed the tears not to fall again.

"Come on, let's go upstairs. You know Dad can't stand girl-talk."

I growled at her, but she helped me off the couch and up the steps to her childhood bedroom.

We sat on the bed together, and I put my hands on my stomach. I was still mad at her. Her not picking up her phone and not coming to the hospital gutted me. It made me realize that I always dropped everything for my sister. I was always there to pick up her pieces, but she never returned the favor.

The person who always picked up my pieces was Nolan, and I was being an asshole to him.

"I'm sorry," Gemma spoke first.

I clenched my jaw and nodded.

"You're really mad, aren't you?"

I squeezed my eyes shut. "I needed you, Gem. I was breaking apart, and I needed my sister, but you didn't even bother to text me back. It was the very least you could have done."

She frowned and bit her lip. "I'm sorry, Avs."

"I needed you, and you weren't there."

She screwed up her face. "You don't need me. You have Nolan."

"I needed my sister. I always drop everything for you when you have a problem, but you never return the favor."

"I'm really sorry, Avs."

"You should be! I'm pissed off at you!"

She bit her lip and put a hand on mine. "But you don't need me."

"Yes, I do! I needed my sister to tell me everything was going to be okay when I thought I was gonna lose the baby."

"But you didn't need me because you had Nolan. I know he was there for you, holding your hand through it all."

I sighed and ran a frustrated hand down my face. She was right; Nolan had done that. He put on a brave face for me and had been the shoulder I should have leaned on, but instead, I treated him like a Grade A asshole.

"I think my marriage is over," I admitted in a quiet voice and wrapped my arms around myself.

"What?" she shrieked.

"Nolan and I got into a big fight that night, and we haven't been talking."

She grabbed my hand. "Oh, Avs. What happened?"

"My normal insecurities."

She raised an eyebrow and gestured with her hand for me to go on.

I sighed. "We ran into his ex-wife."

"So?"

I gave her a look.

She nudged me with her arm.

"She's gorgeous."

My sister held out her hand and gestured to me. "Is she pregnant with Nolan's baby? No. Did he drop everything for her? No. Did he actually express his feelings for her? A big no! That's why they got divorced."

"They got divorced because he wanted kids."

She shook her head. "Dec told me it wasn't just that. They were extremely unhappy. Dec thinks they only got married because Nolan was stressed about keeping a roof over their heads. You know Nolan, he would rather chop off his hand than tell someone how he feels. When I first started working at the brewery, I thought he hated me because all he did was grunt. Dec had to tell me that meant I was doing a good job."

"It's not the same thing."

"Why not?"

"Because I baby-trapped him."

My sister pursed her lips and sighed. "Avs, I love you, but you're making this into nothing. Nolan loves you."

I felt the tears fall, and my sister jumped into action to get the tissues. I dabbed at my eyes, and Gemma rubbed my back soothingly. I leaned into my sister. This is what I needed from her last week. I needed her to comfort me.

"Can I blame this on pregnancy brain?" I asked.

She wiped away my tears and shook her head. "No, I think you need to grovel. Nolan looked so sad when I showed up tonight. Like he was waiting for you. I've never seen him look that way before."

I felt an ache in my chest. "I'm scared I'm gonna lose her, and then he won't want me anymore."

"Her?"

"We're having a girl. I was going to tell you at dinner, but then you ditched me."

She gave me a sheepish look. "I'm sorry. I was a complete space cadet. You have every right to be mad at me."

"I AM mad at you!"

She slapped my arm. "You're supposed to say 'No, Gem, it's okay, you're my sister, and I love you.' I'm trying to apologize."

"Geez, who raised you? You suck at apologies."

"You did. So do better with your actual kid."

I frowned and held my growing stomach with care.

"Aw, Avs, I was just teasing."

"What if I had lost the baby?"

"Stop thinking about it!" my sister exclaimed. "If it happened, you and Nolan would have gotten through it together. He's always been there for you."

"He's always put my pieces back together."

She helped me up. "Go home and do some groveling. If he's still mad, you could always get down on your knees and—"

I fixed her with a glare, and she burst out in laughter.

"What? I'm not wrong, am I?" she asked with a cheeky grin.

I continued to glare.

"Are we good?"

"You might need to grovel a little."

She pulled me into a hug. "I'm sorry. My phone died, and then I fell asleep. I'm sorry I wasn't there, but I will be going forward, okay?"

I nodded. "I still need you, Gem. You're my sister."

"I'm sorry. I'll do better."

I pinched her side. "You better, jerkface."

She laughed and slapped my hand away. "Go home and talk to your husband. He snapped at me like three times yesterday."

I grimaced. "Sorry."

"He's so grumpy!"

"He's my grump," I muttered.

"Then go make-up with him. Geez, everyone is walking on eggshells around him lately."

I frowned. "I'm sorry. That's my fault."

"Then do something about it!"

I hugged her tightly, and we walked back downstairs. I

said goodbye to my dad and Gemma and then went out to my car. On the drive back to Drakesville, I thought about what they both said.

Dad was right. I always ran at the first suggestion of trouble. The thought of losing the baby and Nolan at the same time made me irrational. It made me look for enemies that weren't there. It wasn't fair for him to deal with that.

Everyone talks about how hard marriage is, but I thought it was a myth. I thought that was just what people in awful marriages said. I didn't want a divorce, but I needed to fix the rift between Nolan and me.

The house was dark when I got home, and Nolan was nowhere to be found. I sighed as I lay in bed and set my alarm. I would have to wait for the morning to make things right. I might call out sick because repairing my marriage and making sure my husband knew he was my everything was way more important than teaching Beowulf.

CHAPTER TWENTY-SIX

NOLAN

I slid into bed late and tried not to wake Avery. Since we visited the hospital, things between us haven't been great. I was trying to give her space, but I wasn't sure how much longer I should do that. I didn't want this fight to linger on. I wanted to fix our marriage before it got more messed up.

I made a lot of mistakes in my first marriage. Kath and I didn't want the same things, but I also never told her how I felt. If I wanted to spend the rest of my days with Avery, I needed to fight for her.

When I asked if she would be home for dinner, it was because I wanted to fix things. When she told me she was at her dad's, I went back to the brewery and worked my ass off. Mostly just to keep my mind off the fact my marriage was crumbling.

Avery stirred as I got into bed.

"Nolan?" she whispered.

"Shush, go back to sleep."

Her eyes popped open. "No. We should talk."

"In the morning. Go back to sleep," I urged and kissed her forehead.

She shook her head. "I'm sorry."

"I know."

"No, I'm really sorry."

I curled around her and kissed her neck. My hand went protectively to her stomach. The thought of losing our baby had been scary, but everything was fine now. Avery went to the doctor the next day, and they thought nothing was wrong. They weren't sure why it happened, but since it was just some spotting, it wasn't cause for concern. I didn't blame her for freaking out. I had been freaking out, too.

She put her hand over mine, and I heard her sniffle.

"Oh, Avs, don't cry," I cooed at her.

She shifted, so we were face-to-face in the dark of our bedroom. "I'm sorry for fighting with you. For making you think you weren't enough for me. I felt like I wasn't enough for you."

I caressed her cheek. "I know you were scared about losing our baby. But, Avs..."

"What?"

"Did you really think if you lost her, I would have left you? I was scared too."

She squeezed her eyes shut, and I wiped the tears from her face. She reached up a hand and covered mine with hers. "I've been horrible to you. I'm sorry."

"We were going through a hard time. It happens. But I don't want it to keep on happening, okay?"

She nodded.

"How about we talk about it in the morning?"

She shook her head. "I want you to know that I love you,

and I'm sorry. I saw what I wanted to see. My dad says I always run at the first sign of trouble."

"Did you see Gem?"

"Yeah... I realized something."

"What's that?" I asked through a yawn.

"I pick up my sister's pieces, but she has never done that in return. The person who always puts me back together is you."

I gave her a small kiss. "Avery, you're the light in the dark world for me. I should have told you how I felt a long time ago."

"Really?" she blubbered.

"Yes, really. I'm never getting married again. You're it for me. Can we go to bed now?"

She laughed and wiped her face. "Sorry."

"You have work tomorrow."

She peered at me and gave me a naughty grin. "Maybe I'll call out sick."

I eyed her suspiciously.

"I need to spend time with my husband, who I have been very mean to lately."

I groaned into her neck. "You're killing me right now. I'm so tired."

"Really?" she laughed.

"Yes, really. Can we please go to sleep?"

She pushed me onto my back and kissed me goodnight. "Okay, we'll talk more in the morning."

I let Avery sleep in because, honestly, she needed the rest. The past week had been stressful for me, so it must have been worse for her. She didn't need the extra stress; it wasn't good for the baby.

I had a quick breakfast and eyed the Christmas tree still up in the living room. While things had been tense between us, I hadn't wanted to nag Avery about it being time to take down the decorations. We should probably take care of that today, but I'd talk to her about that when she woke up.

Instead, I went into the nursery. I finished painting it earlier this week and had been working on putting together the furniture. I hadn't asked Avery if she wanted to help because we hadn't been on speaking terms.

I wiped the sweat from my brow as I finished putting the crib together. I looked over my shoulder when I heard footsteps in the hallway. Avery stood in the doorway, biting her lip nervously while she held her pregnant belly.

"Did you call out of work?" I asked.

She nodded. "Yeah, I just called out. I need a mental health day. The kids will live without me." She walked into the room and surveyed the work I had done. "Oh wow, Nol. You did all this?"

"You weren't talking to me. I needed something to fill my time."

She frowned. "I'm sorry."

"I know."

She smoothed her hands across her belly, and then her smile lit up her entire face. "Oh!"

"What's wrong?"

She shook her head. "Nothing wrong. I think I felt the baby."

I crossed over to her and put my hand next to hers. I didn't feel anything, but the way the smile spread across her face and her eyes lit up, I knew she could.

"I can feel her," she whispered.

I bent down and kissed her belly. "Hi, Peanut, you causing trouble for your mama?"

She laughed. "I have a feeling she's gonna be daddy's girl."

I kissed her stomach.

Avery ran a hand through my hair. "I was so scared of losing her, of losing you."

I stood up and gave her a quick kiss. "You're not gonna lose me. I promise."

She nodded but said nothing more.

"Hey, can we take the Christmas tree down now?" I asked, changing the subject.

She gave me a look of horror. "No!"

"Avs, come on, it can't be Christmas forever."

She pouted and then got a glimmer in her eyes. "What if, and hear me out, we make it a holiday tree? We could switch it to Valentine's tree and then St Patrick's and Easter!"

I shook my head at her. "You can't be serious."

She laughed and shrugged. "Maybe..."

"We're taking it down today."

"Okay, fine. I still can't believe you put it up, to begin with."

I pushed her hair behind her ear and stroked her cheek. "All for you. Everything I do is for you."

Her eyes got shiny at that. "Oh, Nolan."

I waved her off. "Come on downstairs. I'll make you breakfast."

I led her out of the nursery and down the stairs. She took a seat in one of the kitchen chairs while I fixed her breakfast. I already ate, but I made another pot of coffee. I got eggs out of the fridge and began scrambling them. I popped the bread in the toaster while I worked.

I only turned around when I heard Avery laughing. "What?"

"You're humming again."

I shrugged. "I never realized I did that until you pointed it out. My mom used to do that."

"She would have been proud of you, Nol. Both of them would be."

I shrugged while I finished breakfast and set down a plate in front of her. I poured coffee into two mugs and handed one to her. I was honestly surprised she hadn't growled at me before she got her coffee. I took the seat across from her and sipped my coffee slowly.

She looked at me over her coffee cup. "Nol?"

I grunted as I drank my coffee.

"I'm sorry," she muttered.

I nodded, but I still didn't understand why she had reacted that way when she saw Kath.

"Why did seeing my ex-wife bother you so much? I told you Kath and I are still friendly."

She grimaced. "Because Gem told me you looked a little too comfortable on New Year's Eve."

"Avs, we were talking about you."

"What?"

"There's a photo from our wedding hanging on the wall, and she said we looked happy. She told me to not make the same mistakes I made with her. That I should tell you how I feel once in a while."

Avery sat back, and her mouth formed a little 'O.'

I laughed. "Were you jealous?"

She muttered under her breath.

"Seriously?"

"Yes," she grumbled.

"Why?"

She sighed and ran her hand through her hair nervously. "She's so gorgeous, and I'm so... not."

"C'mere," I growled.

She jumped at the gruffness in my voice.

I crooked a finger at her when she didn't get up right away. She pushed her chair out and walked over to me. I pulled her into my lap and cupped her face. "You're sexy as hell, you know that, right?"

She shook her head.

I trailed my hands down her curvy body. "You've always been sexy to me. Even more so now that you're carrying my child. I don't give a fuck about Kath."

She grimaced. "You're not gonna think that when I'm as big as a house in a couple of months."

I framed her face with my hands. "Avery, I'm always gonna think that. But you gotta know that Kath's my past, and you're my future."

"You don't want to get married again."

I pointed back and forth between the two of us. "This, us, is my forever. I want you forever and always."

Tears welled up in her eyes. "Nolan..."

"Baby... please stop crying," I groaned.

She laughed through the tears and rested her head in the crook of my neck. "I'm sorry, I can't help it. You're the asshole who had to get me pregnant."

We laughed together, but when she smiled at me, I knew it was going to be okay. Our daughter was fine, and in a few short months, she would be here with us.

"I have to tell you something about Kath, though."

I furrowed my brow. "Did she say something to you? Is that why you freaked out?"

She shook her head and bit her lip. She looked nervous to tell me something, and now I was worried.

"Avs, just tell me."

"You know how you said you wanted kids, and she didn't?"

I nodded. That had been a sore subject my entire marriage with Kath. "Yeah?"

"I didn't want to tell you, but Kath and Grayson have a son. He's one of my students, one of my best students."

I tipped back my head and laughed. She scrunched up her nose and looked at me, confused for a second. "Do you mean Tyler?"

"You know Tyler?"

"Avs, when did I get divorced?"

She shrugged. "I thought it was a long time ago."

"It was only five years ago. He's her stepson."

Her eyes widened in surprise. "Oh! Nol, I didn't want to tell you because I thought it would break you. It made me so mad, and I wanted to protect you."

"That's why I love you. You care so much about those you love; you only want to protect them."

"I was so angry for you, and then when we were at the hospital, I don't know... I let my insecurities get in the way."

I lifted her left hand up and kissed it. "You're the one wearing my mother's ring, and you're the one carrying my child. She's nothing to me now."

"Promise?"

"Promise, baby. You're my light."

She lifted her head up and pressed her lips to mine. I wound my hands through her hair while she devoured my mouth.

"You're too good to me," she whispered when she pulled away.

I placed my hand on her still-growing belly. "Want me to blame it on pregnancy hormones?"

She laughed. "Let me make it up to you today."

I cocked an eyebrow at her. "Oh yeah, how are you gonna do that?"

She gave me a sly smile and ran a finger down my chest. "I can put on the red lingerie for you again."

I gulped, and I felt my cock thicken against my leg. She grinned at me, so I knew she felt it. "Oh, yeah?"

She nodded. "You want that?"

I gripped her hips and ground her against my rock-hard dick. "What do you think?"

She giggled.

"You're a naughty girl, calling off work so you can have sex with your husband."

She stroked my beard. "My sexy, patient husband who has a big dick."

I couldn't help the laugh that bellowed out of me. I loved her so much, and I couldn't wait to spend the rest of our lives together.

"I love you so much, Avery Jensen."

"No, Avery MacGregor," she corrected.

I beamed at that. "Okay, Mrs. MacGregor, get your ass upstairs and put on that red lingerie."

She grinned at me. "I love you so much, and I'm sorry I almost ruined our marriage."

I cupped her face. "You're my wife, my last wife, and I'm never getting married again."

"But—"

I put a finger to her lips. "Avery, I'm not gonna say our marriage will be perfect. Marriage is a give and take. I was married before, and I didn't try for her. I didn't work at it, but I'm not doing that with you. I'm not saying I'm gonna be the perfect husband, but I want to try for you."

Tears pricked her eyes. "Oh, Nolan. I'm sorry for the

way I acted, for pushing you away. You didn't deserve that. I'm not a perfect wife, but I want us to be a team. I want us in this together."

I slid my hand between us on her belly. I wish I felt the baby like she had, but I knew that would come soon. "We're a team. You made me see I don't have to shoulder the burden all on my own. It's you and me against the world, okay?"

"I love you, and I can't wait for you to hold our baby in your arms. I can't wait to spend the rest of my life with you."

"You're my light, and I'm never letting you go."

"Don't let me go," she whispered.

Then I slanted my mouth on hers again.

NOLAN
CHRISTMAS THE FOLLOWING YEAR

"Nol, this is too much," Avery said as she swept her hand across the living room.

"Avs, it's Christmas!"

"Nol, it looks like Santa's workshop blew up in here. Are you seriously wearing that?"

I looked down at my Christmas sweater that looked like a Santa suit and shifted the Santa hat on my head. "What, you're not hot for Santa?" I asked her with a cheeky smile.

She shook her head at me. "You're ridiculous!"

I held our daughter against my chest and looked down at her. She looked so cute in the Christmas onesie that read 'The Best Gift' in green and red font. Avery and I had made the cutest baby ever, and she was the best gift either of us had ever received.

"You hear that, Peanut? Your mother, the 'Queen of Christmas,' thinks it's too much."

Norah cooed and then promptly reached a tiny hand

up to grab my beard. I thought about shaving off my beard after Norah was born, since she wanted to grab at it every time I held her. When I mentioned it to Avery, she threatened to divorce me. My wife certainly loved her beard rides.

"NORAH!" Avery chastised, taking the baby from me. She nuzzled our daughter's nose against hers.

I couldn't believe how big the baby had gotten already. Six months ago, I was in the hospital holding this tiny little thing in my arms and was absolutely scared shitless. But Avery and I were a team. We figured it out together, and now we had the family I always dreamed of.

"No pulling on daddy's beard," Avery cooed as she rocked the baby in her arms.

"She takes after her mother," I mumbled.

"I heard that!" Avery said while she walked over to the Christmas tree and shifted Norah on her hip.

Watching my wife with our daughter filled my chest with warmth. They were everything I ever wanted, and some days it amazed me that both of them were in my life.

Last night, I begged Declan to help me set up the tree and decorate it in the dead of night to surprise my wife. We even recruited Gemma to watch Norah to make sure Avery didn't wake up while we were in the middle of it. We didn't just do the tree; we hung garlands across the fireplace, in the doorways, along the railing of the stairs, and put up all the stockings. The newest one for Norah since it was her first Christmas. We even put the lights on the house. Yes, in the dead of winter and the pitch dark. That probably hadn't been a smart idea, but I wanted to surprise my sleep-deprived wife.

My wife, who loved Christmas with every fiber of her being, but who was looking at me like I had three heads.

Last night, Declan said it looked like the North Pole in here, but I thought he was just being sarcastic.

Avery shifted Norah on her hip, and she stopped dead-center at an ornament on the tree. I knew which one it was; it was the one Gemma made for me. She had painted a round flat circle ornament white with evergreen-styled elements at the top and bottom. In the center, in her neat handwriting, it read 'Norah's 1st Christmas.'

Avery looked back at me with misty eyes. "Oh, Nol, you big softie."

I grinned at her and went over to her. I bent my head to kiss her softly, and Norah squawked at getting squished in between us. I bent down and kissed my baby's forehead. "Only for my girls. Right, Peanut?"

My daughter looked up at me with wide eyes. I laughed when she went to make another grab for my beard, but Avery shifted her onto her other hip.

Such a little stinker. She was lucky she was so damn cute.

"I thought we weren't putting up the tree this year. I barely even made cookies. Being a mom is exhausting."

Parenthood was tiring. When I asked Avery what we should do for our baby's first Christmas, she told me it didn't matter because Norah wouldn't remember, anyway. That had alarmed me because Avery *lived* for Christmas.

I think she had been tired when I asked because parenting was no joke. While she balanced teaching and being a mom, I was a dad during the day, and then I worked all hours of the night at the brewery. My girls drove me to make the brewery even more successful than it already was.

The hefeweizen last summer was a hit. Gemma suggested the name Mac Daddy since we released it right after Norah was born. The unique name intrigued people so much they were buying it all up. We put out a new Christmas beer this year called Wheat Christmas. Avery said it was her favorite, which I knew it would be because I made it specifically for her. I wanted to call it Avery's Ale, but Declan and Gemma vetoed that. Gemma came up with that name, too. She finally agreed to be our marketing director and she was good with that shit.

Avery struggled with the working mom's life, so I had to do something special for her this Christmas. Especially since it was our first anniversary.

"Baby, you love Christmas," I said with a smile.

"I know, but..."

"What?"

"You don't."

I shook my head and put an arm around her. "I didn't use to, but then you came into my life. I told you, you're the light to my dark."

"Oh, Nolan..." she trailed off with a sniffle.

"Come on, Avs, no tears."

She wiped her eyes and looked up at me with a face full of adoration. "I love you, you know?"

I beamed. "I know."

She made a face. She jostled Norah in her arms. "Your daddy thinks he's hilarious. What do you think, Peanut? Do you like what daddy did with the place?"

Norah cooed at her in response.

"I knew it was too much for you this year, but I wanted to surprise you," I said.

"No way you did this by yourself," she said in disbelief as she looked around the living room.

I shook my head. "Nope. I dragged our siblings into it."

"How did I not wake up?"

"One, you drank three beers last night."

She gave me a sheepish look. "That new beer is so good! Thanks for making it for me."

I beamed at her. "And two, Gemma watched the baby while Declan and I did the decorating."

She glared at me. "You little sneak!"

"I did it for you."

Her grin was a thousand-watt. "It was a pleasant surprise, ya big Grinch."

"Not a Grinch anymore," I said and lifted her left hand in mine. "Not since you let me put this on your finger."

"Nolan?"

"Yeah, baby?"

"I'm glad we were careless that night. Thank you for giving me everything I always wanted."

I cupped her face in my hands. "Happy Anniversary, Avs. You're the light in my dark world. You made me love Christmas again. You gave me better memories than the ones that haunted me. You and Norah are my whole world."

I used to hate Christmas. I hated that it reminded me of the worst day of my life, but not anymore. I wondered if we never forgot to use a condom that night if I would be here. If Avery would be wearing my ring on her finger and bearing my name. I didn't want to think about the what-ifs. She was mine, and I was hers, and I'd never been happier in my entire life.

"Merry Christmas, baby," Avery whispered, and then she kissed me under the mistletoe.

***

ACKNOWLEDGMENTS

Whew you all, I was afraid this book might not come out on time, so this has been a journey! But I have a lot of people I'm grateful to for helping me with this book.

I wrote Accidentally In Love two summers ago for Camp Nano. And then I put it away and thought it would be the start of the series I wrote AFTER I finished the Philadelphia Bulldogs Series. Um, joke was on me, because when I realized how much Christmas played a part in the plot, I decided it needed to be released earlier than planned. I'm truly a chaotic writer and nobody tried to stop me, so you're welcome!

There are a lot of people I need to thank for helping me with this book. First up, my author soul sisters, for instead of saying, "No, Danica, please stop being chaotic," they said, "DO IT!" You are all instigators, and I love you for it!

Thank you so much to my betas, Kat Obie, JLynn Autumn, Leah, and Chris. Your guidance on this book was so helpful. JLynn has already claimed Nolan, so prepare to fight her for him!

Thanks to Olivia Blacke for sliding into my DMs and helping me brain storm beer names. Coming up with names that aren't already taken is hard. And if they are taken, I'm sorry, I tried.

Big shout out to my editor Jes for helping me with this

book and falling in love with Nolan. I hope you all love him as much as she did.

And one final special shout out to Leah and Becky at Buzzing about Romance, for always championing my books and helping me. Your support means more than you will ever know.

I really hope you all love this story, and I can't wait to bring you Gemma and Felix's story next.

TRAPPED IN LOVE EXCERPT

GEMMA

JUNE

I blinked and stared at my brothers-in-law while I processed what they had just asked me.

The MacGregor Brothers couldn't look more different, but they had similar mannerisms. While Declan rubbed a nervous hand across his clean-shaven jaw, his older brother Nolan mirrored the reaction by brushing his hand across his big, bushy beard.

"Well?" Nolan asked.

I blinked back at him. "That's the stupidest fucking name for a beer I've ever heard!"

Declan busted up laughing. "Told you!"

Nolan scowled, which was his usual MO anyway. Everyone knew Nolan MacGregor was the biggest grump in all of Drakesville.

I pinned him with a confused look. "Norah's Nectar, really? Nol, that sounds gross!"

Declan tried so hard not to laugh, while Nolan stood up and started pacing around the office. The pacing wasn't new. My sister was heavily pregnant, and the stress was getting to her husband. Lately, he was such a grumpy bear that everyone was walking on eggshells around him.

I got that he wanted to name the new hefeweizen after his baby, but Norah's Nectar was dumb as shit. I chewed on my lip and ran a hand down my tattooed arm as I tried to come up with a better name.

Immediately, a thought struck me.

"Ooh! I got it!" I cheered.

"What?" Nolan growled.

See — grumpy bear!

A smile curled up onto my lips. "Mac Daddy!"

Nolan frowned. "That's so stupid!"

"Nope!" Declan agreed with me. "I like it. It gets people to go 'whoa, what's that?' and pick it up."

"Exactly," I said. "This beer's new. It shows we're experimenting and trying new things. It should have a unique name."

Nolan gnashed his teeth, but then he nodded and walked out of the room.

Declan shrugged. We were all used to Nolan The Grouch by now. Declan went to say something else to me, but then his phone rang, and his brow furrowed in confusion. He held up a finger for me to wait before I darted back out to the serving floor.

"Gemma's coming to get you," he said into the phone.

My eyes widened. By his words, I knew exactly who he was talking to. Oh, shit, it was go-time. Avery was having the baby!

"Go," Declan said when he hung up the phone and

handed me the go-bag Nolan had stashed behind Declan's desk.

"I'm supposed to be on shift. Asher can't handle the bar himself tonight."

Declan swore. "Call Felix. Tell him it's an emergency."

I gritted my teeth and fingered the crystal around my neck. I tried to will away the bad vibes as I thought of Felix fricking Jameson.

I used to like Felix. A lot. He was funny and hot with his eyebrow piercing and sleeve tattoos. Back in January, he asked me out, but then he stood me up. If he apologized, I wouldn't have hated him with the passion of a thousand fiery suns. Instead, he pretended he never asked me out and said it was a joke.

What a douche-canoe.

The worst part? It absolutely crushed me. We had gotten close over the weeks leading up to our date, and my heart did that little pitter-patter every time he was near. Felix intrigued me, and I had wanted to get to know him better. I had hoped going out together, I'd find out more about him. I had already liked what I saw, so when he pretended I meant nothing, it broke my heart. Maybe it was typical 'Gemma Dramatics,' but the hurt of his betrayal rubbed me raw and turned into unbridled hatred.

Declan gave me a warning look. "Just call him."

"Can't you do it?"

While Nolan handled the beer, Declan managed the business side of the brewery. That included managing the front-of-house staff. It wasn't my job to call Felix to cover my shift. Same way, it shouldn't have been my job to handle the social media or work with Felix on the artwork, but Declan was an asshole like that.

"Just do it," he said.

Before I could argue, he rushed out of the office to get Nolan.

I sighed, pulled out my phone, and found Felix in my contact list. I clicked on the name 'Douche-Nugget.'

Felix standing me up wasn't the first time that happened to me. That's probably another reason it crushed my heart into a million tiny pieces when he did it. I'd used dating apps for a while, but if my matches didn't ghost me before scheduling a date, then they stood me up. Just like Felix. A part of me seriously wondered if Felix had cursed me because I hadn't been on a successful date since that night.

I pressed my phone to my ear and hoped the douche in question didn't pick up. I'd rather bother Wyatt or Claudia to come in instead of Felix.

But before I could hang up and call one of them instead, a gruff voice purred in my ear, "Well, hey sweet thing, what can I do for you?"

I rolled my eyes so hard I heard my sister in my head scolding me about my face staying that way. "Yeah. Never mind."

Felix chuckled on the other line. "Hold up now. What's up?"

"Avery's having the baby."

"Okay."

"Can you cover my shift tonight? I need to be with my sister."

I was met with silence for a couple of moments.

"Felix?"

"Yeah. I can do it. But you owe me."

I could only imagine what that meant. But he was doing me a favor, so I couldn't complain.

"K, bye!"

I hung up without another word. I didn't care if I was rude; he was an asshole and deserved it. I noticed Declan leaning against the doorway of the office, staring at me with an annoyed look on his face.

Declan seemed mild-mannered, but he was the most gossipy person at the brewery. He meddled. Wyatt and Lizzie wouldn't have ever gotten married if Declan hadn't pressed Wyatt about it. Nolan never would have told my sister he loved her if Declan hadn't pushed him to talk about his feelings. Okay, that last one was on me too, but Nolan was a special case. The big man would rather chew off his own hand than talk about feelings. Declan forced me to call Felix because he was urging me to bury the hatchet with the other bartender.

"Will you two get it over with already?" Declan asked.

"What?"

He shook his head and walked over to his desk. "Just fucking bang him already so the rest of us can have some peace. We're sick of your banter."

"When he stops being an asshole, maybe I will. I gotta go!"

I rushed out of the brewery and began walking to my apartment on the other side of town. Since Drakesville was so walkable, I never drove to work, but I needed my car to take my sister to the hospital. After Nolan knocked up my sister and moved her into his house, I offered to take over her place. It was a small second-floor apartment, but the rent was astronomically cheaper than what I paid in South Philly. I used to hate that the brewery was in the suburbs, but I'd come to love the small town of Drakesville.

I made the ten-minute walk to my apartment and hopped into my car for the thirty-second drive across the street to the high school. After parking, I jogged inside to find my sister sitting in her classroom, holding her back and groaning.

I never ever wanted to get pregnant. Ever. I couldn't wait to be the cool aunt to little Norah, but I didn't want to be anyone's mom. Ever.

Avery's eyes welled up with tears, and she clenched her teeth. "Nolan?"

I gave her a reassuring smile. "On the way. He'll meet us, okay?"

She nodded, but the color drained from her face. She gritted her teeth again as she pressed her hand onto the small of her back. "Fuck, I can't believe she's coming early."

I laughed. Of course, she was coming early. Norah was my sister's kid, after all. Avery was nothing if not a rule-following punctual lady. AKA the complete opposite of me. "She seems like your daughter already."

Avery glared at me through another grimace, and I took that as a sign to hustle her outside and into my car. Drakesville didn't have its own hospital, so it took ten minutes to drive to the nearest one.

I tried to calm my sister down, but she was freaking out for the entire ride. I opened my center console and pulled out a moonstone necklace, and handed it to her.

She tilted her head at me. "What's this?"

Avery didn't get my belief in crystals. I tried to give her some when she was dealing with morning sickness, but she scoffed at me and called it 'woo-woo bullshit.' Whether or not they worked, they helped me put out good vibes into the universe.

"It's a moonstone," I explained.

"Is this some woo woo bullshit?"

I rolled my eyes, although I wasn't shocked in the least by her comment. "Avs, just take it and channel your stress into it until we get to the hospital. I promise you, as soon as we get there, Nolan will whisk you away and hold your hand the entire time."

"Thank you."

"I know you don't believe in this stuff—"

She cut me off. "I know you do it because you want to help. I love that you do that, even though I think crystals are bullshit."

I nodded and pulled up at the hospital. Just like I said, Nolan met us immediately. He rushed to my car and opened the passenger door to help Avery. He had her wheeled into the hospital before I could even put my car in park. I drove around the lot, searching for a parking spot while trying not to worry about my sister.

I messed up early in Avery's pregnancy when she thought something was wrong with the baby and she couldn't get a hold of me. I was supposed to meet her for dinner, but I was spiraling after Felix stood me up. I flaked out on her and fell asleep with a dead phone, so I never saw her pleading texts until it was too late. I never told her what happened because I felt so guilty about not being there for her. Since then, I had been trying to make amends.

After parking and walking into the hospital, I found Declan and my dad sitting impatiently in the waiting room. We sat for hours while Nolan was in the room with Avery. I paced so much that Declan had to push me down into my seat. Avery had been so afraid of something happening to the baby her whole pregnancy that I wanted the birth to be perfect.

I rubbed at my rose quartz necklace and tried to put happy thoughts into the universe for little Norah. I wanted my niece to be brought into the world surrounded by love.

"She's gonna be fine," Dad reassured me.

"She was scared," I admitted.

"She's got, Nol. You're not the one giving birth," Declan said.

I nodded in agreement, but I still wished I could be by Avery's side. Nolan was holding her hand and telling her everything was all right, but I needed my sister to be okay.

It was late by the time Nolan came out, looking exhausted but with a big grin across his face.

I jumped up at the sight of him. "Can we see them?"

He nodded, and we all followed him into the room, where Avery lay in the bed with the baby in her arms. She looked wrecked, but wore the same happy smile on her face as when she married Nolan.

"Oh my god, she's so cute," I squealed.

Nolan glared at me.

"What?" I asked him.

"Be quiet. She's fussing," he said in a low growl.

Man, was little Norah going to have it hard as a kid. Nolan was going to be a total helicopter parent.

But then I watched Avery hand the baby over to him, and Nolan's entire demeanor changed. The baby wrapped a tiny hand around his finger, and the big guy was glowing.

Holy shit, Nolan had feelings!

"You good?" I asked my sister.

She nodded and handed me back the moonstone necklace, but I shook my head and pushed it back into her hand. "Keep it."

I made that necklace a while ago, but I wasn't sure when to give it to her. The universe gave me the sign today when she was freaking out.

We stayed visiting, watching my dad rock the baby, until she wailed uncontrollably.

"All right, get out!" Nolan said to all of us.

Avery and I laughed together, and I hugged her goodbye.

"Thanks for being here," she said and squeezed my hand.

"Of course. I can't wait to spoil Norah rotten."

She smiled at me. "Love ya, sis."

"Love ya, too. I'm so happy for you."

Tears pricked her eyes. "I never thought I'd get everything I ever wanted with Nolan."

I wiped her tears away. "The big guy loves you something fierce. Never ever forget that."

She nodded and watched as Nolan rocked the baby, trying to calm her down.

As I was leaving, I glanced at Avery and Nolan one last time. I'd never seen either of them look happier before. I had to tamp down the jealousy boiling to the surface. I hoped one day I could find my person like my sister had. If only Felix Jameson hadn't cursed me.

You can find the full book HERE

ABOUT THE AUTHOR

Danica Flynn is a marketer by day, and a writer by nights and weekends. AKA she doesn't sleep! She is a rabid hockey fan of both The Philadelphia Flyers and the Metropolitan Riveters. When not writing, she can be found hanging with her partner, playing video games, and reading a ton of books.